# Sorrowline

By Niel Bushnell

ANDERSEN PRESS • LONDON

First published in 2013 by
Andersen Press Limited
20 Vauxhall Bridge Road
London SW1V 2SA
www.andersenpress.co.uk

3 5 7 9 10 8 6 4 2

British Library Cataloguing in Publication Data available.

ISBN: 978 1 849 39523 6

Printed and bound in Great Britain by
CPI Group (UK) Ltd, Croydon, CR0 4YY

For Diane, with all my love.

# Sorrowline

'There are many Realms. The Earth, everything on its surface, all that dwells beneath it, and the mysterious heavens above, are but one Great Realm. I have seen many others, the strangest of which is the dark landless Realm of Oblivion. The most beautiful, and the most unattainable of all, is Otherworld.'

Extract from *On the Nature of the Concealed Realms*
by Magnus Hafgan

# PROPHECY

Rouland wiped the blood from the length of his sword on the heavy curtains of the Parliament Chamber.

Around him, splayed on the floor, were the Ealdormen of Ealdwyc, their faces frozen into hideous death masks commemorating the terror and anguish they'd felt as Rouland had impaled each one in turn.

He walked amongst his victims, stopping to close their petrified eyes. He owed them that much, he supposed. These men and women had formed the High Assembly of the First World, representatives of the noble families that had reigned for centuries. They had been his peers. Some, he had even considered his friends.

The sword glowed softly in his hand. It had been a long time since it had feasted like this. Rouland felt its impatient tug and made a mental note to place it somewhere safe. It was getting far too strong, but he knew he would need it, if the Prophecy was to be believed.

The Prophecy. Rouland cursed to himself. It was because of the damned Prophecy that he had been forced to annihilate the Parliament. He felt anger surge up through him and he kicked the nearest body. It was Durer. Once, years ago, he had been his closest ally, their friendship sealed in battle. But Durer's voice had become the loudest in dissent. He had openly challenged Rouland's term as Prime Ealdorman. In retaliation, Rouland had killed everyone in the Parliament, saving Durer till the end. But murdering old friends had not held the pleasure he had thought it would. He looked at the bodies, one on top of another, and he felt suddenly alone.

All because of the Prophecy.

The door clicked open and a dark figure entered, a lean woman in a close-fitting suit of armour. Rouland felt his mood lift at the sight of his faithful servant, Captain Alda de Vienne, and his wicked, beautiful face cracked with a smile.

'I'm done,' he said unemotionally. 'Hang the bodies on the gates so all can see them.'

Captain de Vienne nodded as she inspected the room.

'You understand why?' Rouland asked, his tense exterior eased in the private company of de Vienne.

'The Prophecy,' de Vienne replied. 'It is upon us at last?'

Rouland fell into the high chair at the end of the Parliament Chamber and threw his legs over the side. 'It is sometime in September 1940 – everyone is in agreement on that point – and the month and year are upon us now. I have studied all of Hafgan's work, even those volumes lost to us, and if my calculations are correct the Prophecy will begin today. I am convinced of it.'

'The boy from upstream will arrive today?'

'So the Prophecy tells us: a boy from upstream, from the future, will come among us and bring an end' – he gestured around him – 'to all this.' It was more than logical deduction, Rouland conceded to himself. There was a growing feeling, an apprehension deep within. He could feel the shifting tides of destiny all about him, coming together in a crescendo of events. Things were happening.

His eyes moved quickly. 'I will not allow my reign to end. You and your sisters must begin your search. He will be with us soon.'

Captain de Vienne bowed, then left Rouland alone with the corpses.

The Parliament Chamber became silent. Rouland was aware of the sword again, glowing, throbbing. He pressed it into the nearest body and allowed it to feed from the last scraps of life-force before he stood to leave.

Now his great mind began to calculate the multitude of events that could unfold from this moment onwards. Then, for a brief instant, he thought about the boy. Some-where upstream, ahead of him in time, was *the boy*. The boy from the Prophecy. Rouland tried to picture him, to imagine what he might look like, what year he might live in. He realised the futility of his mind-game and felt foolish for trying. Rational thought took over again and he returned to his plans.

He pulled the sword from the body and stared into the shadows. An elongated caped figure grew out of the dark corner. As it bowed its shrouded head to Rouland, a trail of smoke drifted from within its feathered hood.

'Come,' Rouland said to the Grimnire as he walked out of the Parliament Chamber, 'we have much work to do.'

# 1

## DEPARTURES

The day Jack Morrow left this world was abnormal in its beauty. The summer sun painted the grey city in vivid colours that hid its rot and decay. Yet in spite of it all Jack felt a sickening anxiety gnawing at him. Today was not like all the other mundane days. Today was different.

'What happened to you?' Jack's father stared at him from the entrance of the cemetery, his face a mix of concern and anger.

Jack's exhausted mind tried to conjure up something convincing, something his father might actually believe, other than the truth. But his father was an expert at the little lie. He could tell them with conviction, and spot them in others with ease. Lying was pointless, he decided.

'I'm all right,' he mumbled.

His father frowned. 'Who was it?'

'Dad, I'm fine.'

Jack's father stared at the bruise on his son's face, at the smear of blood and sweat that marked his T-shirt. 'Was it Blaydon again?'

'It's nothing.' Jack thought about his missing mobile phone, stolen in between punches, and shuddered. His father had bought it for him and Jack couldn't face telling him about it yet. And this wasn't the first time. He seemed to attract the attention of the school bullies more often than he deserved. He stood apart from his schoolmates, had never fully been allowed into their trust.

Inside the walls of the old graveyard, hidden in mournful shadows, the air was cooler. The mature trees repelled the warmth of the bloated sun, while all around the grey sea of London's high-rise buildings soaked up the fleeting moment of colour. Not too far away the laughter of children's play wafted in on the dry air, momentarily overpowering the perpetual drone of traffic. It was the last joyous bellow of summer, the last moment before Jack's life unravelled.

They walked on, neither speaking. Jack's stomach was in knots. The moment was coming when he'd have to tell his father about the phone. They sat at their usual bench, on autopilot. In front of them was the grave, the headstone that pulled them together when everything else was trying to drag them apart.

'I have to go away for a while,' Jack's father said eventually, his voice filled with a cool apprehension.

Suddenly Jack's worries over the phone were forgotten. 'Away? Where to?' Though he already knew the answer. He had watched and listened these past few months and he knew the dirty secret at the heart of his tiny, deformed family: his father was a small-time thief – and not a very good one, by all accounts. The visits by the police, by lawyers and social workers, could only mean one possible outcome: his father was going to prison.

'How long are you going away for this time?' he asked.

'A long time, son.'

'Why? Why can't you just be a normal dad?'

'It's complicated. Grown-up stuff. You'll understand one day, Jo-Jo.'

'Dad, I'll be thirteen in a fortnight.' Jack flushed as hot angry blood filled his cheeks. No one called him Jo-Jo any more. It had been his mother's nickname for him, and the name had died with her.

Overhead, an aeroplane banked lazily towards City Airport, whining and growling as it slowed for landing. Jack looked up at the cobalt sky and the blinding light forced his pupils to shrink to a tight dot under his dark eyelashes. He was tall for his age, taller than most in his class, and his wiry frame made him appear uncomfortable and awkward, no matter how he sat. His cherry-brown hair needed cutting; it was too thick, too long for this heat. Besides, its uncontrollable wave was all the more apparent the longer it got. But he'd lost interest in his appearance. It was easier just to stop looking in the mirror.

Jack's father put his hand on his son's shoulder. 'You remember your Aunty Lorna? You met her a few years ago.'

'No,' Jack lied. He wasn't going to make this easy.

'Well, she remembers you, and she's looking forward to you staying with her in Brighton while I'm away. It won't be so bad...' Jack heard the doubt in his father's strained voice.

'Dad, I don't want to go. I don't want to move in with anyone else. I want to stay with you.' Involuntary tears rolled down Jack's red cheeks.

'You can't! Don't make this any harder than it already is.' Jack's father stood quickly and paced up and down the avenue of graves. 'I'm sorry, I have no choice. Aunty Lorna's coming tonight to pick you up. We need to get all your things packed before she gets here.'

In the past Jack had stayed with his nan, but she had been ill since last year and they'd moved her into a nursing home. She was too old, too forgetful, too poorly to take care of him any more.

He rubbed the tears from his cheeks, then watched them fall into the coarse dirt below, turning it a dark brown. His world was crumbling around him.

'You won't be able to come here for a long time, Jack. But me and your mum will still be with you. You know that, don't you, son?'

'Mum's dead.'

Anger flashed over his father's face. He opened his mouth as if to shout at Jack, then his face unravelled. He walked over to the granite headstone. 'Look at your mum's grave. Remember it. Picture it in your head. No matter how far apart we all are, we can still remember being here, together. Do you see?' He came and sat down again.

Jack didn't understand. Everything seemed so pointless and trivial. He looked up at his mother's headstone. He already knew every curve, every letter. He'd spent hours sitting beside it. Sometimes he'd talk to her as if she was there with him, listening. Some days – the bad days – it was difficult to picture her face. He would fight to hold onto his vague memories of her, yet still they fell away, like a precious thing slipping through his open hand. He wanted to hold onto her for ever, to keep every image vivid, every colour clear, every smell pure. But when things got really bad, when it felt like he'd forgotten who she was, he'd come here to be close to her again.

Jack left his dad on the bench and walked towards the grave, his legs feeling weak and heavy. He knelt next to the headstone and let his fingers trace the letters embedded in the rock. There was a flash of white light deep inside his mind, sudden and cool, like a heavy curtain pulled away from a brightly lit window. Jack recoiled. For a moment he had felt he was falling into the stone, sinking through its surface. The sensation was followed by an empty sadness, as if his body longed to continue into the gravestone. The experience was shocking and exhilarating and he looked to his father, but his dad was still just sitting on the bench, lighting a cigarette, oblivious to his son's encounter.

Jack's hand moved back towards the stone, almost of its own will, making contact with the hard surface again. The flash returned, cooler and stronger this time, and a yearning to enter the stone flowed from the back of his mind, outwards to the rest of his body. Tears fell uncontrollably as new memories of his mother erupted in his mind. He saw himself, as if through her eyes, new-born and fragile. He felt the weight of his tiny body cocooned in her slim arms. Suddenly it was his second birthday and he could smell her subtle perfume mixed with cigarette smoke. Jack stared at this forgotten child, this echo from his own life seen from a new perspective. He wondered how he could remember this.

Then it was Christmas Day, the taste of burned potatoes caught his throat, and he heard her laughter. *Her* laughter, like it was yesterday. Every instant of that day burst onto his senses like an explosion. It was the last Christmas they had spent together as a family, before things had fallen apart. Everything came at once. All the moments of his life jostled in front of him, unbidden, viewed through the prism of his mother's mind. It overwhelmed him.

He slumped onto the stone, its hard surface rubbing against his cheek. Already, these memories seemed to be slipping away. He wanted to follow them, follow them to their source. His mother was so close, all he had to do was to reach out and she would be there.

Jack reached.

Jack's father shivered; the air had abruptly turned cooler. The sun disappeared behind a thickening band of cloud, and the summer seemed to go with it.

He looked up. Jack wasn't at the gravestone. He stood quickly, searching in every direction at once and his stomach lurched as he realised with a sinking dread that he was completely alone.

# 2

## THE STRANGER

Jack lay shaking. Cold sweat covered his skin, sticking to his T-shirt and jeans. His stomach ached, bile coated his mouth and tears stung his eyes. He coughed. The sensation cut at his dry throat.

What had just happened? He must have fallen, or fainted, he supposed. He remembered kneeling by his mother's grave, his hand touching the stone. He remembered the flood of memories and the cool light inside his head. And then? He wasn't sure.

He blinked, the milky fog cleared and he focused on his surroundings. There was an eerie stillness about the cemetery, and a damp mist put a chill into his bones. The sky had changed, darker and cooler, and the sun clawed at the horizon, rising slowly in the cracks between buildings. But it was more than that. The trees looked different, smaller than he remembered. And his mother's headstone was missing, the earth smooth and untouched. A shiver ran through his body. He looked around again. There was no sign of his father; the bench was empty.

Instead, he saw another person leaning in the gloom of a tree.

'Don't worry, it'll pass in time,' a deep, old voice spoke softly. Jack rubbed his eyes and focused on the ageing man, who was now walking out of the shadows towards him. He had the haggard look of the homeless, his long coat was tattered and dirty, and his face bore fresh burns and scars. He limped as he neared Jack, like a soldier returning from the front line. A pungent smell preceded him, a mixture of sulphur and charcoal that reminded Jack of Bonfire Night. The old man approached cautiously, his limbs stiff and worn, like the rags hanging from him. He looked like the walking dead, Jack thought.

'It's all right, Jack, I'm not here to hurt you.' The man spoke calmly, holding up a charred hand. Jack froze for a moment, taken off guard by the stranger's intimacy. How did the old man know his name? And where was his father? Why had he left him alone?

'Questions,' the old man continued, as if reading Jack's thoughts. 'So many questions. And very little time for answers, unfortunately. So, straight to it.' The old man looked this way and that, full of nervous tension, scratching at a dark tattoo that blemished his leathery neck.

Jack propped himself up against a gravestone, his head spinning from the effort. He stared again at the old man's burns and wondered what had happened to him.

'Get your breath back, Jack,' the stranger continued, stepping closer. 'You've had quite a shock.'

As the gap between them lessened, Jack's nagging fears grew more intense. 'My dad's here, he'll hit you if you come any closer,' he said as defiantly as he could.

The old man stopped and looked Jack squarely in the eyes. 'But your dad isn't here. You're alone, Jack. And you're not where you think you are. Or should I say you're not *when* you think you are. You've travelled back in time. To the day your mother died.'

Jack raised his eyebrows in disbelief. This burnt figure had to be insane, he thought.

'Look about you, lad!' The old man was suddenly in front of him, his movements uncomfortably fast. 'Use your eyes. Use your brain. You know I'm telling you the truth, deep down you know.'

'Keep back!' Jack waved his fists at the stranger.

'Don't waste time!' The old man grabbed Jack's wrists, restraining him without effort. I've too much to tell you to waste time! You have a rare gift, Jack; you're a Yard Boy, a voyager through graveyards. You can travel through the Sorrowlines. They're tunnels, tunnels through time. Every grave, it's connected to the date of the person's death by a Sorrowline. Yard Boys like you, Jack – they can open up a Sorrowline and travel along it, into the past.'

The old man eyed the shadows, and then checked his watch.

'My name is David Vale,' the old man announced gruffly, 'and I'm your grandfather.'

Jack laughed. The statement was absurd. His grandfather had died long before he was born.

The old man let go of Jack, his wiry eyebrows knotted in frustrated anger. He paced up and down nervously, checking the graveyard.

'You're *not* my grandfather,' Jack replied, looking for the best exit.

The stranger pleaded, 'Jack, I am! I was there when you were born. I've watched you your entire life, Jack, knowing that this day – today – would come.'

Jack gazed intently at the old man. The face was unknown to him, and yet, hidden beneath the burns and the scars, there was an unmistakable resemblance to a picture of his grandfather that he'd found hidden in a box of his mother's possessions. In the photo he had been a middle-aged man, with a wild fire in his eyes. This ageing stranger had none of that. But there was the same broad jaw, the same bent nose (had it been broken?), the same protruding cheekbones and brow that made the eyes appear deep and wayward. Could it really be?

'I'm . . . I'm going home.' Doubt took hold. He needed time to think, he needed to find his father.

'Are you listening, lad?' the stranger boomed anxiously. 'I'm your grandfather. I'm here to help you!'

'My grandfather's dead.'

'Your mother told you that to protect you. Me and her, we had our differences, see. But you and I *have* met before, Jack, or at least we will. This is 2008. The year 2008. You've come back through your mother's Sorrowline. You felt the memories, didn't you? You felt the pull of the past, drawing you in. That's the Sorrowline, calling you.'

Jack stared back at the empty space where his mother's headstone had been a few moments ago. The memories lingered still. It was as if they tugged at his soul, yearning for him to rejoin them. He forced himself to look away.

'You say this is 2008?' he said cautiously.

'Yes.'

'Prove it.'

'But you already know, Jack. You even know what day this is. You ride through a Sorrowline, you just know the date, you *feel* the date.'

Uncertainty and doubt crushed his thoughts, and yet Jack acknowledged a truth in the stranger's words: he knew the date. He couldn't explain it; he just knew it as surely as he knew he had two hands. One date dominated Jack's thoughts: the 6th of June 2008, the day of his mother's death. He shivered involuntarily. But still he would not allow himself to believe this stranger's tale. This couldn't be David Vale, his grandfather, could it? Was he really in the past? A part of him believed it all without question, yet the turmoil in his mind remained.

Suddenly a new idea took him: if this were true, if he really was in 2008, then—

'I know what you're thinking.' David interrupted Jack's thoughts. 'You're thinking you can save your mother.'

Jack looked away. How had the old man known?

'Your mother is already dead.' David's gravelly voice faltered. 'She died about five hours ago. I was there and I couldn't stop it.'

A wave of grief came over Jack unexpectedly. It was like he had lost his mother all over again. He looked at the empty plot, picturing the gravestone that wasn't there, and for the first time his doubts eroded completely, leaving only resigned acceptance and a profound feeling of loss and futility.

'You're not safe here. You have to go back to 1940.' David's voice ripped Jack from his despair. 'You have to find me, the *younger* me. I'll be a few years older than you. We'll become friends and I can explain it all to you then.'

'Explain it to me now,' Jack said urgently.

'There isn't time. Your life is in danger. They're not just after me and your mother. You're involved. You need to hide. You can't go home; they might be waiting for you there. The trick is to go back and find me. I can keep you safe, but not here. You can hide in the past.'

'Who?' Jack asked. 'Who's after me?' He really wished his dad were here right now.

Movement in a dark corner of the graveyard caught

David's eye. He grabbed Jack's T-shirt and pulled him upright.

'We're out of time. They've found me,' David said.

'Who?' Jack asked.

'*Dustmen.*'

Nearby, a breeze disturbed a cloud of dirt. It rose up into the air and then stopped, suspended unnaturally in a thin sinuous column of filth. More dirt and dried leaves lifted upwards to join the thin strand. As it thickened it twisted and turned upon itself, forming the rough shape of a body.

The body raised one of its swirling legs of dirt and began to advance clumsily towards David and Jack. From the shadows two more figures appeared, their speed increasing with each step. Jack looked over his shoulder, wide-eyed with terror; another tornado of dust was forming close to the graveyard's main gate.

'You have to go, now!' said David, his face white.

'Where?' Jack pleaded. 'Where do I go?'

'To 1940. I can hold the Dustmen off for a bit, but if they pick up your trail you'll be as dead as me.'

'I-I don't understand! I can't do this alone!'

The first Dustman opened a space in its head out of which a siren wailed. The sound, a deep screech like metal drawn over stone, stung Jack's ears. It howled for a second time, then its rudimentary mouth disappeared again into the swirl of dust that made up its head.

'It's letting them know it's found us,' David said.

'What do they want with me?'

'They're from Rouland. Quick! There's a gravestone down there goes back to December 1940,' he wheezed. 'The tall one with the broken corner. Feel your way in, like you did with your mother's headstone.'

'I don't know...I can't...'

'You *do*, Jack. You *have* to! Trust me. You're stronger than you know.' David threw his tattered jacket to one side and pulled out a long, twisted weapon made of metal and ivory that looked to Jack like an improvised shotgun. David pressed a small switch and a choir of deathly noise erupted from its funnel. The sound ripped the nearest Dustman apart. Almost at once the fallen dust began to swirl again though, reforming, advancing...

'Help!' Jack prayed for the familiar sound of a police siren to flood the graveyard, for passers-by to rush to their aid, but the graveyard was deserted, the nearby streets muted in dawn's slumber.

'Why can't you stop them?' he pleaded with David. 'What are they?'

'Dust and dirt. I can't kill them.' David looked at Jack again. 'Go, now! 1940. Follow the Sorrowline and find the young me at the Hanging Tavern, it's on Morte Lane in Wapping. Follow the river to the west, you'll find it.'

For the briefest of moments David stared at Jack, his bloodshot eyes filled with tears. His words seemed to falter on his cracked lips. 'Jack, you *have to protect the Rose*. I'm sorry. Now *go!*'

Before he had time to digest the words, Jack felt David's cindered hand push him forward. His legs took over and he scrambled away from the old man and the unearthly creatures. He heard David shoot his weapon again, a Dustman's shrill cry replied, then another joined the horrible chorus. Above it all David was screaming.

Jack ran headlong towards the gravestone David had pointed to. He slid into it, almost knocking it over. He put his hand to the surface, feeling about desperately. Nothing. He checked the engraving: the date was in 1940, yet he felt nothing as he had at his mother's grave. His dark hair blew about his face as the air rushed up past him. He turned his head to search for David and gazed straight into the empty face of a Dustman. Jack screamed, scrambling to his feet. The Dustman raised his arm high into the air and swung for Jack's head. He ducked instinctively and began to run again. The Dustman's arm smashed through the old gravestone, sucking up the masonry and debris into its swirling bulk. It raised its foot and marched after him, moving its makeshift body faster and faster.

Jack fell behind one of the large tombs, catching his breath for a moment. The strange creature approached his hiding place, drawing up the air into a roaring tempest.

His mind raced. There was no way he could get to 1940, not now this squalling creature had shattered the headstone.

He was running again, zigzagging through the gravestones, searching for another escape route. He tried to focus on the lettering cut into the headstones as they blurred past, all the while knowing that the inhuman Dustmen were advancing on him from all directions. The stones were a mismatch of the old and new, the grand and the modest, the rich and the poor. The nearest one had a date of 1969, the next 1954. He ran deeper. Behind him he felt the air moving uncomfortably quickly, like a small cyclone chasing him down.

He turned a corner and tumbled down a small bank, hitting his back hard against a large ornately carved gravestone. The wind was close behind. He was about to rush to his feet when he noticed the date shouting out at him from the stonework. The letters read, *13th September 1940*. This one, he thought, this one would have to do.

The empty cry of a Dustman deafened his ears and he turned to see one looming large over him. Its body shifted, and two new arms grew quickly outwards. Again it bellowed, this time the tone lower, like a victory roar.

Jack stretched his thin dirty fingers and touched the rain-worn stone. It was cold, damp and covered with a fine moss, but Jack could feel further than just the surface. He sensed a river of mourning behind the rock. In a fit of impulse and desperation he pushed. The cool trickle of the Sorrowline responded, opening to allow him passage, and Jack felt himself vanish.

The Dustman lashed out, not knowing why it wasn't holding the boy. For a moment it surveyed the scene, then somewhere deep inside its primitive soul it made a decision. The Dustman bellowed out a long, slow, pathetic whine. All of the Dustmen in the cemetery heard it and fell to the ground, nothing more than dust and dirt once again.

# 3

## THE HANGING TAVERN

Everything was white.

Jack was aware of fleeting images, white upon white, each full of pain and laughter and hope. As one formed it instantly merged into another, becoming a kaleidoscope of mourning. Memories passed him by. The memories of the dead.

Jack was in the Sorrowline.

He saw the lost fragments of a life that resided here, tiny echoes of greatness. They appeared to him all at once, like a film downloaded into his brain. But the sequence was jumbled up, one instant overlaid onto the next.

Jack tried to pull the memories into focus: this grave – this Sorrowline – was formed by the death of a man, a tailor in his early twenties. He had died swiftly, Jack saw, his future ripped from him by another. A woman mourned him. No, two. One young, one old. They had stood on this very spot and shared their grief. A mother and a wife. No, not even a wife, a fiancée with her hopes shattered.

A great wave of grief flooded out in every direction, almost overwhelming Jack.

Foreign memories invaded his thoughts and tried to embed themselves as if they were his own. He felt sick. His mind shut down and he screamed out with the pain, but he couldn't make a noise. His first journey into a Sorrowline had been mercifully brief, but this time it seemed without end, the years mocking him as he travelled back in time.

The sounds and images faded away, and Jack felt a loss like no other. This was beyond physical tears, beyond physical pain.

He felt colours of crimson burning into his mind. And then he felt a void, like he'd dropped into a giant bubble whose surface was too far away to perceive. The colours drained into blues and other cool tones. There was a mighty shock wave and the Sorrowline seemed to crumple in on itself. Air rushed past him at a violent rate, his world went black and his ears popped, as if he was reaching back to the surface from a long dive in the school swimming pool.

Then an empty nothingness consumed him.

Jack opened his eyes. They stung and refused to focus properly. It was night and he was wet, cold and hungry. He was exactly *where* he had been before – sitting in the same graveyard where his father had told him he was leaving, the same graveyard where a stranger had claimed to be his grandfather, the same graveyard where creatures made of dust had tried to kill him. The last thought filled him with terror and he looked around, dreading what he might find. He was blissfully alone.

An almost-full moon bathed the graveyard in blue twilight, illuminating the subtle differences. It was emptier, younger. The air was coarse, gritty and full of soot. And the old gravestone – the tailor's gravestone – was gone.

Jack focused on the world outside of the graveyard. The silhouette of the nearby houses and buildings appeared stunted and malformed. The streets were darker; sparse, dimmed gas lights picked out tiny portions of the blackness with their soft glow. Columns of smoke rose upwards from almost every chimney, blotting out the stars above. Distant voices shouted, horses' hooves trotted over cobbles, dogs barked. But the roar of traffic, the cacophony of engines, the urban noise that he knew so well had been reduced to a single car making its way home.

So this was 1940, he thought, hardly able to believe the sensory evidence that flooded over him. It was absurd, after all. He couldn't possibly have travelled in time. He was dreaming, or in a coma. Somehow that was easier to accept.

He took a deep breath, and the air felt gritty and smelled of wood burning. After his journey here and his encounter with David Vale Jack felt a surreal calm, like the

25

aftermath of a storm. He laughed to himself, his fears forgotten in the wonder of this moment.

A bright flash lit up the sky in the north, tearing through his moment of calm. Seconds later, another flash erupted much closer and a giant fireball spewed upwards into the sky. Somewhere nearby a siren cried out like a dying animal, its endless wail like nothing Jack had heard before.

He gazed up; the sky was full of aeroplanes, their distant drone barely audible. Around them flashes and explosions tore the sky apart. One of the planes burst into flames as a wing tore free, leaving the body to spin uncontrollably towards the ground. It dropped below the line of dark buildings and a massive explosion erupted into the air.

Jack ran under the cover of a nearby tree as an old fire engine sped past the edge of the graveyard, its bells ringing. Flames licked the sky all around him, a perfect portrait of Hell on Earth. He felt like his heart would burst from his chest.

'This can't be real,' he whispered to himself. But his eyes defied his common sense. This vista's gut-wrenching terror was more authentic, more tangible, than anything Jack had ever witnessed before. He remembered his English history well enough: this had to be the Blitz, the bombardment of London by German forces during the Second World War.

He swallowed his fear and stepped out of the graveyard, into a world that was both familiar and strange. Wapping lay to the south, and somewhere amongst its narrow streets was a pub called the Hanging Tavern. But the great city was younger, and any landmarks familiar to Jack were either missing or in darkness. In his time, 2013, this area had been full of new housing developments, expensive apartments and glass-fronted office blocks. Things were very different now. Mills and factories lined the narrow streets, many on fire, belching thick smoke into the night sky. He suddenly realised that his own home, an unloved East End flat, didn't exist here, not for another fifty years at least. The thought sent a shiver down his spine. He thought of his father, adrift from him in the future. What did he think had happened to Jack?

He pointed himself at the river and began to run towards it. He saw few others on the streets. Only the drunk or the foolish remained outdoors, each one a grey silhouette of drab clothing, their faces aged by the terrible burdens of war.

Finally the Thames came into view, and with it a crisp breeze that brought much-needed clean air into Jack's lungs. He saw fishermen trying to tame a fire that had taken their boat and he watched for a moment as the old vessel rocked back and forth on the lapping water, the fierce flames eating into the wood. Hot points of ash blew violently about the dockside, singeing his clothes and skin.

27

He retreated, not quite sure where he was going. In front of him was a row of taverns and drinking holes, separated by small shops selling maritime equipment, trinkets and dried foodstuffs. All were closed and dark, but the reflection of the burning city in their window-fronts disturbed him, and he moved on. He saw more vehicles here, but their designs were foreign to him, like something that had fallen out of an old film. He passed a squat grey van, the logo for a breakfast cereal painted proudly onto its side. The rear door had been forced open and its contents obviously looted. A lone empty box of corn flakes remained. Jack picked it up, suddenly fascinated by this minute detail. His father ate this same brand every morning, always standing, looking out of the window at the London skyline.

A distant explosion rumbled through his feet. He put the torn box down and continued on his way, following the street as it hugged the river heading west, past trawler men and sailors who looked on helplessly at the inferno. He turned into a side street, its buildings miraculously spared from the carnage. He saw one or two revellers, drifting from bar to bar, drinking until the bombardment didn't matter any more. They stared at him as he passed by, pointing and laughing, and he looked down at his clothes: a pair of tatty jeans, which were too short and a light blue T-shirt that did nothing to stop the cool wind blowing in off the wide curve of the river. His jeans were torn and muddy from his race with the Dustmen, and dried blood now streaked the front of his T-shirt.

Then he saw his trainers and understood why people found him so amusing. Like his phone they had been a present from his father, an expensive treat to make up for his repeated absences. Jack had taken great delight in choosing them himself: they were booted trainers with a thick rubber sole, and very, very white.

The path sloped upwards and zigzagged past more shops, houses and pubs, none of which Jack recognised. Ahead he came to an empty crossroads. He stood at the junction, not knowing which way to try. He felt lost and alone. Most of all he felt afraid, and he wished he were at home, in his tiny bedroom where it was safe and warm.

'What the bloody hell have you got on?'

The voice was loud and confident. Jack expected it to belong to another drunken worker, but as he turned round he was surprised to see a teenage boy studying him. The boy was dishevelled and dirty-looking, his black hair ragged and unkempt. He wore a long tatty coat that looked like it had once belonged to someone in the British Army. Underneath was a pair of grey trousers, too big for his hungry frame, kept in place by braces that pinched into a once-white shirt.

'What're they?' the boy enquired, pointing at Jack's trainers. 'Never seen shoes that white outside a loony bin! You one of them asylum geezers? D'you escape?'

Jack hesitated; he thought it best to run away, to stay hidden. But this was just a boy, not much older than him.

'No,' Jack said, trying to keep his voice calm. 'They're just clothes.'

The boy scrutinised Jack as he fished out a pipe and a bag of tobacco from his jacket pocket.

'Never seen nothing like that before. You from London?' The boy spoke with a broad East End accent that gave his words a lyrical quality.

'No,' Jack lied. 'I'm just visiting.'

'You want to be careful, dressed like that,' the boy said as he lit his pipe. 'There are some funny sorts around here.' He smiled at Jack and began to walk away.

'Wait,' Jack said at last, throwing caution to the wind. 'I'm looking for the Hanging Tavern.'

The boy stopped. He turned round slowly, studying Jack anew.

'You?' he said. 'The Hanging Tavern?'

'Yes,' Jack replied.

The boy laughed. 'You wouldn't last five minutes in there.'

'I can take care of myself.'

'Course you can!'

'Do you know the way or not?' Jack demanded, frustration welling up inside him.

'That way,' the boy said, pointing down the street. 'Turn left onto Morte Lane, you'll see a fork in the road.

You can't miss it.'

'OK, thanks.'

'But as I'm going that way anyway I can take you there.' The boy coughed out smoke into the night air. 'Probably for the best, what with you looking like a madman and all.'

The boy walked past Jack, smiling through a haze of pipe smoke. 'You coming or not?'

Jack reluctantly followed.

'So,' the boy said, 'what you want with the Hanging Tavern?'

'I'm meeting someone there.'

'Who you meeting? I might know 'em.'

'David Vale.'

An impossibly broad grin covered the boy's face. 'Davey? Davey Vale? You know him?'

'Not exactly,' Jack replied, wondering if he had told this stranger too much.

'Does he owe you money? Are you gonna, you know...' The boy mimed a boxing match, bouncing lightly on his feet as he threw punches towards Jack's face.

'No, nothing like that,' Jack said, dodging his fists.

'Fair enough,' the boy said. 'He's a tough nut is Davey. You wouldn't want to cross him. Heart of gold, though. He'd do anything for a friend. Salt of the earth.'

The bombing had shifted to the north and west. Overhead the glow of burning buildings lit up the clouds of smoke, yet an uneasy calm settled over Wapping.

They stopped at a tiny opening between two large warehouses. A battered sign hung from the wall of the alleyway: *Morte Lane.* Further in, the gap widened and the path meandered to the left, hugging the profile of a long derelict building. Ahead, the road parted. In the middle of the two paths, breaking them apart like the prow of a mighty ship through water, was a pub.

'Here we are: *the Hanging Tavern.*' The boy gestured to the building like a circus ringmaster.

The Hanging Tavern's walls had long since deviated from straight and true, the twisted beams leaned outwards dangerously, pulling the walls and tiny windows with them.

'That'll be ten shillings.' The boy held out his dirty hand to Jack, his fixed grin never wavering.

'What?' Jack said sceptically.

'Ten shillings: for getting you here. Who knows what might have happened to you if I'd have left you behind. OK, call it five and we'll part as friends.'

'Shillings?' Jack said. He went to pull some coins from his jeans pocket before realising that all he had was twenty-first-century money. 'I haven't got any money,' he mumbled.

'I knew it. I bloody well knew it!'

'You never said you wanted paying.'

The boy thought about this, rubbing his chin theatrically. 'True, very true. And you've got stupid shoes, so I should have known better.'

He stepped forward and slapped his hands onto Jack's shoulders, his pipe gripped between his ever-smiling teeth. 'Tell you what, how about we both slope round the back way? We can sort this out over a drink.' The boy smiled another broad infectious grin. Jack couldn't help but smile back.

'What's your name, anyway?'

'Jack Morrow.'

The boy put his arm round Jack as he guided him to the side of the Hanging Tavern. 'Hello, Jack, good to meet you. My name's David, but everyone calls me Davey: Davey Vale.'

# 4

## A TIME-TRAVELLER'S TALE

'You did what?' Davey asked doubtfully. He sat opposite Jack in a discreet booth at the back of the Hanging Tavern. Electric lamps cast soft pools of smoky light over the huddled patrons and their hushed conversations. Not far away a radio crackled with lazy big-band music, drowning out the 'all clear' siren that lured relieved drinkers from their shelters.

A long bar separated the tavern into two halves; the front part was scattered with small round tables where Jack saw men who looked like workers from the nearby shipyards mixed with traders offering black-market goods to those who could afford them. Their conversations were loud, bawdy and full of relieved laughter. The patrons sitting on the other side of the bar – where they were – were quite different. Some might have been mistaken for homeless beggars, or perhaps visitors from overseas who had laid anchor on their way to somewhere more exotic. Others were dressed in much finer clothes, and looked completely out of place in the East End. One booth was home to three men dressed in smart military uniforms, each with a winged lion emblem on their chest. In another, a thin man stroked his unnaturally long skull with equally long fingers as he read a children's comic. Further along, a beautiful woman sat with a badly scarred old man who had an elaborate clockwork device where his left hand used to be.

And yet these outlandish people went unnoticed. Two different worlds separated by a bar and a few stools.

'Hey, madman!' Davey smiled. 'Are you listening? How'd you say you got here?'

'I travelled through time,' Jack said hesitantly.

Davey's eyes narrowed. He toyed with his wooden pipe, emptying the tobacco into an ashtray and replacing it with a fresh stash. 'Time travel, eh? Really?'

Jack shrugged, feeling small.

'But here you are, as real as raisins,' the older boy said as he gripped the pipe between his teeth and lit it with a match. Puffs of rich smoke circled around the booth, making Jack cough.

'You know that's bad for you, don't you?' Jack said, feeling uncomfortably judgemental.

Davey laughed behind the smoke. 'Life is bad for you.' He sucked on the pipe again, staring intently at Jack. 'How'd you do it? How'd you travel in time?'

'*You* told me how,' Jack said, waiting for a reaction.

'Me?'

'I travelled through a Sorrowline.' Jack heard the words coming from his mouth, but he hardly believed them. It was all just too strange, and yet he saw the reaction on Davey's face and he knew the older boy believed his story. He shook his head and pressed on. 'I met you, but you were an old man, and—'

Davey interrupted, 'Me? Old? Never! Forever young, that's me!' He leaned in closer. 'How old?'

'I don't know. Quite old. It was in 2008.'

Davey suppressed a scornful laugh.

Jack scowled in return. 'You – the older you – told me to come back here to 1940 and find you. He said you could help me.'

'Why would I help you?'

Jack hesitated. This teenager was supposed to be his grandfather, and he'd travelled here on his word, but he was also a stranger, a roguish chancer. He needed to be sure he could trust him, but there was no one else here to turn to.

'I don't know,' Jack said. 'Ask yourself.'

Davey looked on doubtfully. 'Sounds all a bit far-fetched, don't ya think?'

'Look, the older you sent me here. I know it's crazy, I can hardly believe it myself,' Jack said firmly. 'This sort of thing isn't meant to happen, is it?'

'Not to normal people.'

Jack frowned. 'What's that supposed to mean?'

'Normal people go to church, or school or work. Normal people read the paper and listen to the radio. They dance, they get drunk, they sing songs. But they don't travel back in time. Only Yard Boys can travel in time.'

Jack's eyes widened. 'That's what the older you said. That's what he called me. What does it mean?'

'Yard Boys travel in time, through Sorrowlines, see? So, you're from upstream? From the future?'

'I suppose I am. But it's not the future to me; it's my present. This' – Jack gestured at their surroundings – 'this is all history to me: the past.'

Davey nodded slowly, as if he'd arrived at some new understanding. 'And what am I supposed to help you with?'

'We were being chased.'

'Who by?'

'Dustmen.'

Davey put down the pipe, his smile faded. Quietly he asked, 'What have you done?'

'Nothing,' Jack said. 'They were after you as well.'

Davey's face turned a pallid grey. 'Those things don't go after just anybody!' His tone had changed; the bravado was gone, replaced with an uncomfortable apprehension. 'This is serious stuff, Jacky-boy. What happened to me?'

'I don't know. I ran, like you told me to. You used some sort of gun against them, but it didn't do any good.'

'*Them?*' Davey gasped. 'How many?'

'I'm not sure, at least four.'

'*Four!* You were attacked by four Dustmen? What did this gun look like?'

'It was long and made of metal. It didn't fire bullets; it made a blast of air.'

'Sounds like a chronohorn. That's what I would have used.'

'You did,' Jack said, realising the absurdity of what he was saying.

'Then what happened?'

'I told you, I ran. I found a gravestone, like you said, and that brought me here.'

'So, you're First World?'

'What?'

Davey eyed him sceptically. 'You really don't know?'

'No!'

'See the bar? This side is First World. The other side, that's Second World.'

'I don't know what you mean,' Jack said with a hint of frustration.

'How many people do you know who can travel through Sorrowlines? Only Yard Boys can do that, and they belong to the First World. Me, the other people you see here: all First Worlders. You?' He scrutinised Jack carefully. 'Maybe you've been Second World until now, but if you can open up a Sorrowline you are most definitely a First Worlder.'

'What are you talking about?' Jack said angrily. 'None of this makes any sense!'

Davey chuckled. 'That's how First Worlders want it. It's like a big secret club, a secret world hidden everywhere. The First World is where the real power is, but we don't like to shout about it, so it's kept hidden.'

'Is this the First World?' Jack asked, nodding to the bar.

'This? The Hanging Tavern?' Davey replied. 'Well, yeah, I suppose so. The Tavern is one of the places where the two worlds come together, if you like. A crossing point, where trade can happen. The sort of place the noble families come to slum it with the likes of you and me. Know what I mean?' Davey nudged Jack, laughing.

Jack smiled doubtfully.

'But it's nothing special really,' Davey continued. 'Just a place, just a pub, but they serve a decent beer. You should visit Ealdwyc some time, then you'd understand. That's the capital city of the First World. Beautiful place it is, and underground 'n' all. Now that's real power.'

Jack noticed that the two sides of the bar didn't mix at all. 'Can the people from each world not see each other?'

Davey sighed, half laughing. 'Course they can! But most people look away when they don't understand something. They just leave us be, just as we let them go about their own business too. See?'

'Sort of. But I'm not staying,' Jack said firmly. 'I don't belong here. I just want to go home.'

'You're a Yard Boy, Jacky-boy! This is exactly where you belong.' Davey jabbed his finger onto the tabletop to

39

reinforce his words and Jack shrank back into the booth, alone with his fear. Davey chewed the end of his pipe. 'Well, I did the right thing sending you back to me,' he continued. 'Glad to hear I'm still brilliant, even if I am old. And if you really are a Yard Boy, and a good'n by the sound of it, I'll need to get you to see the Journeyman.'

'The Journeyman? Will he be able to get me home? Can he stop the monsters?'

Davey screwed up his face, mocking Jack's nervous fears. 'Is it past your bedtime, little fella?'

'Shut up!' Jack's eyes narrowed. He could probably take him, he mused.

Davey's stony eyes didn't blink. 'I'm happy to have a scrap, if it'll make you feel better, but it won't fix nothing.'

Jack turned away.

'Better.' Davey smiled. 'A Journeyman, he looks after Yard Boys. He trains 'em, gives them jobs, that sort of thing. He'll know what to do with you.' Davey blew out on his pipe, sending fresh plumes of smoke circling over their heads. 'Being a Yard Boy,' he continued, 'it's a good living. Regular work, good pay. Dangerous, of course! Most are dead, or worse, before they're twenty.'

'I don't want a job!' Jack said quickly. 'I just want my family safe.'

Davey smiled again. 'Calm down, little chap, plenty of time. We'll get some drinks in, then we'll go see the

Journeyman.' He waved at the barkeeper, a heavy woman leaning against the end of the bar.

She approached the booth and slammed two pints of ale onto the table, sending beer and foam slopping into the wood.

'Thank you, Betty,' Davey said sarcastically.

Betty grunted, her thick eyebrows contorted in disgust, and returned to the bar.

'Are we allowed to drink this?' Jack asked, looking cautiously at the dark glass.

'We're First World! We can do what we want! If you can pay for it you can drink it.' Davey took a large gulp from his glass and urged Jack to do likewise. He took a small sip. The sharp taste stung his mouth and he put the glass back down on the table.

'Do they sell Diet Coke?'

'Die it what? It's ale or whisky here. And the whisky is watered.'

'I don't have any money,' Jack said. 'I already told you that.'

'I know, but we can soon fix that, if you're as good as you say. I'll get these.' Davey gestured at the drinks in front of them. 'Once you're working for the Journeyman you can pay me back.'

'I already told you, I'm not staying here, and I'm not working for anyone.'

'Fine. You can sort out those Dustmen on your own.'

Davey smiled and finished his drink, ending with a long deep burp. He pointed to Jack's drink. 'D'you want that?'

'No,' Jack said, happy to be certain about something, no matter how trivial. Davey took the glass and drank down the contents in one gulp.

'Look,' Davey said sympathetically, 'you'll be safer with the Journeyman, he can show you how to use your talents.'

Jack sighed heavily, his eyes focusing on nothing. Then his grandfather's words in the cemetery came back to him. 'Do you know anything about a rose?'

Davey suppressed a laugh. 'What you on about now?'

'You, the older you, back in 2008, you said something about a rose. I have to protect the rose.'

'What from? Greenfly?' Davey shrugged nonchalantly. 'I don't know nothin' about a rose.'

'Maybe it's to do with the Dustmen,' Jack guessed doubtfully. 'Or maybe something to do with the place you mentioned.'

'A place? What's it called?'

'Runeland...' Jack said, uncertain if he had remembered it correctly. 'Runeland...or maybe Roudland.'

The distant rumble of an explosion rattled the bar. Jack looked back to Davey and saw that the colour had drained from his face. The older boy opened his mouth, his lips were dry and he spoke in a broken whisper. 'Could it have been *Rouland*?'

Jack thought, running the word over in his head.

'Yes, that sounds right. You said the Dustmen were from Rouland.'

Davey closed his eyes, grimacing.

'Do you know where it is?' Jack asked.

Davey looked past Jack, a flash of nervous tension on his features. Jack followed his gaze: Betty was walking towards their table, rolling her sleeves up as she approached.

Davey stood up quickly, a restless terror in his eyes. 'I know *who* it is. Rouland isn't a place. It's a man. Come on, we have to get to the Journeyman, right now.'

Before Jack could say anything Davey had disappeared through the door. He scrambled to his feet and ran to follow. As he reached it a heavy glass shattered on the wall close to his head. He turned to see Betty advancing on him, her hefty arm raised ready to throw another glass at his head.

'Two pints!' Betty growled, her face contorted into an angry grin. 'And you can pay for that broken glass 'n' all.'

'Davey!' Jack shouted, but the older boy was gone and Jack was on his own again.

# 5

## THE PALADIN

The cellar was a cool space, full of vintage bottles and kegs of beer. Its thick stone walls kept the air dry and crisp even in the tight fist of summer. In between the disorganised barrels stood Jack, hunched and nervous. From somewhere in the tavern above came the sound of muffled laughter, vibrating through the oak beams. He yearned to be back up there, anywhere but here in this dingy space.

In front of him was a small round table, its rickety legs propped up on one side with folded paper. The table was covered in receipts and bills, illuminated by a small gas lantern. Behind the table sat a chubby-looking man who scrutinised Jack as a farmer might study a prize cow at market. His tailored suit had been expensive once, but its glory days, like those of its owner, were long forgotten. His name was Castilan and he was the landlord of the Hanging Tavern. When Jack couldn't pay for the drinks, Betty had dragged him down here and thrown him in front of this little man.

Jack wanted to get out of there as quickly as he could, but fear grounded him to the spot. Maybe he could fix this, make it right somehow, he mused. 'I could wash dishes,' he offered, 'or clean the floors, or something...' His voice trailed off as Castilan raised a stubby hand in front of him. He leaned forward into the lamplight, casting deep shadows over his chubby face.

'You know Vale?' Castilan asked, his contempt for the name barely hidden.

'Davey? I only met him an hour ago,' Jack said.

'*How* do you know him?'

'I don't.'

'Don't mess with me, lad,' Castilan said impatiently. 'Your clothes...' He waved a finger at Jack. 'Where are you from?'

'From London – here,' Jack replied clumsily, instinctively wanting to keep his time-travelling from this stranger. 'I just want to go home. My dad can pay for the drinks, if you'll let me—'

'Lies!' Castilan thumped his fist onto the little table. 'Your clothes, your voice. You shouldn't be here.'

Jack tensed.

'What should I do with you, eh?' Castilan leaned back into the shadows.

'Please, just let me go.'

'What year were you born, boy?'

Jack was lost.

'Lies again.' Castilan laughed wearily. 'Lies! In your mind and almost on your lips. There is some truth there, but so much else as well. I could spend a long time in your head, Jack.'

This was the second time a stranger had known his name, and it was as unnerving now as it had been before.

'How do you know who I am?'

'Your mind is an open book to an Operator, even one with my meagre talents. You must learn to protect your thoughts.'

'You can read my mind?'

'That's what an Operator does! Are you stupid? Oh, my skills are modest, I'm sorry to say, hardly worthy of the title, but I can pick up some of your thoughts.' Castilan closed his eyes, concentrating. 'The raw emotions are there for all to see. You are lost. You are far from home. You are not of this time. A Yard Boy! Excellent! And you are being hunted. Monsters? Yes! Dustmen, indeed. Terrible business. And more! A warning? Protect...' Castilan opened his eyes again. 'The Rose? Rouland?'

The urge to escape was overwhelming. Jack's eyes fixed on the stairs, and the small door at the top.

'The door is unlocked, I am not keeping you.' Castilan smiled.

Jack hesitated, then walked quickly to the stairs.

'Of course, you could walk out of here, with your

thoughts shouting out for any Operator to read,' Castilan continued, 'but I could help you, Jack, teach you how to shield your mind. Protect you from Rouland. Believe me; if Rouland's after you, you'll need protecting.'

Jack walked slowly back to the table, and the lantern flickered as he approached, sending hard shadows dancing over the ceiling.

'What...what do you want?'

'Me? I am but a humble landlord, a small-time businessman. I may have some influence, some minor talents, but that is all. Perhaps we can do a deal. My guidance, my tutelage; in return you work for me.'

'Doing what?'

'Oh, nothing too dangerous, I'm not a Journeyman. I'd treat you well. Together we could—' Castilan froze. His smile evaporated and he looked up, alert. 'Visitors,' he whispered.

Jack had heard nothing. Then, after a moment, there was the sound of heavy boots walking through the bar above. The cellar vibrated softly and dust escaped from one of the large wooden beams.

'They're looking for a boy.'

'Me?' Jack trembled.

'I can't tell. Perhaps.'

The noise of raised voices pulsed down from above. The shrill vibration of smashing glass made Jack jump.

'What should I do?' Jack's eyes pleaded with Castilan.

Castilan looked as confused and afraid as Jack felt. 'There's only one way in or out of this cellar.' He nodded at the stairs. 'We're trapped here.' He turned his head, as if listening intently. 'There are three of them. They're coming down here.' He rapidly removed his tatty jacket and threw it at Jack. 'Put that on, and quick.'

As Jack wrapped himself in the oversized jacket the door at the top of the stairs opened and three tall, lean figures walked down the rickety stairs. His breath caught in his throat as he tried to take in these eerie beings. They were dressed identically in layers of tightly fitting medieval armour and leather. Over their armour they each wore a flowing dark robe the colour of dried blood. From their belts hung long swords that clanged against the stone wall as they descended, sending tiny sparks falling into the darkness. Each wore a beautiful metal helmet with the shape of a cross embossed into the faceplate. The ancient surface was as smooth as black ice. Jack thought he saw writing just below the surface, embedded into the metal, but it disappeared again as the figures approached.

'Paladin,' Castilan said, the word choking on his lips. Then, without warning, he stood and swung his arm at Jack, hitting him squarely on one side of his face. 'Foolish boy!' The blow stung and knocked Jack to the ground. 'I said *two* cases of the twenty-one vintage, not four! I don't know why I bother to keep you here. You're nothing better than useless.' Castilan kicked Jack as he tried to get up. He fell back onto the floor, the breath knocked out of him, and stared up in disbelief, uncertainty and confusion filling his mind.

The Paladin watched impassively.

Castilan brushed his bristly hair back from his face, straightened his suit and smiled at the Paladin.

'I am sorry you had to see that, Captain de Vienne,' Castilan said, charm oozing from every pore. 'My sister disappears to Magog and leaves her stupid son with me! He's supposed to be helping out but he's costing me a fortune.'

The Paladin pulled at a buckle and the faceplate opened with a barely audible hiss. Jack watched as the helmet parted, folding away into the neck of the Paladin's armour to reveal the face of a young woman inside. She shook her pale beautiful head, freeing her dark ponytailed hair.

'We are looking for a boy,' said the captain, her voice thick with an accent Jack couldn't quite place. Was it French?

'You can have this one.' Castilan smiled, rubbing his hands together. 'He's for sale. Forget what I said earlier, he's not too bad once you get him broken in.'

The Paladin captain looked at Jack lying on the floor. 'This is your boy?'

'My nephew, Erasmo. He's good at carrying things.' Castilan looked at Jack and said, 'Erasmo, get up off the floor, you stupid boy.'

Jack stood cautiously. As far as he could tell, the woman was accepting Castilan's lies.

Castilan grabbed him roughly around the jaw, forcing his mouth to open. 'He's got good teeth, see? He might look a bit thin, but...' He turned to Captain de Vienne. 'Make me an offer. I'll settle things with my sister when she comes back.'

The Paladin looked at Jack. 'We are not buying.'

'Oh come now, Alda, everything has its price,' Castilan said, his voice like oil.

Captain de Vienne scowled at Castilan. 'You will call me *Captain.*'

'Suit yourself,' Castilan replied coolly. 'What d'you need a boy for, anyway?'

'Our master seeks him.'

'What for?'

Jack's heart thundered in his chest.

The Paladin captain stared at Castilan, her gaze unblinking. 'Do you have any other children here?'

Castilan sighed heavily. 'No, not any more.' He rubbed his soft chin, as if to recompose himself and returned Captain de Vienne's steely glare. 'Do you want this one or not?'

Captain de Vienne turned to study Jack. 'No. You will tell us of any strangers who pass this way. We seek a boy, about twelve, perhaps thirteen years of age.'

'You can count on me,' Castilan said quickly. He

50

nodded and picked up two bottles of red wine, handing them to Jack. 'Right, lad: give these to Betty, and don't drop them, or I'm posting you to Magog. In pieces.'

Jack took the bottles as he gawped at the Paladin. Somehow, for now, it seemed he was safe.

'Come on! I've got customers waiting!' Castilan shouted.

Jack started to walk towards the staircase. The Paladin captain stepped aside and allowed him to pass, then she turned to Castilan and said, 'If we find any deception we will return.'

Castilan nodded and grabbed a bottle of wine from a dusty case. 'Here, take this with my compliments, one of our best. It's always a pleasure, indeed an honour, to be visited by the Paladin.'

Captain de Vienne looked down at the bottle with distain. 'Thank you, no. We do not . . . drink.'

Jack reached the top of the stairs and for a brief instant he hesitated, holding the door open a crack to hear the Paladin. Then, regaining his senses, he closed the door quietly and took the bottles to the bar. Betty looked up, surprised to see Jack emerge alone from the cellar.

'What's happening?' she asked.

Before Jack could answer, the cellar door opened again and the three Paladin walked out, helmets back in place. The hushed First World conversations ceased, all eyes watching as the trio left the tavern.

There was a stinging clip to the back of Jack's head. He turned round to see Castilan, red-faced, standing behind him. He grabbed Jack and pulled him close. 'A decent bat to the head: it's as good a way as any to stop you thinking too loudly when people are listening. Remember that, lad!'

Jack nodded quickly.

'Jacket!' Castilan demanded. Jack removed it and held it out to the landlord.

Castilan snatched it back. 'I don't know what you've done, but you've got a lot of very powerful people very angry. This game's too rich for me. It's not worth the risk any more. I want you out, and I don't want to see you back here again.'

Betty protested, 'He's not paid for his drinks yet!'

'He's leaving,' Castilan hissed. 'And you tell your friend Davey he's barred.'

He pushed Jack away and let go of his T-shirt. Jack turned towards the door, unsure where he was going.

'Thanks,' he said to Castilan.

'Get out. Run till you can't run any further. And don't look back.'

Jack nodded and walked to the door. His jaw tensed as he peered outside; there was no sign of the three Paladin. But the city was bigger, unfamiliar and terrifying now that he was alone again, and he shuddered as he ran into the confusing streets. He didn't know where to go or who to go to. He thought about heading back to the cemetery, back home, but something was keeping him here.

Not far ahead the tight alleyway took a blind turn to the left. As Jack passed it he felt a pair of hands drag him into a shop doorway. He fell to the floor, his shoulder bruised against the door. Standing over him was a wiry figure silhouetted by a gas lamp.

'Where the hell have you been?' asked Davey.

# 6

## BETRAYALS

Jack rubbed the sleep from his blurry eyes. He hadn't felt tired, but when Davey insisted they rest inside an abandoned warehouse his impatient frustration had quickly given way to a deep slumber. He woke at about six, he guessed, just as the dawn light was striking the Thames, its dirty waters lapping gently against the dockside.

The fires were under control, for the most part, but columns of dark smoke marked the spots where homes had become coffins. The sky was an ashen grey, but the most persistent of the bright stars lingered. Jack had never paid much attention to history, it had all seemed so long ago, so dull, so lifeless. Yet, here he was, somehow dropped in between the pages of the past. His heart beat faster as he watched the pillars of smoke. His teeth felt rough from the sooty air, and the side of his head ached where Castilan had thumped him to distract the Paladin. History was far from dull, he mused.

But the river was busy, even at this hour. The tide was

on the turn, and the line of boats broke the glass-like surface into soft crisscross patterns.

Jack was tired; he'd lost track of how long he'd been awake, his body clock in time-lag, yet still the unreal visage of the city amazed him. The skyline, so different to the one he knew, somehow quashed his remaining doubts. He was in the past, with his teenage grandfather.

Davey sat next to him eating a bacon sandwich he had snatched from an all-night café, seemingly unperturbed by the bizarre chain of events that had thrown the two boys together.

'Sure you don't want some?' He held up the last of the sandwich to Jack.

Jack shook his head with defiant spite. He didn't want any favours from Davey right now. His empty stomach rumbled.

'Suit yourself.' Davey took one large bite and the sandwich was gone.

'Why did you leave me back there?' Jack tried to sound casual, but his anger filtered through.

Davey smiled. 'You'll have to think on your feet if you're gonna make it here, Jack.'

'I don't want to make it here, it's not safe.' Jack thought of home, of his father. What must his father think had happened to him?

'Safe? Course it's not safe! That's why it's fun. Who wants a safe life? You've got to stop thinking like a Second

Worlder and live a little before the Paladin get you.' Davey shuddered. 'You'll be doing a lot less living then.'

Jack asked, 'What are the Paladin? Police?'

'Not exactly – more like a very elite private army.'

'For who?'

Davey threw the paper bag from his sandwich onto the ground. The cool breeze lifted it up and propelled it over the water. 'Rouland. They work for Rouland.'

'Who is he? Can he help?'

'Rouland is lots of things, none of 'em any good.'

'Like what?'

'He thinks he's some sort of scientist, but no one ever came out of his labs alive. All you need to know is that he's powerful and he has the Paladin in his pocket.'

'But why is he after me?'

'I don't know, mate. The sooner we get you to the Journeyman the better.'

'I should go home.'

'It's not safe there, is it? You like playing with Dustmen?'

'What are they?'

'Dead things,' Davey said cautiously. 'An echo is all, left behind by the living. An Operator, a good 'un, can play that echo and make it work for 'em. See?'

'No.' Jack sighed. There was too much to take in. 'Not really.'

Davey frowned. 'It's simple! They're hate and fear and anger, and that's all. There's nothing alive in there.

You can't talk to 'em, you can't beg for mercy. All you can do is run and hide and hope they don't kill you.'

'But I don't understand how—'

'Stop talking like a girl!' Davey interrupted. 'If you just listen to me you'll be fine. I'll look after you, won't I?'

'Look after me?' Jack scoffed. 'You just left me.'

'I took the heat away from you, that's all. If we'd both been in the Hanging Tavern when the Paladin turned up we'd be as good as goners, wouldn't we?'

Jack hesitated, and then nodded doubtfully.

'All right then,' Davey said. His smile couldn't disguise the irritation in his voice.

Jack closed his eyes, trying to make sense of this new world of Paladin and Dustmen and Journeymen and Operators. He had so many questions, so many doubts. Suddenly his life before today seemed grey and mundane, full of petty arguments over unimportant things. He yearned to return to that safer, insignificant existence.

But Jack was different, and he knew it. He didn't know how, but he felt apart from the other kids on the estate. Even his few friends at school seemed to be at arm's length, little more than passing acquaintances. He lacked the tight pack of friends that should be sharing his life, the sort of friends that would endure for decades to come. There was definitely something different about Jack, something abnormal, something alien.

'When can we go to this Journeyman?'

Davey walked over the coarse pebbles to the edge of the lapping water. 'In a minute. I need to pee first.'

Jack scanned the skyline once more; he couldn't get over how it was all so very different from the London he knew. St Paul's was still where it should be, and he could see the tower of Big Ben further down the river, but much of the rest was different. The Gherkin, the Shard, Canary Wharf and the gleaming towers of Docklands had gone. The city looked humble, low and wide.

'I learned about this time, about the war,' Jack said.

Davey looked round, interested. 'War? You know about the war?'

'Yeah. We get taught it in school.'

Davey looked unconvinced and turned back to the river. 'What war are we talking about?'

'World War Two. You know, Germany and Hitler, and all that stuff.'

'Not my war, mate.' Davey casually buttoned up his trousers, tucked in his grubby shirt and brushed some crumbs off his long coat. 'I got my own worries.'

'What could matter more that this?' Jack gestured to the smoking wounds of London.

'Rouland.' Davey turned his back to the river and walked towards the grey streets. Jack watched his grandfather-to-be, and then he ran to catch up with him.

\* \* \*

Billingsgate Fish Market was full of noise and chaos even at this hour. The smells of thousands of different fish mixed together and bled out into the nearby streets. Jack had never seen such a vibrant, lively place, even in 2013. Market traders from a dozen different stalls raised themselves up on stools and tables, shouting their prices over the bustling crowd. The noise was deafening. Below them buyers made notes, shouted back counter-offers, sometimes agreeing and striking a deal, sometimes moving on to another stall. The raw language was almost as striking and rich as the smells that infected Jack's sinuses. He laughed to hear it used so liberally and without malice.

They walked through the crowds of chefs and restaurant managers. Here and there were well-dressed men, the heads of the large family houses keen to find the best catch for their master's supper.

One fishmonger, a heavy man with a smouldering cigarette hanging from his lips, threw a giant salmon straight over Jack's head. A young boy, no older than Jack, caught the flying fish nimbly and wrapped it up for a customer.

'Where are we going?' Jack shouted above the noise.

'Not far now,' Davey answered. He led Jack towards a secluded blue door, away from the hustle and bustle, knocked on the wood and waited.

After almost a minute had passed Jack said, 'Try again.

They might not have heard.'

'Patience,' Davey said. 'They heard.'

Another minute went by before Jack noted the heavy clunk of a key, and the door opened. A rush of air whistled past him and then a figure appeared out of the dark doorway. He was a tall, thin man, dressed in a white shirt with a high collar buttoned up tightly to his chin. His hair was long, well-groomed and greying at the temples. Jack's eyes trailed up to the man's face, and the air left his lungs in an automatic scream.

The man had only one eye. A dark void marked where his right eye should be. His left eye seemed oversized, a massive rotating white dome that looked like it might fall from his head at any moment. The milky pupil stopped its nervous searching and locked onto Jack. The man grunted, his hairy nostrils flaring open like a horse's and Jack recoiled from him, bumping into Davey.

'Calm down!' Davey whispered into Jack's ear. 'You'll make him angry.'

The man smiled, revealing a row of razor-like teeth. Uneven grooves pitted their yellow enamel, as if they had been filed down with a sharp tool. Wordlessly he waved his taloned fingers, beckoning them inside.

Davey hit Jack in the chest. 'Relax, all right? It's just Harodon. He won't bite.' Davey nodded casually to the man. 'All right, Harodon? Busy today?'

Harodon grunted noncommittally.

'Well, can't stand 'round here gassing all day, big man.' Davey sighed. 'Places to be, people to eat.'

Harodon grinned at this last remark, flashing his shark-like teeth, then turned to lead them through the door. Davey pushed Jack forward, into a damp corridor filled with sinister orange shadows.

Ahead, Harodon stopped at the door to a service lift, opened the squeaking metal gate and beckoned them inside. He held out his open hand to Jack.

'What does he want?' Jack asked Davey.

'Pay him.'

'With what?'

The long spidery fingers flicked impatiently at Jack, and his giant eye flitted downwards.

'I'm sorry,' Jack said nervously. 'I don't have any money.' He stared into the empty socket, horrified and fascinated.

Harodon pointed to Jack's feet and grunted again.

'Give him your shoes,' Davey said.

Jack looked down at his white twenty-first-century trainers. 'But my dad got me these.' He remembered the numb helplessness he'd felt when Blaydon had taken his phone – that felt so long ago now.

'Give him them!'

The strange figure grunted aggressively, his teeth seeming to grow as his mouth widened. Reluctantly Jack unlaced his trainers and handed them, his hands

61

trembling, to Harodon. He took them eagerly, letting his fingers caress the rubber soles. Then he was gone, leaving Jack and Davey to close the lift door. The carriage juddered upwards.

'My feet are cold,' Jack said.

'*Shhhh*,' Davey replied.

The lift lurched to an abrupt stop. Davey steadied himself quickly and pulled open the metal door. In front of them was another single door. Davey knocked and entered.

They stepped into a compact office full of an astonishing array of antiques and collectables. A large three-piece suite, reclaimed and restored, sat along two walls. Butted up next to it was a grand oak table, its six high-backed chairs stacked on top in a fragile pyramid that seemed to sway menacingly in Jack's direction. A large chandelier dominated the near corner, its shards of light reminding him of a tacky Santa's Grotto. Everywhere, massive framed paintings leaned in rows, like giant dominoes waiting to be toppled, making Jack feel confined and uneasy.

At the heart of the hoard sat a young man who read from a newspaper spread out in front of him on an artist's easel. The man must not yet be thirty, but his dark, scarred face hinted at a violent past. He wore an open shirt, the sleeves rolled up, with a brown waistcoat. The man looked at Davey, his face fixed and unreadable. Suddenly he held a large gun in his hand – Jack hadn't seen him draw it. He pointed it at Davey.

'You better have the money with you, Davey-boy.' His voice was clipped and well spoken, with only the slightest hint of his Caribbean origins audible.

Davey put up his hands. 'Steady, Titus, I've brought you better than that.'

'You can't be trusted.' Titus's eyes flitted to the stranger in his office. 'Who's this?'

'This is Jack. He's got the gift: he's a Yard Boy.'

Titus laughed. 'You always say that. You told me *you* had the gift. You took my money and accepted a job you couldn't deliver. If you have any gift at all it's the power of persuasion. I must be losing my marbles to fall for your prattle. Why I entrusted you with such an important job I'll never know.'

Jack's hopes sank. Everywhere he turned he seemed to end up in the mess of Davey's odd life. He felt the urge to leave, but his fear and uncertainty kept him in place.

Titus smiled a bloodless smile. His finger tightened on the trigger.

'Titus,' Davey pleaded. 'Jack's a Yard Boy, I'm sure of it. My finder's fee'll settle our score.'

'I have Yard Boys, Davey.'

'But not many. You know how rare they are.' Davey suddenly smiled, seemingly oblivious to the gun pointed at him. 'But if you don't want him then maybe we should go to one of your competitors instead. I'm sure Will Aitken would have Jack here in a heartbeat. Always admired old Aitken: top Journeyman.'

Titus brooded, his eyes narrowing. 'I'd kill you both first.'

'Yeah, he's been creeping onto your patch, old Aitken has, ain't he? But you don't want a turf war, do you? What you want is new blood, like Jack here. And this one's different, Titus. He's from *upstream*. From the future. More'n seventy years, by my reckoning.'

'Impossible!' Titus scoffed, but Jack was relieved to see that the nose of the gun dropped slightly. 'No one can go that far.'

'I tell you, he can.'

Titus considered this for a moment, then he placed the gun carefully onto the easel in front of him.

'He can travel forward?'

'That's what I reckon, yeah.'

Titus rubbed his chin, a thin calculating smile growing on his lips.

Jack tried to take in what they were saying. He'd never thought he was special, but Davey seemed to think he was. Special enough to trade. He stared at Davey in disbelief. 'You've sold me?' he whispered, aghast.

Davey shrugged a feeble apology and turned away.

'You, boy,' Titus said loudly. 'Do you know who I am?'

'The Journeyman?' Jack's voice was quiet and feeble.

'Do you know what that means?'

'No.'

'It means that if you really do have the gift, if you really are a Yard Boy, then you work for me. All Yard Boys work for a Journeyman.'

'What...what do Yard Boys do?' Jack enquired hesitantly.

'Yard Boys retrieve things: lost objects, rare artefacts, but information is the most precious commodity they trade in. You would be amazed what someone will pay for information lost to time. All jobs go through me, then I give them out to my boys, depending on their individual skills. I make the deals, collect the money, make sure everything is tiptop. My boys are well-fed, looked-after, healthy.'

'I don't want money. I want to go home, and I want those monsters to go away.'

Titus was instantly suspicious. His finger tracing the contours of the gun in front of him. 'Monsters?'

Davey stepped in, his eyes darting between Titus and Jack. 'Bad dreams is all, Titus, nothing more. Hazard of the job.'

Jack's burning anger rose up from deep within him. He pushed Davey away with an unexpected strength. Davey stared, wide-eyed, and stepped back from Jack.

'It was Dustmen,' Jack announced to the Journeyman.

Titus shivered involuntarily at the mention of those creatures.

'Dustmen,' Jack continued. 'Four of them. They

attacked me in 2008.' Jack hesitated, uncertain if he should reveal Old David's role in all of this. 'They tried to kill me. I ran through a Sorrowline to here.'

'See, he's from upstream,' Davey said nervously.

Titus, his eyes wide with fascination, stepped out from behind his treasures. 'So he claims. If you are what you say you are . . .'

'He is,' Davey said.

Titus ignored Davey. 'But none of my Yard Boys come from more than a year or two upstream, Jack. Your claim is almost too huge to be taken seriously. And yet, you have an honest face. I think I would know if you were lying to me. You have an air of truth about you, certainly more than your friend here.'

'He's not my friend,' Jack said, glaring at Davey, wondering as he did whether Titus could read his mind as Castilan had.

'Oh, this is most excellent.' Titus rubbed his hands together, his large teeth exposed. 'Two young friends, one betraying the other. I thought today might be dull, but not a bit of it. And if you really are being hunted by Dustmen they must want something. Something you've found, perhaps?'

'I've taken nothing,' Jack said.

'No, not yet at least. But then our line of work has a habit of being somewhat non-linear. Effect precedes cause, if you take my meaning. You obviously have done,

66

or will do, something that has piqued the interest of some powerful people.'

'He mentioned a rose,' Davey blurted out desperately.

Jack scowled at Davey.

'A rose, you say?' The Journeyman's eyes widened. There was a long silence while Titus digested this. 'Wait here.' Titus pushed past Davey and left the room. The subtle click of a key locking sent a shiver up Jack's spine.

'This ain't good,' Davey mumbled to himself.

'You sold me out!' Jack snapped.

'I had no choice!'

'You don't grass on your friends.'

'Grow up, Jack! This ain't school. This is real life.' Davey pulled at the locked door. 'And I think Titus has just sold us *both* out.'

# 7

## FAMILY PORTRAIT

Davey climbed over the stacks of antiques, their value reduced with each misplaced foot.

'What are you doing?' Jack said.

'Looking for another way out.'

'There's only one way out of here, and you managed to get it locked.'

'At least I'm doing something!' Davey let a row of framed pictures clatter back to the wall, then he paced back and forth like a trapped animal, a mirror of his older self.

Jack watched him with a palpable disgust. 'How could you just trade me like that?'

'Stop whining like a baby.' Davey pulled on the door handle for the sixth time. 'You saw how the Journeyman reacted when I mentioned the rose. He's off to sell us out.'

'Just like you did!' Jack said grimly. 'And he knows what it is, doesn't he? He knows what this rose thing is.'

'Yeah, I think maybe he does.'

'But we don't!' Jack shouted. 'Even though it was you

in the future that told me about it!'

'I'm not that old man!' Davey retorted.

'No, you're not. At least he tried to help. I trusted you,
Davey!'

'Well, more fool you!' Davey growled. 'It's just business,
that's all. I owed Titus money, and he would have killed
me if I didn't pay him back. Then you turn up, sticking out
like a sore thumb, with your tale of the future, and I see my
chance to make a few bob. Who would blame me? No one
ever did me no favours, no one's gonna look after me, are
they? So I have to look after meself. And don't pretend like
you care for me, either. You're no different to everyone
else. If the tables were turned you'd do the same. Don't
fool yourself that you care.' Davey pulled out his pipe and
chewed on the end.

'I *do* care!' Jack said.

'Yeah?' Davey said accusingly. 'Why would you care
about me?'

Jack's hand swiped at Davey's pipe, knocking it from
his mouth. 'Because family means something to me.
Because I'm your grandson, and you're my grandfather,
you idiot!'

Davey, for once, seemed speechless.

'You're the only person here I should be able to trust,'
Jack continued, his voice trembling with anger. Davey's
betrayal had brought his fears to the surface. His father –
lost to him somewhere in the future – was leaving him.

His mother had done the same. Now he had foolishly latched onto Davey, and he had paid the price for his naive trust in a stranger. He felt used. His fists landed on Davey's chest, hammering out a defeated rhythm. 'You're the *one person* who's supposed to be on my side. But you're not. You've sold me out to save your own skin. So much for family.'

'I...I didn't know.' Davey's eyes were like a dam holding back a lifetime's pain. Jack saw the front, the cockiness, the bravado fall away to reveal the scared, lonely boy underneath. 'I didn't know,' Davey repeated.

'Don't you have any family, Davey?' Jack probed cautiously.

Davey hesitated. 'I...no, not no more.'

He was about to say more when the lock clicked and the door opened. Titus stepped into the room.

'Gentlemen,' Titus said, his charm almost concealing an undercurrent of apprehension. 'I think a deal can be done.'

'What kind of deal?' Davey asked.

'I have called on an associate; he will be here very shortly. He will be able to help the Yard Boy here, and your debt will be settled.'

'In return for?'

'Information, nothing more. He wishes to know about the Rose.'

'Who is it?'

70

'He will be here soon enough. He will introduce himself to you then.'

'Rouland,' Davey said bitterly. Jack trembled at the mention of that name again. He found himself close to the Journeyman's easel, with its newspaper spread out over it. That's when he saw the gun. Without thinking he grabbed it and tossed it in the air towards Davey. At the same time he called out to him. Davey turned round and, in one fluid movement, caught the gun in his hand, cocked it and pointed it at the Journeyman's head.

'I think we're leaving now,' Davey said, his signature smile returned triumphantly.

Titus smiled back. 'It's not loaded.'

Davey considered the weapon. 'I didn't plan on firing it.'

A confused expression flashed over the Journeyman's face as Davey pushed him backwards. Titus fell onto a vast canvas, ripping through its painted surface and becoming wedged inside the frame. Davey pulled the Journeyman's handkerchief from his pocket and stuffed it into his protesting mouth.

'A pleasure doing business with you,' Davey said. He pulled open the door and looked at Jack. 'Come on!'

Jack stood his ground. 'First I want your shoes.'

'What?'

Jack pointed to his shoeless feet.

'We don't have time for this,' Davey said, nodding at

Titus, wriggling to be free from the frame.

'So get on with it.' Jack laughed angrily.

Davey pulled off his shoes, muttering to himself, and threw them at Jack. 'There, happy now?'

Jack quickly pulled on Davey's shoes. They were too big for him, but it didn't matter – Jack had had his victory.

Outside, the grey ashen sky alluded to the early morning sun, its autumn light still hidden behind the broken buildings.

Jack and Davey ran through the rubble-strewn streets, away from the noise of Billingsgate Market, away from the Journeyman.

'Can we slow down?' Jack asked breathlessly.

'No,' Davey said.

'What now? Where are we going?'

Davey didn't reply. His lack of shoes didn't seem to hinder him, and Jack struggled to keep up as Davey bounded over fallen roof slates, bricks and timber.

They approached Monument tube station. Davey leaped down the steps, into the dusty ticket hall with its rich smells of new wood mixed with pipe tobacco. This looked like no tube station Jack was used to. There were no automated barriers that would open at the swipe of a travel card. Instead, a row of ticket machines and a weary ticket inspector were all that lay between them and the platform. Wartime posters blurred past Jack's peripheral vision: 'WHAT TO DO IN AIR RAIDS', 'DESIGNATED SHELTER THIS WAY', 'IS YOUR JOURNEY REALLY NECESSARY?'. The two boys dodged the inspector, who feigned momentary annoyance, and they ran down towards the platforms. Jack's chest ached, red needles pricked at his lungs, but somehow he kept at Davey's heels.

They ran down one of the wooden escalators, pushing past fatigued workers, ignoring their indignant shouts. At the bottom, with the platform ahead of them, Davey finally slowed to a brisk walking pace.

The narrow platform was full of people. Some were commuting to work: cleaners, labourers, shop owners, all trying to hold onto some sense of routine. Others looked to have been here all night, sheltering from the bombs falling outside. Families huddled together for comfort, some with small children. A young courting couple flirted and laughed, to the annoyance of those around them. Here and there were old men, solitary and red-faced with whisky on their breath. Jack followed Davey as they passed the disorganised crowd.

'What are those?' Jack asked, pointing to the small boxes that most of the passengers carried over their shoulders.

'Gas masks. For when the bombs come. This is the seventh night in a row,' Davey said, his face severe.

'The Germans?'

Davey nodded and pulled out a packet of cigarettes.

He offered it to Jack.

'No thanks,' Jack said.

'It's like everyone's gone mad. They're all rushing to sign up. I'm rushing the other way.' Davey lit the cigarette, his hand trembling slightly, and threw the spent match away. He took a long, deep drag and blew out thick grey smoke as he crouched down against the wall.

'Why are we down in the tube?' Jack said, hunkering down beside him.

'Needed to get away from the Journeyman. Need time to think.' Davey's voice dropped to a barely audible whisper, his eyes darting in every direction. 'I'm sure the Journeyman sent a message to Rouland, about you and that rose. So, the Paladin, they'll be—'

'The Paladin will be looking for us.' Jack remembered the piercing eyes of the captain in Castilan's cellar and shuddered.

Davey nodded grimly. He finished his cigarette and flicked it onto the tracks; its red glow shone out defiantly, then faded into the darkness.

Jack whispered, 'But they can't find us down here, can they?'

'Not if we got away quickly enough, but if they saw us, if they followed us . . .'

Somewhere an old man coughed violently, his wet rasping echoing along the curved tiled walls. Davey squinted to see the sound's origin and movement caught his eye; at the end of the platform were three cloaked figures. They advanced towards them with a menacing grace, past the perplexed masses. A young girl spotted them and cried out in fright, pulling at her father's hand. The father, oblivious to the approaching danger, hushed her protests. But Jack and Davey could see them coming.

'Come on, we're leaving.' Davey pulled Jack up by the arm – his grip uncomfortably tight – and retreated further along the platform. The sheltering masses tutted and complained as they passed – some even blocked their way – but nothing would slow Davey's progress until he abruptly ran out of platform. He released Jack's arm and jumped onto the track.

Jack hesitated.

'This way!' Davey shouted. 'Now.'

Voices rose on the platform as people began to wonder at the commotion. Someone bellowed after them and a policeman's whistle blew. Jack looked back, just in time to see the three figures erupt from their dark robes. Their ancient armour shimmered in the dim light of the tube and the smooth profile of their helmets was unmistakable: the Paladin had found them.

Jack jumped down onto the tracks. Above him he heard the gasps and cries form into a chorus of shouting voices calling out to them.

'Stupid boys!'

'Where are you going?'

'Get yerselves bloody well killed.'

'Serve 'em right!'

Jack left the voices behind and followed Davey as he disappeared into the dreary blackness of the tube tunnel. Like deathly crows on the wing the Paladin launched themselves onto the tracks after them.

Jack gasped, a primal fear clawing at his insides. His foot caught on one of the sleepers and he tumbled headfirst into the dirt. Davey stopped, his eyes darting from Jack to the approaching menace. He took a tentative step away from him, along the tunnel. Then, to Jack's surprise, Davey ran back and pulled him to his feet.

Jack ran headlong into the darkness. Ahead of him was the indistinct shape of Davey, guiding him onwards at a reckless pace. Behind him he heard the clatter of the Paladin, closing the gap, and in spite of his fear he glanced over his shoulder. The Paladin were almost upon them! He cried out and stumbled into Davey again, this time dragging them both to the ground.

The Paladin captain – Jack recognised her the moment her helmet folded open – drew her sword and spun it around her body. The other two followed her lead and struck menacing poses, their swords poised.

'What do we do?' Jack screamed at Davey.

Davey's face was a mask of indecisive terror. There was no way out. Davey had failed him and Jack was alone again: he could rely on no one but himself. At that same

76

moment he saw a dull white light growing over the brickwork behind the Paladin.

He stood to face them, his trembling fists clenched. He opened his mouth to shout, but his voice sounded weak and hesitant. 'I'm . . . I'm not afraid of you!'

Captain de Vienne paused for an instant, recognition tumbling over her features. 'You!' she cried. 'The boy from the tavern!'

There was a rumble like summer thunder. Almost without thinking, Jack grabbed Davey and pulled him away from the tracks. They smashed into the bricks of the tunnel wall, tucking their bodies into a shallow recess as Captain de Vienne turned to see what the great noise was coming upon them. At the same moment the white light filled the tunnel and a tube train appeared from round the bend and struck the Paladin with all its force, dragging their broken bodies under its wheels and along the tracks. The train screeched, sparks cascading from its wheels as it tried to stop. The front carriage lifted up and unbuckled from the rails. Jack heard the screams from inside as it tipped over onto its side. The train slowed, metal grinding into metal, and then stopped in a cloud of smoke.

Three twisted bodies lay on the tracks, still, silent. Jack felt sick at what he saw.

Suddenly a fractured arm rose up into the air. With a sickening click the arm righted itself, its fingers twitching.

77

'One of them is alive,' Jack gasped, watching with morbid fascination.

'No,' Davey said, finally finding his voice. 'They're all dead. They've been dead for a very long time. Come on.'

The two boys ran back through the tunnel, towards the station. People swelled along the platform, attracted by the commotion. Jack and Davey ran on, past the shouting men, past crying children and frightened women, up the escalator to the surface.

They were too far away to hear the rattle of armour as the Paladin recovered, one twisted bone at a time.

# 8

## THE WELL OF ANTEROS

Jack hated running. Sprinting at school was fine, and his height made him a natural at hurdles. But distance running was not his thing. It made his chest wheeze. Bile and saliva filled his throat. His legs trembled and threatened to give way under him. Running and Jack just did not mix, so the half hour spent following Davey in and out of alleyways and lanes was particularly painful. But he dared not stop.

From time to time the river appeared at their left as a fragmented vision between buildings, but Jack was too uncomfortable to take everything in. The night's air raids were over hours ago, yet an air of panic still prevailed over London; the claxons and sirens of fire engines, ambulances and military vehicles wailed over the rooftops.

Abruptly the alleyway joined a wider concourse. Jack recognised it instantly, even with its numerous illuminated billboards switched off.

'Piccadilly Circus,' he said to himself.

Most of the buildings were as he knew them, but the

famous fountain and its statue of Eros stood in the centre of a great roundabout. The Saturday morning traffic trundled by continuously, as if on some vast conveyor, and the war-weary population mostly went about their business in an insular haze, though some passers-by did stare quizzically at Jack's unusual clothing, making him want to change into something more appropriate to his surroundings.

Davey and Jack navigated through the traffic, ignoring the honking horns, to the centre of the roundabout and the fountain. Jack immediately scooped handfuls of the cold water to soothe his rasping throat.

'What are we doing here?' he asked, not expecting an answer.

'The Paladin are coming for us, right? We need to get out of sight.' Davey walked around the fountain, inspecting the structure.

'What are the Paladin? How could they survive that crash?' Jack said.

'There are twelve of them. They're dead knights, some call 'em OnceDead, hundreds of years old, brought back to life by... by Rouland. They work for him. You can't stop 'em, you can't kill 'em, and if they find us we're as good as dead. So, we need to go even deeper,' Davey said, nodding to the fountain.

'Deeper? But we've just come up from the tube.'

'And the Paladin found us. So we're going deeper. We're leaving the Second World behind. We're going into the First World. Hopefully we shouldn't be so easy to track amongst other First Worlders.'

Jack looked doubtfully at Davey. 'Hopefully?'

Davey shrugged. 'Best I can do right now.' He pulled a coin from his pocket. It flashed in the morning sun, its golden surface embossed with an image of a winged lion. He threw it into the air. It tumbled into the water with a small splash.

'Right, in we go,' Davey said as he stepped onto the fountain's edge. The water seemed to shimmer, and an ethereal glow lapped over its surface. Davey jumped into the fountain, fell into its shallow water – and disappeared completely!

Dumbfounded, Jack looked about, expecting the unusual sight to attract the attention of the usually oblivious commuters. He wondered how so many impossible things could go unnoticed. He climbed onto the edge and peered into the water. He could see the bottom of the fountain clearly. The water was no deeper than half a metre, yet there was no sign of Davey. Had he abandoned him again? Jack asked himself.

He looked about him at the city, at the cars carrying on in their arcs around the fountain; he was anonymous and ignored at the heart of the capital.

The urge to return home had been buried by the wonder of the past, by the terror of being pursued. His mind was a fog of doubts, yet an idea had been growing somewhere deep down, an idea so toxic and enticing he hardly dared think it. If he could travel through Sorrowlines, if he really could live in the past then maybe, just maybe, he could go back to 2008, to a time when his mother was still alive. Maybe, he thought, I could see my mother again. He shook his head. The idea troubled him as much as it excited him. And yet, he surmised, by following Davey, by trusting in his distrustful grandfather, by riding on this dangerous wave of adventure, he might just fulfil this forbidden hope.

He put the notion out of his mind and looked back to the shimmering water, then he stood on the fountain's edge, took a deep breath and plunged into the chilly water. Almost immediately his feet hit a hard floor and he rolled over in sawdust. He was in a low circular room; carved pillars around its perimeter supported a beautiful stone ceiling and above him was a large opening that matched the size of the fountain. A wide column of carved stone and metal extended down in the centre of the opening, supporting the statue above it. It cut through the plane of water, which hung like an inverted pond impossibly above his head. He stood up and put his outstretched hand to it, sending ripples over its cold surface.

'Water,' said Davey. 'It's just water.'

Jack turned to see Davey behind him, the dawn light spreading over him in a dancing dappled pattern. He looked down at his clothes in wonder. 'But we're not wet.'

Davey grinned. 'Clever, ain't it?'

'Where are we?'

'This is the Well of Anteros,' Davey said enthusiastically. 'It's a junction. A hidden doorway. The water is a barrier; if you have the right key it lets you through.'

'The coin?'

'Was the key, yes. It's First-World currency.'

'Is this magic?'

'Science. I don't know how it works.' Davey shrugged. 'But someone did once. They built this as a way between the First and Second Worlds. There are dozens of junction chambers all over London. A lot of them are closed off now, more every year.'

'Are we still in London?' Jack wondered if there were places like this in his 2013 city.

Davey shook his head. 'We're under it. About six miles under it, from what I can remember. We're close to Ealdwyc, the First-World capital.'

'Can we be followed?'

'The door'll close soon, but we can still be tracked by the Paladin. So we need to go deeper.'

A drop hit Jack's forehead. He looked up to see the water fizz and boil for a second before it disappeared completely, revealing a solid expanse of carved stone.

'There,' Davey said. 'Closed. Now, let's go!'

Jack nodded half-heartedly and followed Davey out of the junction chamber and into a long arched tunnel.

Recessed lanterns puffed into life as they approached, lighting the ancient corridor, then extinguishing automatically behind them as they passed. The gaslight picked out alcoves in the corridor. In them sat rows of human skulls piled one on top of another. Jack felt his stomach turn over. 'Davey, where are we?'

'Catacombs. This is where the First World's dead are brought. Been down here for centuries.'

Each skull had an inscription on its cranium: a name and dates. Some had ornate floral patterns painted on the bone; others were painted entirely red. The red ones were smaller and Jack supposed these must have belonged to children. One or two adult-sized skulls were cobalt-blue.

'What's with the blue ones?' he asked lazily.

'Bad people, criminals, that sort of thing. If Rouland was dead they'd use a bucket of blue paint on his skull.'

'Tell me about Rouland,' Jack said at last. 'Everything.'

Davey sighed heavily, like a parent preparing to deliver bad news. 'He's ancient, hundreds of years old, so they say. He's Chief Scientist and Prime Ealdorman of the High Assembly, or he was. Rumour has it he's gotten rid of the High Assembly completely, leaving him in charge. I don't take too much notice of politics, but I know things are getting worse.'

'Worse? How?'

'I dunno. It's like people have given up. I don't think

about it too much, but it's getting harder to move around without the right permits, without bribing people or keeping as low a profile as you can. Rouland is letting the First World fall apart, and he don't seem to care.'

Jack shivered. His mind throbbed from trying to make sense of what had happened to him as they carried on, past row after row of skulls. The deeper they went the more broken and decayed the skulls became until only powder filled the alcoves. And on they went, deeper and deeper. The air became dense and hot, and he found it hard to breathe properly. It tasted dusty and stale on his tongue, and left a metallic tang in the back of his throat.

'I need to rest,' he said.

'It's not far now. We're nearly there.'

*Nearly where?* Jack looked ahead, and he could see a bright light at the end of the tunnel where it opened up into another chamber. He picked up his tired feet and forced them along the length of the corridor, stepping finally into a circular space from where he could count a dozen other tunnels leading away into darkness. Above, the walls stretched up out of sight, the ceiling hidden in the grip of a grey mist. The decoration in the chamber was finer and more elaborate than it had been in the long tunnel, and several large metal caskets sat in alcoves around the sides. Twelve columns ran upwards. On each stood a statue of a knight in armour, like a frozen guard of honour.

Davey studied the numerous exits. 'This way,' he said, picking one of the tunnels. 'If we get as far as Newton Harbour we should be safe. I know a captain who might help us.'

As they approached the exit a heavy slab of stone dropped into place, blocking the tunnel completely. Jack glanced nervously at Davey. Without hesitation Davey tried for another tunnel, and another stone slab blocked their path. Behind them Jack heard the grind of stones dropping over the other tunnels, falling in a chorus of despair, until only one tunnel remained open. Jack stared down its length, his heart pounding with terror, and heard the distant pad of feet coming towards them.

'Not good,' Davey said under his breath. 'Not good at all.'

Jack froze. The slow footsteps grew louder, echoing up into the high chamber. The dim shadows inside the tunnel grew more distinct until Jack could see a tall man approaching them. He was in his early forties, athletic, strong and sculpted like a statue, with a thick head of silver-white hair. A stunning suit of black armour moulded itself to the contours of his bronzed skin, its surface made of jet with ribbons of gold, silver and lead that circled around it in dazzlingly intricate patterns. A long red cloak fell from his shoulders, trailing behind him on the floor. Under it a sword hung at his waist; its design aligned itself to the weapons of the OnceDead Paladin. Behind him, almost hidden in the darkness, unnoticed in the wake of the armoured man, was a slender creature draped in a mass of cloth and feathers, dirty smoke spewing from the void of its hooded face.

The man approached, his hawk-like eyes glistening and sparkling like infinite pools of oil. He looked directly at Jack, making him feel naked, as if this stranger had just peered into his very soul. He shivered, transfixed as the visitor crossed the chamber like a suited god. He ignored Davey, his terrible focus completely on Jack.

'Who...who are you?' Jack asked, his voice barely a whisper.

The man smiled.

'Ah, but you already know my name,' said Rouland.

# 9

## THE CARLTON CONVERSATIONS

Jack awoke with a start.

He was on a large circular bed. Exquisite silk sheets were stretched perfectly over the mattress and a mountain of pillows caressed his aching head. His twenty-first-century clothes had gone, replaced with clean trousers, braces and a crisp white shirt. Last summer his father had insisted he dress up for a family wedding and he had felt hot and uncomfortable all day. His trousers had itched and he had been glad when he had finally been able to dump the clothes in a pile on his bedroom floor. But these were somehow different; these clothes felt good.

He sat up slowly, wondering if he was still in 1940. He was alone, and he yearned for the reassuring, annoying presence of Davey at his side. No longer underground, he was in a stately room full of opulence and grandeur. The expansive bed dominated the chamber, but it was a large enough space to also accommodate a giant wooden wardrobe and a matching dressing table without feeling in the least bit cramped. A vivid-red sofa rested along one wall and a beautiful antique lamp nestled in a corner. To the left of the bed was a door. To the right, behind translucent curtains that swayed in a cool breeze, was a pair of French doors, which led to a large balcony. The morning sun bled through the open doors, fracturing and reflecting off the grand surroundings until everything appeared to glow. For a moment Jack thought he might be dead.

He lowered his feet over the side of the bed and felt smooth fibrous fur between his toes. He looked down and saw the skin of a tiger, its mighty head and paws still attached. Next to the beast was a pair of socks and shoes, which fitted him perfectly. Jack stood up, a little unsteadily at first, and tried the door. It was locked.

As he began to walk towards the balcony he wondered how he had arrived here. He recalled standing in the chamber deep under the streets of London. He remembered the tunnels closing off their escape. And then he remembered Rouland standing inches from his face, serene and god-like.

The next part was harder to recall. He thought Rouland had touched him, or perhaps it was something on his breath. The trigger didn't matter; whatever had happened had pushed Jack into a sleep like no other.

He stepped out into a fresh September morning. He was overlooking London, the green splendour of Hyde Park and the Serpentine winding lazily through autumnal trees. The city was scarred and fragile after the previous night's air raid. The skeletons of burnt-out buildings clawed at the sky, throwing up trails of ash and smoke, oddly beautified by the glorious sun.

The rich chimes of Big Ben echoed over the park. He counted eleven. He had slept for longer than he thought. In spite of the strangeness of his surroundings, of the events of last night and the gap in his memories, he felt no panic whatsoever, only awe and wonder. As he took in the wide panoramic view the magnitude of it all came into sharp focus. The past was not a dead thing to him any more, a frozen event hidden behind the tedium of a school textbook. It was vivid, living, full of colour and sound. He felt at home here, amongst the smoke and the ruins, like a falling star that had buried itself deep into some unmapped corner of the world. The memory of his home on the estate, of school – even of his father – seemed fleeting now. His life in the present was fading into his past. And yet he felt no fear, no remorse at its passing. He wondered why.

He saw three aeroplanes flying low over the city, Spitfires heading back to base, their propellers screaming a song of defiance. They flew so close, so low, that he saw the pilots inside their cockpits. Jack laughed involuntarily. His eyes followed the Spitfires as they arced past and, with a start, he saw that he was not alone on the balcony.

Rouland sat in a reclining chair with a book on his lap. His armour was gone; instead he wore a tailored suit and a long overcoat.

'A stunning sight, is it not?' he said, without looking up. Jack watched his hand lift a large hourglass sitting beside him. Rouland turned it over, watching the white sand fall from one glass bulb to the other. A narrow, satisfied smile dragged itself over his face as his terrifying eyes locked onto Jack. 'How are you feeling? It's Jack, isn't it? Your friend asked after you.'

'Where's Davey?' Jack demanded.

'Davey is nearby and quite safe.'

Jack tensed. 'Where are we?'

'Why, the Carlton Hotel, of course,' Rouland said. 'The Second World has few things worthwhile, but this is one of them. Luxury should be embraced whenever possible. Do you not agree?'

Jack said nothing.

'I am sorry that this suite is somewhat . . . humble,' Rouland continued. 'An unexploded bomb landed close by last night. We are fortunate that it did not detonate, but it still caused considerable structural damage, and my master suite is being cleaned.' Rouland gestured over the balcony. Below in the street Jack saw a wide crater where the bomb had landed. Fire crews had erected a perimeter fence, around which passers-by gazed at the unexploded device.

A butler appeared on the balcony pushing a silver trolley laden with bacon, eggs, sausages, cheese, bread, pastries and two large steaming pots: one of tea, the other coffee. The butler set a small table with cups and plates.

'Thank you, Graham,' Rouland said. The butler bowed and left. Rouland smiled and poured tea into a china cup, which he offered to Jack, then he poured a coffee for himself and sat down at the table.

'Please, sit, and I will answer any question you wish to ask of me.' His hand stroked the glass of the timer as the sand fell relentlessly.

Jack looked at the plates of hot food and felt his stomach yearning.

Rouland smiled. 'Don't worry. I've not gone to all this trouble just to poison you. After all, there are a dozen ways I could have killed you while you slept.'

Jack wondered if this was meant to reassure him. He hesitated for a moment, then pulled up a chair and helped himself to several sausages, which he ate with a ferocious appetite.

'That's better.' Rouland laughed. 'First, my name is Rouland Delamare. I am a gentleman of the First World. You have had quite an adventure, Jack. My Paladin have not had such exercise in some time.'

Jack gazed up from his plate. 'Why are you chasing me? I've done nothing.'

'No, that is true,' Rouland mused, 'but your arrival here is not without its portents. And I believe you mentioned something about a rose?' Rouland's manner was genial and relaxed, but Jack felt a shiver of terror crawl up his spine.

'I don't know what you mean,' Jack replied evasively.

Rouland smiled, his mouth narrowed to a thin line of irritation. 'Come now, Jack. You spoke of the Rose to Titus, the Journeyman. I would rather this conversation was civilised, and I think you would too.'

Jack put down his half-eaten food. His feet twitched under his seat.

'Very well,' Rouland said at last, 'we shall do this your way. I seek the Rose of Annwn. It is not a mere flower, as you know it, something that grows in the earth. This is an element of pure energy, a primal object older than the stars. It is a living thing that can commune with a man, become one with him and reveal the secrets of the universe to him. Its power is confined only by the imagination of the one who wields it. Worlds turn on the power of the Rose, Jack, a power greater than any army the surface of this pathetic realm has ever known. So, I would be most grateful if you would tell me what you know of the Rose.'

'Really,' Jack said quickly, 'I don't know anything. I was warned about it, that's all.'

'Warned? By whom?'

Jack looked about him nervously. There was nowhere to run. 'By a man, a stranger.'

Rouland rose up from his chair and leaned over Jack. 'What did he say?'

'He told me to protect the Rose, that's all I know.'

93

Suddenly Rouland grabbed hold of Jack's jaw, his dark eyes invading his. Jack felt an uncomfortable pressure deep inside his head. 'Please! what are you doing?'

Rouland ignored Jack's cry, his focus elsewhere. This was very different from when Castilan had entered his head. Now the pressure inside Jack's mind grew stronger, and a burst of images erupted from his subconscious. He saw Old David in the graveyard, his cracked lips uttering a final warning to Jack. Then the pressure lessened and Rouland slumped into his chair, breathing heavily. Jack felt exhausted too, unable to raise himself up. But, in that last moment of contact, he had felt something else, an emotion left behind by Rouland: fear.

Rouland muttered to himself, his eyes wild, 'The Prophecy...' He took a steadying breath and focused on Jack. 'You...you have an unusual mind, Jack, unique in fact.' His words were laboured and deliberate. 'And you are from upstream. A Yard Boy from the future. From such a long way away. 2008.' Rouland smiled as his heavy breathing lessened. 'Who? Who was the old man? Who was the man I saw in your memories?'

Slowly Jack regained his strength, as if it had been hiding deep within him. Anger grew with it, until his fear was overwhelmed. 'I won't tell you.'

'You refuse me? You defy me?'

'Yes!' Jack said stubbornly.

Rouland stood quickly, his movements reminding Jack of a predatory cat, and stared at the view. 'Would you believe me if I told you I am over five hundred years old? It is a mighty thing to contemplate, I would imagine. I do not know exactly how long I have lived – my memory is infuriatingly perfect, yet my first days are shrouded in fog. But I do not lie when I say I have lived for at least a millennium. In that time only a very few have dared defy me. None still live.' Jack sensed a tone of weary regret in Rouland's words. 'I have walked this world and lived many lives. I have seen everything that a man can dream of seeing, and many things he would never wish to. I thought I had witnessed everything, but you, my young friend, are something quite new.'

Jack could feel the dark eyes of Rouland upon him, studying him with a scientist's scrutiny. 'What do you mean?'

Rouland wiped his mouth with a napkin. 'You have not been raised as a First Worlder – although that is what you most certainly are – and you are not familiar with our legends, our prophecies. I see that now. The Rose existed on the shores of Annwn, an island of the Realm of Otherworld. There are many realms, you understand. The one you see before you is a tiny fraction of what is out there. Some we know of and have charted. Others are elusive and hidden. The foremost of all these concealed realms is Otherworld.'

'Otherworld?' Jack asked, while his brain scrambled to see a way out of this situation.

Rouland paused for a moment. When he spoke again his voice was softer, calmer. 'Imagine another Earth, a perfect Earth, in another dimension, another realm. That is Otherworld, a place of beauty and peace. I tried for many years to reach Otherworld. The way there is hidden and treacherous. Many thought me mad to try, but eventually I stumbled briefly upon it. What a sight it was, a place of eternal summer without death, without fear or pain, where a day lasts for a thousand years. I was already old when I found a way to Otherworld, but there I was young again, and all things were new. The Rose was the source of that power, so I took the Rose and for a while it lived within me. But without the Rose Otherworld fell into decay. War was inevitable, a great and terrible war, and my claim to the Rose temporary. The Rose was taken from me, lost, and I was cast out from my beloved Otherworld and had to return to this grey, cruel realm you see before you.'

Jack saw tears in Rouland's eyes and heard the loss in his broken voice.

'Without the Rose I can never return there. I have survived for hundreds of years, a gift from one lungful of air from Otherworld. Those around me have died, but I am cursed now to prevail, my memory intact so that all things are old to me.'

Jack asked, 'What does all this have to do with me?'

'In recent years a new legend has emerged, that the Rose was found again and is now hidden in this realm, somewhere upstream. I never thought these tales to be true, until today. For I believe you have touched the Rose, Jack.'

Rouland stared intently, his dark eyes fixed like a hawk's. 'As soon as you arrived in this time I smelled it on the air, and now you are with me here, its perfume is almost too much to tolerate. You have the scent of Otherworld about you.'

Jack shivered.

'I can learn some things from your mind, Jack, without doing any damage to your brain. But if you resist me, the damage would be severe. You felt the pressure, yes?' Rouland paused and a heavy expression of sympathy clouded his features. 'You know, a child's skull is a curious thing,' he continued in a hush. 'It can hide a great many things. But once the bone is removed it is much easier to read the secrets of the mind inside. It is not a simple procedure; the patient must remain alive and conscious throughout the surgery. I have practised this many times, often on minds even younger than yours. I am skilled enough to make the suffering a concise thing, but I will not pretend to you that it is anything less than a terrible end to a young life. No one wants to die, Jack, but I believe your mind holds the key to the location of the Rose.

So, your limited options make your decision an easy one: you will help me find the Rose, and in turn the Rose will lead me back to Otherworld.'

Jack fought his impulses to run, to bang on the door until someone came to rescue him. Because he knew no one would help him.

Rouland's oily eyes narrowed. 'You will find the Rose for me, Jack, or I will destroy you, your life and all that you hold dear. Somewhere inside your mind is the key to the Rose. Either you can discover it yourself, or I will remove it with a knife. Please forgive my ultimatum. I usually despise such brute force, but for this I would do anything. I am a reasonable man, Jack, a gentleman of some refinement, but know this: *I would move worlds to have the Rose.*'

'But I can't help you,' Jack pleaded. 'I don't—'

Rouland's fist abruptly hammered down onto the table and the plates rattled with aftershocks from his barely contained rage. Jack stared, wide-eyed, as Rouland slowly composed himself again, a tight smile replacing the fury that had robbed him of his beauty.

'Forgive me,' Rouland soothed.

Jack heard again the tremble in Rouland's voice and believed he was quite mad.

Rouland stood up slowly. 'I am sorry, Jack. It is a terrible burden for you to bear and I wish it were given to one with malice in his heart. It is unfair that this has come down to you. But life is unfair, doubly so for matters of the Rose.' He folded his napkin and placed it neatly on the table. As he walked to the door he added, 'Please enjoy your breakfast; if you wish for anything, use the bell on the table. You have until the sand runs out of the hourglass to make your choice. Good morning, Jack.'

Rouland closed the door behind him. The room suddenly seemed abnormally large, as if a terrible storm had passed, leaving a great silence in its wake.

The sand in the hourglass fell impassively through the glass, the pile growing larger in the lower bulb with every passing second.

Jack put down his cup. The tea had gone cold and he had lost his appetite.

# 10

## ON THE TILES

Jack's thoughts raced. The only way out of the suite was through the locked door, behind which, he was sure, Rouland's people waited. Jack's head turned slowly towards the balcony and his mind filled with terrible alternatives.

He was at least five storeys up. A low brick wall surrounded the balcony, beyond which the wide rooftop sloped downwards at a steep angle. To his left he saw other balconies jutting out of the rooftop, and a dangerous notion offered itself up to him: perhaps he could escape through one of the other balconies. Jack felt instantly sick.

Then his eyes fell on the hourglass sitting where Rouland had left it. Only a fraction of the sand remained in the upper bulb – time was running out fast.

His mind was already made up: he would not help Rouland. So his life was in danger if he stayed here a moment longer. Jack looked back at the locked door and then to the sloped rooftop. His heart thumped in his chest as he took the first step onto the balcony wall. Tentatively he put his foot onto the tiled roof, then shifted his weight and pulled the rest of his body out, using his hands to cling onto the slope. The tiles groaned and creaked under his weight and he felt horribly unstable, his mind filled with dizzying images of the street far below.

Carefully he began to shimmy across the tiles, slow and awkward like a drunken spider. A tile under his right foot cracked and slipped free. Impulsively he pulled up his foot, causing his other foot to slip down and, with a terrifying realisation, he could feel his body moving down the rooftop. His fingers splayed over the tiles, desperate for purchase as the edge of the roof approached rapidly. Jack gasped, certain he was going to slide right over. Desperately he dug his knees into the tiles while at the same moment his white fingertips found a protruding edge and gripped it with all his strength. His body slowed, then stopped, and somewhere far away he heard the sound of the dislodged tile smashing into the road below. His left foot touched nothing, hanging beyond the gutter at the edge of the roof.

Slowly, cautiously, he began to claw his way back up the tiles towards the next balcony, until he was only a few metres away from it. He reached out with his hand and grabbed hold of the perimeter wall. Sweating and breathless, he scrambled clumsily over the wall and landed in a heap on the balcony floor. He lay there for a moment on his back, breathing hard and looking up at the blue midmorning sky, before he got to his feet.

The balcony led to another suite, similar to the one he had woken up in. A face looked back at him through the French doors, mirroring Jack's own expression of surprise.

'Davey,' Jack whispered.

Jack pulled the doors open and ran inside.

'You're all night?' Davey said, his voice sounding incredulous.

'Yes, just about,' Jack replied, thinking about his close call on the tiles. 'Are you locked in here?'

'Yes. They've left me alone for now. Rouland came in for a moment, but once he knew your name he left.' Davey gestured towards the balcony. 'You climbed over the roof? You're either brave or an idiot.'

Jack ran back out onto the balcony and surveyed the rooftop. There was a third balcony further along the building. 'Want to be an idiot with me?' he said to Davey.

Davey caught up with Jack and looked over the balcony. His face went pale. 'Over?'

'Do you have a better idea?' Jack waited for a response; he really hoped Davey might come up with something easier, something safer. But Davey just shrugged. Jack took a deep breath, steadying himself, steeling his mind. It was up to him now. 'Then it's the roof.' He climbed back on the tiles, praying the trembling in his legs would not grow any stronger, and edged across the rooftop.

Davey watched him for a moment, then climbed over the wall and followed him out. Jack stopped at a high chimney stack, the smoke of the first lunch sitting drifting out of it, and waited for Davey to catch up.

A noise caught his attention: there was someone on the first balcony, someone searching for him. The man was dressed in a butler's uniform and he had come to retrieve the breakfast tray. Jack pulled Davey towards him and they both disappeared behind the chimney again. Jack heard raised voices, the butler shouting at someone inside the suite. After a long moment of silence Jack peered round the chimney stack. The butler was gone.

'Now!' Jack staggered forward towards the third balcony, with Davey right behind him. They were both on their feet this time, the slow safety of using hands a forgotten luxury. They landed on the balcony at speed, fell to the ground and rolled over each other until the perimeter wall stopped them.

This suite had French doors, like the rooms they had been locked in. Jack pulled at a door, dismayed to discover it was locked from within. Davey quickly picked up a small potted plant and raised it over his head.

'Wait!' Jack gasped. 'What are you doing? If they're inside they'll hear us.'

Davey looked at the windows, then at the potted plant. He nodded in agreement and put the pot down. Quickly, he pulled out the metal wire that supported the plant and ran to the door. 'Quietly does it.' He smiled as he worked the wire into the keyhole and with expert dexterity teased the lock open. Davey then ran into the suite, towards the interior door. Jack hoped it was unlocked, prayed it would lead them away from this madness. Slowly Davey turned the handle: the door was unlocked. He tentatively squinted through the thin gap, then quietly closed the door.

'Paladin are outside,' he said with a sigh. 'Rouland must own this entire floor. We need to think of something else.'

'Such as?' Jack asked, frustrated and afraid.

Davey ran back onto the balcony and frantically looked over the edge. Jack followed him to see what he was looking at. Two floors below was a large open terrace, so big that it had a bubbling fountain at its centre.

'There,' Davey pointed.

'How do we get down there?' Jack asked breathlessly.

'We jump.'

'Jump? We'll die from this height.'

Davey rooted around in his pockets and pulled out a shining coin. 'Not if we use this,' he said with a defiant smile. 'Remember Piccadilly Circus? Remember the fountain?'

Jack saw the winged lion emblem on the little coin. He looked back over the wall at the small fountain far below. 'You want us to jump into that? From here?'

'Yes.'

'How do you know there's a junction chamber under the fountain?'

Davey nodded to the coin in his hand. 'It's tingling. Trust me.'

Jack stared sceptically at Davey; the coin looked completely still and lifeless to him. Then he tensed at the sound of voices coming from the corridor outside the room.

Davey ran back inside and pulled at a large wooden cabinet, shouting, 'I need your help!'

Jack ran in and got behind Davey. Together they pushed until the antique cabinet wobbled, then fell with a thunderous bang, blocking the doorway.

'So much for being quiet!' Davey said as he picked up cushions and chairs, throwing them on top of the cabinet. The door banged against the cabinet as someone tried to get in. 'Get the bed sheets!' he shouted, in between tossing several hand-bound books onto the growing mountain of furniture. Jack pulled the crisp sheets from the bed and dragged them over the cabinet, where Davey took out his matches and lit the corner of the bedding. He then set fire to one of the books and threw the flaming rectangle onto the pile. Within moments the flames spread, taking hold of the material, and smoke rose, to cling to the ceiling, thickening into a dark mass. The banging on the door increased and the cabinet shook from the blows.

'That should keep them busy for a few minutes.'

As the fire grew so did Jack's doubts. The only way out

now was either back on the tiles or straight down, and parts of his brain seemed to shut down as adrenaline flooded his body. Davey was yelling over the banging and the fire, pulling him back towards the balcony wall. Jack's eyes focused on the fountain and, for a moment, he froze. Then he turned and realised that he could see people on the other two balconies – figures in armour that glinted in the morning sun.

Davey also saw them and quickly threw the coin over the side, aiming it with precision at the small target below. He held out his hand to Jack and counted to three, watching the coin tumble towards the fountain. It hit the water with a small splash. At the sight of the shimmering ripples Davey screamed, 'Jump!'

Jack took Davey's hand and felt his arm tugged outwards. His legs pushed feebly against the wall and he was airborne. Behind them the Paladin scampered over the rooftop towards them, like armoured insects hunting their prey. A shadow flickered over Jack as the Paladin captain leaped free of the roof, into the air above them with her arms outstretched.

Jack looked down at the approaching terrace; the fountain seemed to be off to the right. They were going to miss it. Davey jerked his arm and Jack's weight shifted him to the right, just enough. They hit the water precisely, with barely a centimetre to spare, forcing a column of water upwards.

Jack felt the cold water hit him hard against his face, then air was rushing past. His eyes cleared, and he saw Davey still beside him, laughing with relief as they dropped serenely onto the ground. They had fallen through the fountain's surface and landed softly on the dusty floor of a junction chamber.

Jack looked up at the fountain portal set in the high ceiling. Through the disturbed water he saw the falling Paladin, her shape dancing through the ripples, growing larger and larger. How long would *this* gateway stay open?

Captain de Vienne drew her sword and pointed it down in front of her, but the water shifted, contorted, and then transformed into solid rock as the portal closed in on itself.

Jack heard a terrible scream. The beautiful sword of the Paladin fell from the ceiling, embedding itself upright in the ground between the two boys, Captain de Vienne's severed hand still clasped tightly round the hilt.

# 11

## ELOISE

Jack stared in disbelief as the sword swayed gently between him and Davey. The hand holding it jerked and shuddered, as white blood trickled from the clean cut where a forearm had been seconds ago, then released its grip and fell to the ground, immobile.

Jack gasped. 'Don't they ever give up?'

'The Paladin?' Davey replied as he stood, looking around the circular chamber. 'No, they'll do anything for Rouland. When you're already dead you tend to lose your fear. Come on, we have to close off that portal completely before they reopen it.'

'How long have we got?' Jack asked, brushing the dust from his new clothes.

'Not long.'

The space was similar to the junction chamber beneath Piccadilly Circus, but this one looked partially ruined. One side had collapsed inwards and a slope of rubble snaked towards the fountain portal in the ceiling. Davey climbed over the rubble pile and began to lift up slabs of rock, throwing them aside.

Jack heard something. He looked up to see a small coin appear momentarily from the ceiling before being vaporised into golden dust. The portal shimmered and the stone turned to water. Light flooded in from the opening, and drops of disturbed water fell onto Jack's face. A shape appeared above the rippled water. Without thinking Jack took the sword and pulled it out of the ground.

'Davey, they're coming!' Jack shouted, swinging the heavy sword up in front of him as he took several steps back.

Davey pulled a heavy slab to one side, almost unable to take its weight. Beneath was a mass of cables. He pulled them up towards him and shouted at Jack, 'Cut it!'

'Which one?'

'All of them!'

Jack lifted the sword and ran to Davey, throwing all his weight behind the blow. His thin arms struggled to hold on as the sword arced down and struck the cables, rending them in two. Sparks flew from both ends of the cables, and electricity arced up the sword, throwing Jack backwards across the chamber. Above them the water flickered and became stone once more. The chamber became dark, save for a dying glow from the broken cables.

'Davey?' Jack called out weakly.

'I'm here,' Davey said, his voice sounding far off and breathless.

'Are we safe?'

'Yeah, I think so,' Davey replied. 'Junction chamber's dead.'

Something moved to Jack's left. There was the noise of metal on stone. 'Jack, is that you?' Davey whispered.

'No,' Jack said, wondering where the sword might be. He stood and moved cautiously towards Davey's voice.

'We're not alone,' Jack whispered.

'I know.'

Suddenly the room lit up, so brightly that at first Jack couldn't see where it was coming from. As the light faded Jack gazed in awe at its origin: the Paladin sword glowed as if alive, a sinuous dancing green energy playing over its blade. While Jack and Davey watched, the light climbed up the hilt, up an arm that now held the sword, towards the pale face of a helmetless Paladin. She studied the sword in her hand like it was something long forgotten. The warrior's slender frame seemed to change in the unearthly incandescence, growing, feeding, healing. Her skin had the same cool pallor as her Paladin sisters, but her eyes flickered with a rich blue sparkle that softened her face. An unkempt mane of long dark hair fell about her face and shoulders like that of a wild beast. She looked no older than seventeen, but she was OnceDead, and her age could not be guessed at. Her ancient armour hung about her, its surface pitted and perforated.

'How did she get in here?' Jack whispered.

'I think she was here before us.' Davey pointed to the heavy manacles that hung from her wrists and ankles, broken chains swinging back and forth from them.

The Paladin, still seemingly in a daze, lowered the sword and looked directly at Jack. She opened her mouth and motioned as if to speak, then coughed, cleared her throat and tried again. Slowly, uncomfortably, the words began to form. 'I am forgiven . . . at last?' Her voice had just a hint of a French accent. It grated like a forgotten, disused instrument. Her pained eyes pleaded with Jack for a response.

'Yeah,' said Davey, 'you're forgiven.'

The Paladin turned to see him; at the same time Davey hit her over the head with a piece of broken masonry. The blow was heavy and the Paladin staggered backwards. At first she looked confused, but then in a moment she had Davey by the throat, his feet dangling off the ground.

'I spit on you and Rouland,' she said, her vice-like grip tightening, intent on snapping Davey's neck.

'Wait!' shouted Jack, struggling to make his mouth work. '*Rouland* didn't send us, we're running *from* him!'

The Paladin appeared to consider this for a moment, then turned back to Davey. Her grip faltered and she dropped him, gasping for air, to the ground. She took an uncertain step backwards and collapsed on the floor next to Davey, tears flowing from her mysterious eyes.

Davey coughed for air as the colour returned to his face. The Paladin's cool stare settled on Jack. 'I am Eloise de Montauban,' she said, wiping her face and pushing away her dark filthy hair.

'I'm Jack, and that's Davey.' Jack's heart pounded in his chest, willing him to run away from this terrible hunter. 'Are you a prisoner here?' Jack nodded at Eloise's broken shackles.

Eloise said slowly, 'Yes, I suppose I am. I have been here for a long time, a very long time, alone in the darkness.' Her voice faltered. She gathered herself and continued, 'I am weak, but this sword is healing me.' She still held the glowing blade, its light throbbing like the pulse of a vivid heartbeat. 'The Paladin and the sword are one. This sword is not my own, yet it still replenishes me.' As she spoke she raised the weapon into the air and struck at one of the metal bands. It cracked in two and fell to the ground. Eloise swapped the sword into her freed hand and continued to break the shackles from her limbs.

'Who put you here?' Jack asked.

'My master. I disobeyed him. More than that: I raised an army against him and I was defeated.'

'How long have you been here?'

'I do not know. I have no sun, no moon. What year is this?'

'1940. September,' Jack answered.

As the words sank in, fresh tears flowed freely down

her cheeks. Her lip quivered. 'Far too long,' she said.

Jack went to Davey's side and whispered in his ear, 'What do we do about her?'

Davey shrugged. 'This is a new one for me.'

'Where are we, anyway?' Jack asked.

'It's another junction chamber,' Davey said. 'I thought I knew them all, but this is one I've never mapped before.'

'It is forgotten,' Eloise said. 'You are the first to come this way since I was imprisoned here. Was it you who brought the thunder upon the chamber?' She pointed to the collapsed wall.

'It must have been the unexploded bomb, outside the hotel,' Jack explained.

Davey stared up thoughtfully at the ceiling. 'Can't be too far below the surface here.'

'There's a war going on up there,' Jack said to Eloise. 'A bomb did that.'

'I am grateful,' she said. 'The thunder freed me from my chains.'

'Ah, I get it!' Davey paced excitedly. 'This place must have had a coin wall over it, and the Nazis have knocked it out.' He grabbed Jack. 'Don't you see? The coin wall keeps people like me – like us – out of junction chambers, keeps them private.'

'It is Rouland's doing, to keep me here,' Eloise said mournfully.

Davey continued, hardly listening to Eloise. 'If that

113

bomb hadn't switched it off last night we'd have just jumped into a normal fountain!' The idea amused Davey greatly and he laughed as he spoke. '*Splat!*'

'And you think that's funny?' Jack was disgusted. 'You're sick!'

'I feel fine!'

Eloise walked slowly towards one of the tunnels that led off the chamber.

'Hey, she's leaving,' Jack said, his anger fading. 'Where's she going?'

'How should I know?' Davey said.

'And what about Rouland?' Jack asked. 'He's going to find a way in here to look for us, isn't he?'

'Yeah, probably. He won't give up, that's for sure.'

'So maybe we should be following Eloise,' Jack suggested with a tone of urgency.

'Follow a Paladin?'

'She fought against him, and if we're going to fight Rouland too we'll need some allies.'

'Fight Rouland?' Davey said with concern.

'Like you said, he won't give up,' Jack observed grimly.

As Eloise walked further down the tunnel the light in the junction chamber faded rapidly, leaving Jack and Davey in darkness.

'Are you coming?' Jack asked as he ran to catch up to the light before it disappeared for ever in the labyrinth of tunnels.

# 12

## TAVERN TALES

'You remember the Rose?' Jack asked pensively.

Davey screwed up his face. 'The one you were told to protect? Course I do.'

Jack nodded grimly. 'In the hotel Rouland said it was called the Rose of Annwn. He said it was from a place called Otherworld.'

Davey scoffed, 'Otherworld don't exist. It's a child's fairytale, nothing more. I believe what I can see with my own eyes.'

Jack laughed, amazed at Davey's viewpoint. 'But the things you've seen, they were fairy stories to me until I met you.'

Davey began to reply, stopped, then shrugged his shoulders. 'I'll believe it when I see it.'

They walked along the dark tunnel, following Eloise from a distance, like two cautious sheep.

'It's what Rouland wants,' Jack said. 'He says I've touched it. He wants me to find it for him.'

Davey looked surprised. 'We jumped off a building for a rose?'

'It's not an ordinary plant,' Jack replied feistily. 'It's something powerful.'

'We still jumped off for something we don't know nothing about.'

'We wouldn't have been there if you hadn't sold me out to the Journeyman.'

There was a long uncomfortable pause, then Davey replied, 'Things were different back then.' He looked at the floor. 'I'm sorry. If I'd have known who you were...'

'Your grandson,' Jack said.

'Is it true? Am I really your grandfather?'

'I'm afraid so.'

Davey managed a half-smile. 'I've not had a family for a long time, not really. I must be a big let-down for you.'

'Yeah, you could say that,' Jack said softly. 'Where are your parents?'

'Long gone.' Davey sniffed casually. Too casually, Jack thought. He wanted to ask more, but he sensed Davey's growing discomfort with the subject. 'What am I like? Am I an OK grandfather?' his friend asked.

'I don't know,' Jack said hesitantly, considering every word. 'We'd never met until the day you sent me back here.'

'Welcome to the family, for what that's worth!'

Ahead, Eloise stopped in front of a huge arched doorway. As Jack and Davey caught up with her she inserted her sword into a slot in the archway and a set of massive metal cogs pulled the heavy door open. Stinking grey water flooded through the opening, the rising water not slowing until it lapped gently about their knees.

Davey had been quiet for several moments. When he spoke his voice echoed off the curved brick walls. 'I don't know nothing about this rose, Jack, but if I can help you then I will, all right?'

Eloise stopped abruptly. She turned to face the two boys. 'You hunt the Rose?'

Jack shivered. Since all this began he'd felt as if he was always one step behind everyone else, the new boy on the first day of school. He looked back at Davey and saw a flash of the same frustration in his face, hidden behind the smile and the bravado.

'Depends,' Davey replied with a bold shrug. 'You know what it is?'

'The Rose of Annwn,' Eloise said impatiently. 'Is this what you seek?'

Davey seemed to stall, uncertainty colouring his grubby features. Jack looked back at Eloise and decided he had to give in to trust. 'Yes,' he replied. 'Rouland wants me to find it for him. I can't help thinking that it's got something to do with my family, my mum . . .'

'Your family?' Davey said.

Jack's mouth dried up. He wanted to say more. He wanted to tell him about his mother, about her death, about Old David's sacrifice. And beneath it all was the notion that a time-travelling boy might be able to stop

117

things that had already happened, to save people who had already died, to put his family back together again. He looked to the ground before Davey could see the pain on his face.

'What happened to your family?' There was an urgency in Davey's voice, an urgency that Jack could no longer ignore.

'Mum,' Jack whispered. 'Your daughter, I think she's in danger. She . . .' The words caught in his throat. He tried again, but he couldn't bring himself to say it out loud. His mother was dead, and all the angry questions he'd buried were bubbling back up to the surface.

Davey said nothing. He waded over to Jack's side and put an arm round his shoulder. 'I reckon we need to find the Rose before Rouland, or stop him getting to it, don't you?'

Jack looked up and nodded. 'Can we stop it from happening? Can we save her?'

Davey sighed heavily. 'Honestly, I don't know. I've never been into destiny and all that guff. But I reckon we could give it a try.'

Jack smiled, a mix of relief and fear in his eyes.

Eloise had been silent, but now she pulled her sword from the slot in the door and held it up in front of her, its blade glinting in the dim light. 'You oppose Rouland. You will need protection. My sword is yours.'

'Thanks,' Jack managed.

'So, what do you know 'bout the Rose?' Davey asked meekly.

'I know Rouland sought it, that it was precious to him, a thing of terrible power,' Eloise continued. 'Before my imprisonment my knowledge was ... fractured. Rouland saw to that.'

'So we still don't know,' Davey said.

'What should we do now?' Jack asked, a thousand thoughts racing through his mind. 'If Rouland thinks I know something about the Rose maybe that's why Mum dies. Maybe it's all connected.'

'Well, if it's information we need then there's only one place to go: back to the Hanging Tavern,' Davey said with a wry grin.

The Hanging Tavern sat like a dark ghost in a street of dead buildings. The noisy revellers Jack had seen on his first visit here were gone, and the pub seemed hollow and empty without them. He paused outside as an uneasy thought occurred to him. 'What if Rouland's waiting for us?'

'He is not here,' Eloise said, a faraway expression on her face. 'His forces *are* looking for us, but I do not sense anyone loyal to him nearby.'

Jack raised an inquisitive eyebrow. 'How can you be sure?'

Turmoil flashed over Eloise's face. 'I can feel Rouland. I know when he is near. We are safe for now.'

Jack exchanged a cautious look with Davey.

'Let's hope he can't sense her,' Davey whispered.

They circled around the tavern, to the side entrance.

Davey pulled the handle. 'Locked.'

He rattled persistently on the door until, eventually, the formidable shape of Betty unlocked it. 'We're not open till six thirty,' she said, squinting at the visitors.

Davey smiled widely. 'Afternoon, Betty, how are—?'

'You're barred!' Betty snapped.

'I know, I know,' Davey said, his hands held up, 'but we really need to speak to Castilan. It's important.' He gestured over his shoulder at Jack and Eloise.

Betty inspected them through narrow eyes. 'I said you're barred, until you've paid what you owe.'

'I have money.' Davey beamed and produced a thick wallet from inside his coat.

'Where'd you get that?' Jack whispered.

Davey elbowed him in his side, and Jack shut up. Davey pulled out a wad of notes and offered them to Betty. 'I think that should cover what I owe. You do take Second-World currency here?'

Betty took the notes out of Davey's hand and held them up to the light, inspecting each one in turn.

Davey counted out more notes. 'And we'd like some rooms for tonight. And food: your steak special. And drinks. Lots of drinks.'

Betty snatched the wallet from Davey's fingers and took

out more of the remaining notes.

'Hey!' Davey protested, snatching the wallet back.

'Interest,' Betty said gruffly. 'Cas!' she shouted, suddenly spotting Eloise. 'Visitors!'

'I'm busy,' came the distant reply.

'*Now!*' Betty said in a tone that few would argue with. Frustrated footsteps thumped from within.

'What is it now?' Castilan said angrily, appearing at the doorway. As he saw the visitors waiting for him his demeanour changed. He ventured a smile, but was looking around the alleyway nervously. 'You're not welcome here,' he said through gritted teeth, flashing a scowl in Eloise's direction.

'We're not leaving till we speak to you,' Davey said doggedly. 'You want people to see us outside?'

'He's paid,' Betty said to Castilan, 'and then some. He's paid for rooms.'

'Up front?' Castilan replied, dumbfounded.

'Up front.' She waved the bundle of notes at Castilan. Castilan's eyebrows arched upwards in disbelief. He looked back at Eloise and sighed. 'Inside, before you're seen,' he said regretfully.

Jack, Davey and Eloise filed past Betty into the dim bar.

'Quickly, quickly, this way,' Castilan fussed. 'Betty will bring us some drinks.'

'I bloody well won't!' Betty replied gruffly.

Castilan came up close to his wife. She towered over her short, chubby husband. 'Drinks, Betty. Please.'

Castilan spat the words out sharply through narrow lips before gesturing brusquely to his visitors.

They followed Castilan up the uneven wooden steps behind the bar, along a narrow hallway, past several bedrooms and into a room at the far end. Inside was a round table, set for a card game Castilan obviously planned to hold later that night, and several chairs, none of which matched.

The landlord closed the door and rounded on Davey. He grabbed him by the collar and held him tightly against the door. 'What have you brought here, Davey?' He nodded over his shoulder at Jack. 'That boy is trouble.'

'He's OK, Castilan.'

'And is she what I think she is?' Castilan tutted loudly. 'Is she Pala—'

Jack was about to cut in when Betty pushed on the door, hitting Davey on the head. Castilan let him go and Betty entered with a tray of drinks.

'You want me to drop these? Just keep standing behind the door, that'll do the trick!' She bashed the tray down on the table, spilling froth and beer everywhere. As she left she slammed the door behind her.

Castilan shivered, his eyes still fixed on the door. 'That woman! Formidable, isn't she? I'm a lucky man.' He sat at the table, picked up a tall glass and drank the contents in one long gulp. Then he wiped the foam from his face and looked up at Davey and Jack. 'What do you want?'

'Information,' Davey said, pulling up a chair to the table.

'We want to know about the Rose of Annwn.' Jack joined them at the table. 'We need to know how to find it.'

Castilan grimaced. 'No. Not until you explain her.' He pointed a plump finger towards Eloise.

'This is Eloise,' Jack said. 'She used to be a Paladin and—'

'I may have been entombed these last hundred years,' Eloise said calmly, 'but I can still speak for myself, thank you, Jack.' She walked slowly over to the table and pulled up a chair.

Castilan edged back from Eloise, as if he feared he might catch some unspeakable disease from her.

'I was indeed once Paladin,' Eloise continued, 'but no more. I took up arms against my master and for my treachery I was imprisoned and forgotten. Now I am . . . nothing.'

Castilan smiled. 'Nothing can still be trouble.' His eyes fixed on her ancient face.

'You are an Operator?' Eloise asked, cocking her head to one side.

'You could feel that?' Castilan asked with surprise.

'I allowed your crude intrusion. You can see my mind is truthful.'

'Oh, yes, it's as you say. Very interesting.'

Jack wondered what Castilan could see. What horrors

might Eloise have witnessed?

'I would not call the long eternity of my imprisonment "interesting",' she said bitterly.

'Why did you and Rouland fall out? Being one of his killers stop being fun?'

Eloise hesitated. 'My reasons are my own.'

'And I'm supposed to be happy with that? You expect me to trust you?'

'I expect nothing from you. You should do likewise.'

A smile festered on Castilan's face as he studied Eloise. He sniffed the air and his nose wrinkled in disgust. 'What is that awful smell?'

Jack suddenly realised: 'We've been through the sewers,' he confessed.

'You smell like one! Make sure you take a bath before you jump into one of my beds,' Castilan said. He opened a drawer under the table and fished around inside, producing a long pipe and tobacco. He took his time preparing the pipe before lighting it. 'Best if we keep this little meeting brief, and airy.' He stood and opened the small windows as wide as he could, the rich smoke from his pipe drifting out into the night air.

'So... the Rose,' Jack prodded, his face caught in the light from the lantern hanging above him. 'What can you tell us?'

'Not much to tell. Why'd you want to know about the Rose, anyway?'

'Rouland wants me to tell him where it is, or he'll kill me. He thinks I've touched the Rose.'

'Really? And have you?'

'I'd never even heard of it before yesterday. Do you know where we can find it?'

'Why?' Castilan asked. 'You gonna give it to Rouland, like he wants? Think that'll save your hide? He'll kill you either way.'

'I know,' Jack said thoughtfully. 'That's why I want to find it before him. Please, you have to help me.'

Castilan scoffed. 'Stuff of legend, the Rose is. Been a long time since anyone even mentioned it. Hard to remember.'

'You know more,' Eloise said tersely.

'You're an Operator too?' Castilan asked.

'I do not need to read minds to know when you are concealing information from me.'

Castilan smiled. 'I like you more and more. Anyway, if you used to be with Rouland you'll know as much as me about the Rose.'

'My memory is fractured.' Eloise returned his smile, but it seemed like an unnatural action. Jack glanced cautiously at Davey.

'All right,' Castilan said as he returned to his chair. 'I know the Rose is supposed to be from Otherworld and that it was brought here a long time ago.'

'Rouland said he'd been to Otherworld,' Jack offered.

125

'He's dangerous, Jack. He might look like a man, but he can do things that even the best minds of the First World can't fathom.' Castilan puffed on his pipe. 'As for the Rose, well, legend says it was cast adrift, *some-when*.' He paused for effect. 'It still exists but it's upstream. One day, when we catch up with it there'll be a war. Not like this war, with bombs and bullets. This'll be a war of the minds. And the First World's supposed to fall. There's a prophecy, see. It says whoever has the Rose is condemned to rule the First World and bring about its end, and a Timesmith, the Last Timesmith, will make it happen. That's not something you should take on lightly.' He blew out rings of smoke that danced above his head. 'Course, it could all be a load of gossip and nonsense. Thing is, when you can travel through time, prophecy looks more like history in reverse. That's the thing with legends, you just never know.'

'Timesmith?' Jack asked pensively.

'A Timesmith is a rare thing indeed. You're a Yard Boy, right?'

'I suppose I am.'

'So, a Yard Boy can only travel downstream, to the past, yes? They can come back the way they came, but that's it. And there's a limit to how far a Yard Boy can travel. But a Timesmith, that's a Yard Boy without limits, someone who has mastered the Sorrowlines. They can go upstream, downstream, wherever they want.'

Jack turned to Davey, confused. 'But you told Titus you thought I could travel upstream. Were you lying to him?'

Davey hesitated, but before he could explain the door opened and Betty entered again, carrying a large tray of food: hot steak sandwiches and a huge plate of chips. She threw the tray onto the table. Jack's thoughts about the Rose, about Timesmiths and prophecies disappeared as he looked at the steaming food with anticipation.

'Thank you, Betty,' said Castilan.

'Choke on it!' Betty marched out and slammed the door behind her.

Davey was first to grab a handful of food, and Jack didn't wait to be invited either. He picked up a steak sandwich and devoured it with a rage like a wild animal. He stuffed a rough handful of chips into his mouth, burning his tongue and lips as he chewed them. The food tasted good, and the relentless fear of the chase, and the thought that Rouland might find them here, subsided for a while.

Castilan put down his pipe and took a steak sandwich from the pile. Only Eloise abstained, watching impassively as the others ate.

'So,' Castilan said finally, his mouth still full of food, 'how are you going to find this Rose before Rouland, if it even exists at all?'

Jack swallowed. 'I don't know.'

'What about your friend there?' Castilan nodded at

Eloise. 'She must remember something.'

'Rouland has searched this world for the Rose, and it is not here,' Eloise said, her face full of confusion, as if she was hunting down her elusive memories.

'Then maybe the legends are true – maybe it's upstream, in the future.'

'And a Yard Boy from the future might be able to find it,' said Davey, eying Jack intently.

Jack's mind raced with possibilities. 'But it could be anywhere,' he said. 'Where would I start?'

Castilan replied with a smile, 'There are people who can help, people who can find things.'

'He wants us to find a Limner.' Davey pointed accusingly at Castilan.

'What's a Limner?' Jack enquired.

Eloise scoffed, 'Limners are more legendary than the Rose.'

'What's a Limner?' Jack repeated, trying to temper his growing frustration.

'The only person who can help you now, boy,' Castilan said in between puffs on his pipe, 'and almost impossible to find.'

'*Almost?*' Jack said.

Castilan leaned back, his hands behind his head and a smug grin poking out from behind his pipe. 'Unless you know the right people.'

# 13

## THE SMALLEST ROOM

Jack awoke to the noise of Davey snoring like a wounded pig taking its last breath. He opened his eyes and peered through the dim light at the dark shape of his grandfather-to-be in the opposite bed.

He guessed it was about six o'clock. The sun squeezed through the edges of the curtains, but outside the streets slumbered still. He had heard more raids in the night, sirens followed by a tense silence, and then bombs dropping close by. In spite of everything Jack had some-how managed to drift off to sleep, so exhausted that he had slept well. He was also hungry again.

He stood and dressed in the dark, then opened the curtains just enough to see through the window, forgetting the blackout paper that was stuck to the glass, barely letting any light in. He let the curtain close and crept from the room and down the steep wooden staircase to the bar below and the smell of breakfast cooking.

Betty was working at a small stove in a tiny kitchen at the end of the bar. A fine smoke filled the kitchen, bleeding over the ceiling of the bar, as a chorus of sausages spat and sizzled on the stove. Jack's mouth watered.

Betty must have sensed his presence and she turned, her hair down around her shoulders and her face relaxed, feminine, welcoming.

'You still here?' she said roughly, and all illusions of warmth evaporated. 'Suppose you want some breakfast?'

'Yes please,' Jack said politely. He sat down at a nearby table and wished he'd waited for Davey to wake up so he had someone to talk to.

'You're a Yard Boy?' Betty enquired, without looking up from her stove.

'Sort of, yeah.'

'From upstream?'

'Yes. And you, you're First World. Do you have… a power? You know, a gift?'

'Me?' Betty barked. 'No. Should I?'

'Don't all First Worlders?'

'Only some, like you. The rest of us make breakfast and pull pints, that's all.' Betty chuckled to herself as she deposited a feast of fried delights onto a large plate. 'The future, where you come from: what's it like there?'

'Different,' Jack said. 'It's busier, and the buildings are bigger.' His memories of the future were somehow alien to him now, distant and dreamlike. He looked at Betty as she toiled over the stove. 'We've got computers, they're pretty cool.'

'What are they?'

'You know television?'

'Don't have one.'

'Oh, right.' *This is hard*, Jack thought. 'Well, they're a bit like a television, but you can do all sorts of stuff on them.'

'Like what?'

'I dunno, anything.'

'Cook?'

Jack smirked. 'No. It's hard to explain.' He loved his computer. It was one of his favourite things. None of it seemed to matter any more. Everything had happened so quickly, he'd hardly had time to miss his old life. He recalled his box-like bedroom in the flat he shared with his father; it was untidy and noisy, in an ageing tower of concrete, full of fear. There was little to miss, but it was his home. He thought of his father, and of the strained routine that had been their life since his mother had died.

His father had lost his anchor, and in turn Jack had lost the best of his father. He felt only pity for him, for the inevitable chain of events that had led his father to prison.

'Tell me,' Betty said as she placed the heaving breakfast in front of Jack, 'when does this war end? Do we win?'

'Now, now, Betty. You know better than that.' The voice belonged to Castilan.

Jack turned to see the landlord walking down the stairs in a short dressing gown, his pipe already smoking away from the corner of his mouth. Betty growled and went back to the kitchen. Jack shivered.

'The future's like a wild snake,' Castilan said as he walked behind the bar and poured himself a large glass of whisky. 'We can hold down the head, but the tail is going to swing about like a...well, like a wild snake.' He swallowed the drink and poured himself another.

Jack was just about to ask what he meant, but Betty tutted loudly, squinting at Castilan's glass. 'Bit early for that?'

'Time of day is a made-up nonsense!' Castilan grumbled. 'Just like the future! And you should never know too much about your own future. Isn't that right, Betty?'

Betty's grunt was barely audible, but her displeasure was clear. Castilan smiled and turned his attention to Jack.

'I made a few enquiries late last night, and I think I can get you to a Limner.'

Jack recalled last night's cryptic discussions about someone called a Limner. 'That's good, right?'

'Yes!' Castilan replied indignantly.

'Sorry,' Jack said, not meaning it.

'The Limner, he can see things, hidden things. A Limner is the perfect person to find something hidden. Something like the Rose. As with many things in the First World the Limners have disappeared, almost forgotten. But...' Castilan tapped his nose and winked.

Jack suppressed a smirk at Castilan's pompous ego.

'Something wrong, lad?' Castilan asked sharply.

'Yes! No!' Jack said without thinking. 'Where will we find the Limner?'

'You won't,' Castilan laughed, 'but a Boagyman will.' He leaned back, wallowing in his own smug superiority.

'What's a Boagyman?' Jack asked grudgingly.

Castilan's pride deflated. 'What's a Boagyman? You really don't know anything! Aren't you First World?'

'Yes, I am.' Jack couldn't help sounding indignant.

'The Boagymen,' Castilan harrumphed, 'own the smallest rooms in every house in this realm.' He pointed towards a tiny cupboard under the stairs. 'That's his there.'

Jack looked at the small cupboard and remembered a similar one in the flat he had grown up in.

'Sometimes it's a cupboard,' Castilan continued, 'sometimes it's a toilet, always the smallest room. You ever hear noises in the night? Scratches or a cough, maybe a whisper? You ever lose something in a cupboard? Did you ever see something in the dark, watching you?' Castilan gestured theatrically. 'That's the Boagyman.'

Jack shuddered at the thought of meeting such a creature.

'He can travel to any house, anywhere, through those little rooms. They're all connected to the Realm of Oblivion,' Castilan explained. 'He sometimes takes people with him, at a price, of course.'

'How will that help us?'

'The only person who will know how to get to a Limner is a Boagyman.'

'And why are you helping me?' Jack enquired.

Castilan scowled at Jack. 'When this is done I might need a favour or two from an upstream Yard Boy. Know what I mean?'

'No,' Jack replied.

'I help you, you help me. That's how the world works, lad.' Castilan chuckled darkly. 'Let's just see what the future brings, eh?'

'Can you see the future?' Jack swallowed hard.

'Sometimes.' Castilan leaned towards Jack. 'You know what I can see right now?'

Jack shook his head. He felt cool sweat run down the back of his neck.

'I can see . . .' Castilan whispered, 'a big plate of grub coming my way.' He leaned back again and barked at Betty, 'What does a man have to do to get some breakfast around here, woman?!'

Betty turned to face Castilan, her rage simmering under a frozen expression of contempt. 'D'you still want a jaw to eat it with?'

'Betty, my dear,' Castilan soothed, 'some breakfast would be delightful.' He rubbed his chubby hands together in anticipation, enjoying the banter.

Betty threw an egg and two sausages on a plate and

brought it to the table, tossing it under Castilan's crooked nose. As she turned to leave, Castilan grabbed her apron and pulled her back towards him, smothering her in a passionate embrace. Jack blushed. Where was Davey when you needed him?

'Thank you, my dear,' Castilan said as he released Betty and picked up his fork. Betty smiled to herself and returned to the kitchen, spurred on by a hearty slap to her rear from Castilan's hand.

The old ceiling creaked and groaned. Jack looked up and saw Davey at the top of the stairs, weary and dishevelled.

'Here comes the mighty warrior,' Castilan teased. 'Ready for battle?'

Davey grunted as he sat down at the table, his tired eyes inspecting their plates of food. Betty bustled in with a plate for Davey.

The bar door opened and a gust of fresh dawn air stroked Jack's legs. The majestic silhouette of Eloise filled the door frame. She had discarded her ancient armour and now wore a long dark dress, pulled in by a heavy belt round her waist from which hung her mighty sword. Her dark hair was silky clean and pulled back into a loose ponytail, making her look less fearsome and revealing her beautiful pale face for the first time. A hooded cape hung about her neck, and over her shoulder she carried four lifeless foxes tied onto a stick. She gave the foxes to Betty, who accepted them without emotion.

Jack gazed in silent awe. She looked more alive now, animated and vibrant, ready to take on the world.

Castilan's face reddened with consternation. 'Where have you been?' he demanded.

'I have not hunted in a long time,' Eloise said with a flash of a smile. 'It is good to be out again.'

'But I'm the only one with a key to that door,' Castilan protested. 'This is *my* tavern. I know who comes and goes. I know who's here. How? How did you . . .' His voice faded away.

'So,' Eloise asked, ignoring Castilan, 'we must find a Boagyman. Yes?'

Castilan smiled, trying to regain his composure. 'Yes, well, I have that all in hand.'

'This is not necessary,' Eloise said, her French accent suddenly much stronger. 'I have contacted one already.'

'You've what?' Castilan stood, hardly able to contain his anger. Behind him Betty laughed.

'I have agreed passage for myself, Jack and Davey. He is on his way here now.'

'But, but what of the cost?' Castilan spluttered. 'I can negotiate a fair deal. I can—'

'Terms have been agreed.'

Castilan shouted, 'I will not have a Boagyman in my house, not without my say-so!'

Jack did his best to hold in a smile. He felt a growing

admiration for Eloise.

'I am sorry,' Eloise said, her tone unchanged. 'The Boagyman is on his way. Perhaps you would like to explain—'

'No! No, I would not,' Castilan spluttered, alarm flashing over his red face. 'This is a fine way to repay my hospitality, after everything I've done for you.' He turned to face Davey, his hand outstretched.

Davey looked up from his food. 'What? You want more? I've paid you enough.'

'Damages, breakages. Boagymen are never subtle.'

Jack put his hand on Davey's arm and said softly, 'Just pay him, Davey. Don't be an idiot.'

Davey put up his hands, defeated, and pulled out the grubby stolen wallet again. 'OK, I'll pay,' he said. 'But don't think you can rip me off!'

Castilan feigned offence at the comment, but his hand remained outstretched.

Suddenly the room began to shake, as if a fast train was passing by outside. The glasses behind the bar rattled and juddered violently; one fell off and shattered on the stone floor. As the vibrations increased and the floor bent under his feet, Jack could see the walls twist, expanding and contracting as if to allow some large object to pass behind them. The distortion spiralled towards the stairs, and the tiny wooden door underneath them, then the vibrations lessened and the noise died away. As the glasses stopped rattling Jack heard a hiss, like a huge valve being released, and a plume of blue smoke spread out from under the wooden door. The gas dissipated into the air and an ominous calm settled over the bar.

The brass door knob rattled, and then slowly turned anticlockwise. The little wooden door opened and more blue smoke billowed outwards; as it settled Jack saw something emerge from within. A long thin hand gripped the frame, then another on the opposite side. The hands tensed and a shoulder pushed outwards at the top of the door. Next, a booted foot appeared on the stone floor, followed by a long, thin leg whose calf was almost the height of the door. As the body pushed outwards, the frame creaked and threatened to give way before a shabby head emerged and the figure of a Boagyman freed itself from the door. His body seemed to unravel in front of Jack's eyes, his head rising and hitting the ceiling with a thump. The ungainly creature must have been at least nine feet tall and was so thin that every bone seemed to burst out of his earthy skin. His eyes were set deep into his head, shielded by a heavy brow, which cast dark shadows over his face, and his pointed nose capped a dark beard, which melted into a long mane of matted hair that hung about his shoulders in dirty braided clumps. He wore an old pair of overalls, which were far too small for him and made him hunch over like an inquisitive ape.

The bizarre thing coughed, and two twinkling eyes peered out from their deep sockets and looked around the room.

'Morning,' he said with a dry voice. 'Which one of you lot called a Boagyman?'

'Greetings, Boagyman,' said Eloise, stepping forward to meet him. 'My name is Eloise and I summoned you. May I know your name?'

'Torbalan, ma'am.' He pointed to a grubby embroidered patch on his chest; the faded letters spelt out his name.

'Thank you for coming, Torbalan.' Eloise bowed graciously and the Boagyman nodded in acceptance. 'We wish council with a Limner.' As she spoke the lanky creature scratched at the walls and ceiling, sensing his surroundings through his long yellowing fingernails.

'Tricky,' Torbalan said, rubbing his thick beard and pulling it into a rough point. 'I've not seen a Limner since, oh, about 1918, I think. Might have been 1917, come to think of it.' He shook his head, looking puzzled by his own words. '1916, probably. It's not important.'

'Can you find one?' Eloise asked, her voice conveying the frustration Jack was feeling.

'Aye, probably, hang on there.' The Boagyman crawled back into the tiny doorway, his bony bottom rising upwards as he crawled on his hands and knees searching for something. Eventually he stood back up and pulled out a large cloth sack, from which he produced an

139

ancient-looking map, torn and yellowed at the edges. He unfolded it carefully and studied the rune-like images that covered its surface.

'Difficult,' Torbalan said as he sniffed at the map, turning it upside down and holding it to the light. He turned it over again and studied it through squinted eyes. 'Yes, difficult but not impossible.' He paused to consider his statement, a far-off expression on his face. 'Probably impossible,' he said apologetically as he folded up the map and it disappeared back into his sack. Then he stood up as tall and straight as he could, his head rubbing the ceiling, and smiled at Eloise. 'Yes, I'm sure it's almost probably impossible, but let's give it a try, shall we?' He locked his fingers together and cracked his knuckles, which made loud popping noises. 'How many are we?'

Eloise pointed to Jack and Davey. 'Three, including myself.'

'Payment is upfront,' Torbalan said. 'Too much bad debt. Can't trust anyone these days. Very sorry.'

Jack saw the scowl on Castilan's face, but Eloise nodded in agreement and pulled a small knife from her belt. She took her black hair in her hand and cut the entire ponytail off with the sharp blade. She gave the hair to Torbalan, who snatched it from her, sniffing and tasting it like a hungry animal. Jack watched in stunned silence as Torbalan took the hair and put it into the front pocket of his overalls.

'Good quality, very old.' He smiled his approval and turned to crawl uncomfortably back through the small door, dragging his sack in behind him. 'All aboard, please.'

Eloise stooped gracefully and followed Torbalan into the tiny space.

Jack turned to Davey. 'Ladies first.'

Davey's lopsided smile spread over his face. He thumped Jack playfully as he disappeared into the cupboard.

'Thanks for looking after me,' Jack said to Betty and Castilan with a smile.

Castilan scowled, thoroughly displeased with the turn of events, but Betty managed a brief smile before her face returned to its usual stony visage.

'Go on, get going,' she said abruptly. Jack crawled into the cupboard and the wooden door slammed tightly shut behind him.

# 14

## THE PIPELINE

The tiny cupboard was hot and dingy. Jack elbowed and jostled with his three companions for room, desperate to find a more comfortable position. The clutter of the cupboard rattled and took on a menacing spectre; in this tiny coffin the brooms, buckets and junk became oversized and oppressive. The old coats and shoes were burying him and a sudden, uncontrollable wave of claustrophobia washed over him, like a heavy blanket smothering his face. His lungs clawed for air as panic took hold, and his arm fumbled in the dark for the door handle while his lungs refused to work.

Suddenly the floor fell, and Jack along with it. His stomach lurched, and the cupboard's contents disappeared upwards, taking his numbing claustrophobia with them. He screamed, in relief as much as terror.

They fell for several minutes, icy air rushing over Jack's face, soothing his sickness until, with a judder, they came to a halt. As his eyes adjusted to the weak crimson light he saw Davey, Eloise and Torbalan were still close by. The cupboard's walls and ceiling had gone; all that remained now was a small wooden platform with cables and wires connected to its underside. Jack peered over the edge of the tiny floor and another sensation took hold: vertigo. All around them was a void – an endless, dark nothing.

'Where are we?' he asked fearfully.

'This is the Boagyman's province, the Realm of Oblivion,' Eloise said quietly.

Torbalan mumbled under his breath as he rummaged in his sack, searching for something. With a tug he pulled out a glowing lantern on a long stick and dropped it into a hole on the edge of the floor where it cast a warm light down onto the platform. Next he pulled out the old map again and a thick pencil, its end worn and chewed. He inspected the map in the flickering light and began to draw a long spidery line between two rune symbols. Almost immediately Jack heard something coming towards them from the darkness, screeching and wheezing, and a large metallic pipe appeared out of the murk. The snake-like shape grew larger as it approached and he could see a multitude of smaller cables running over its pitted surface, like maggots devouring flesh. Jets of hot steam escaped from the joints along its length as it grew out of itself, each new section thinner than the last until, by the time it had arrived at their platform, it was no larger than a few centimetres across. It pushed itself aggressively into a slot on the underside of the platform, and a huge blast of steam hissed upwards through the gaps in the rickety platform, heating Jack's legs to an uncomfortable temperature. There was nowhere for Jack to move, but the steam cut off abruptly as the myriad smaller cables caught up with the central pipe. With a multitude of clicks, hisses and whistles they linked to the platform until, like ivy growing over a tree trunk, they consumed the main pipe.

The pipe wheezed and groaned as pressure built inside, causing the platform to vibrate, gently at first, then much more forcefully, until Jack was sure that the whole thing could explode. The noise became deafening, with cables banging against each other, steam hissing and metal groaning against wood. He instinctively crouched down, his hands gripping the side of the platform. Eloise and Davey were soon kneeling next to him with only the Boagyman still standing

'Need to build up the pressure!' Torbalan shouted, his voice barely audible over the racket. 'Won't be a moment. Very sorry.' He scribbled something onto the map, and the platform suddenly propelled itself along the pipe, lurching and bucking as it crossed the uneven track.

In the darkness around them Jack caught fleeting glimpses of shapes passing by rapidly – other rooms from a thousand different houses, all somehow connected in the Boagyman's province.

'This must be magic,' Jack said, thinking out loud.

'Not magic,' Eloise replied. 'A treaty made this happen. Centuries ago the Boagymen were a mighty and proud race of architects. They taught the founders of the First World the great secrets of geometry. It allowed enlightened men to build greater and bigger cities, in both the First and Second Worlds. In return they asked for a portion of all of our buildings. So the smallest rooms became theirs to use as a conduit between the realms. Since then the Boagymen's numbers have dwindled, their society crumbled away.'

Torbalan grunted, as if recalling some distant time. 'Weavers. Vermin. They hunt us. They take our souls.'

After several minutes the pipe changed direction and the platform fell straight down, like a car on a terrifying roller-coaster ride. They were jolted in different directions; sometimes down, sometimes up, at one point even twisting over so that, for a moment, Jack felt like they were travelling upside down.

Out of the gloom other pipes appeared, each as long and twisted as their own, and each suspended impossibly in space without any means of support. Sometimes they passed what appeared to be crossings, where two or more pipes would intersect, and Torbalan would draw a route on his map that would take them onto a new pipe.

They passed through clouds of steam, which condensed into raindrops and fell back onto the pipeline; the rain stung Jack's face and stained the platform, leaving behind dark rings of ash. Ahead, a flock of bird-like creatures, dark shapes each as large as a man, fed off the cables, pulling and pecking at their casings. As the platform accelerated towards them the gulls rose sharply into the air, circling overhead, squawking and crowing until they had passed them by.

As they travelled further along the pipeline Jack sensed a growing melancholy in Eloise; looking at her, he saw that the soft lantern light had illuminated moist tears on her cheeks.

'Eloise,' he said, reaching out awkwardly to touch her hand. 'Are you all right?'

She forced a smile. 'I cannot feel him any more.'

'Who?' Davey listened intently. 'You mean Rouland, don't you?'

Eloise nodded as she wiped her face dry. 'He brought me back to life, so long ago now. He gave me his breath; I have always felt him since that day. I have never left his side. Even in my long imprisonment he was never far away from me.' She shook her head. 'But now, here, in this realm, I feel less than whole. The further away I get from him the less alive I feel. I hate him. I wish he were dead. And if he dies I wish that I will also die.' Hope flickered into her eyes.

'I thought you *were* dead?' Davey said.

'I do not live, that is true. Not like you. But to die, to truly cease to exist. To be released from this unending pit of guilt . . .' Eloise shook her head. 'When you have lived as

146

long as I have, had to do the things I was made to do, you too would welcome death with open arms.'

Jack's mind filled with thoughts of his mother's death and he was suddenly angry. 'You wouldn't say that if you were going to die.'

'Jack, I have died before. I know of what I speak.'

Jack turned to Davey and tried to imagine him as the old man he had met in a graveyard, the same old man who gave his life so that Jack could escape. He felt angry and empty, but in spite of everything he'd lost already he knew that life – any life – was precious.

A cold breeze shook him out of his miserable thoughts; he looked up to see the platform fall off the end of the pipeline and land painfully onto another one several metres below.

'I'm gonna live for ever,' Davey said cheerfully.

Jack winced.

'Do not wish for such a thing,' Eloise said. 'Great books always end, and they are better for it. Would you think a great story improved if it never ended? Even the noblest adventure would become tedious, meaningless. The most virtuous hero would be corrupted by time and become something base and hideous. No, we die for a good reason.'

They travelled on in silence until the platform came to a screeching halt. Jack looked at the Boagyman. He was studying his map and mumbling to himself again.

'He's lost,' Davey said.

'No, no, not lost,' replied Torbalan, hearing him. 'Just not quite found. We might have to go to the Lowlands to pick up the trail. Haven't been there since 1880, or 1885. Bad place. Full of Weavers.' He turned the map over and raised his pencil into the air.

'What is a weaver?' Jack asked.

But Torbalan didn't even acknowledge his question. 'You might not like this bit,' he said apologetically. He swung his hand down and stabbed the pencil into the map.

Almost at once the pipeline disconnected itself and ripped away from the platform, knocking it sideways. They began to fall, increasing speed with every second. The air around them crackled and sparked, illuminating the platform with short bursts of blue light. Below them the air ripped open in a whirlpool of gas and lightning and Jack gasped as the furious vortex consumed the little platform. Lightning coursed over it, tiny static shocks stinging his body, and there was a smell not unlike rotten eggs, painfully sharp. The moisture in his mouth and eyes evaporated and he could no longer see anything but white light. Every inch of his body cried out in pain, yet he could do nothing but cling to the platform and submit to it, his eyes clamped shut.

And then the lightning stopped. For a moment he lay very still, catching his breath. He tried to open his eyes again. They felt scratched and dry, like after a swimming lesson, but much worse. Blurry shapes appeared before him: Eloise and Davey.

To Jack's surprise, Torbalan stood upright and peeled a banana he had pulled from his sack. 'Always makes me hungry,' he said as he swallowed large chunks of the soft fruit, before eating the skin as well. He brushed his hands clean and smiled a banana-filled smile. 'Welcome to the Lowlands.'

The air around them swirled with a green mist that reeked of decay. Jack's eyes adjusted and he looked over the platform; they were drifting above an endless lake of dark muddy liquid that constantly bubbled and boiled, spewing out stinking gasps of the green mist.

Torbalan sniffed at the air, then picked up his sack and pulled out a large spherical object that hung from a piece of twisted cord. Raising his hand, he let the sphere swing back and forth freely. It flapped open to reveal a large dilated pupil – a giant bloodshot eyeball that darted quickly in every direction, tugging on its cord.

'He's got a dowsing eye,' Davey said in amazement.

'What is that?' Jack said, disgusted.

'Need it to pick up the trail,' Torbalan explained. 'Dowsing eye will find it.'

Eloise was not looking at the swinging eyeball; she had turned to peer out into the misty void. 'We are not alone here,' she said.

'What is it?' Jack asked.

Torbalan looked up, his deep-set eyes flashed through with fear. 'Weavers.'

'That's probably not a good thing, is it?' Jack said.

'Weavers are abominations, cursed to sail the Lowland Lake,' Eloise said. 'They weave coats from your soul.'

Davey laughed. 'They're going to knit us into jumpers?'

Jack chuckled too, despite the situation. But Eloise's concerned expression made the laughter dry up on his lips.

A bell rang out and the blurred shape of a boat appeared in the mist. It floated above the stinking lake, rising up slowly towards their little platform. The ship was vast; silhouettes of twisted figures lurched about the deck and as the bell rang again Jack could hear the shrill cries of a thousand tortured souls drifting on the mist. No matter how long he lived, he would never forget that sound. He shook as he turned to plead with Torbalan to take them far away. He opened his mouth but panic had caught his breath – he had never felt a terror so powerful. Eloise and Davey seemed to be paralysed too, unable to resist.

The energy to fight drained away from him, leaving only a feeling of grim inevitability.

Yet Torbalan toiled on, the eye still searching, looking for the right way to go. The Weavers' ship bore down on them, its wooden prow breaking through the mist as echoing voices shouted out orders. And all the while the unending sorrow of the lost souls cried out, louder and louder, closer and closer. This was a million times worse than travelling through a Sorrowline.

Jack could take no more. He fell forward, his head banging off the wooden planks. He felt the bodies of Eloise and Davey land heavily next to him, all of them prone, immobile and helpless.

Torbalan dropped to his knees, the crying beginning to affect even him. His hand was still stretched out in front of him, and the dowsing eye swayed rapidly while his other hand gripped his pencil tightly, its tip hovering over the map spread out on the platform floor.

The Weavers' ship's bell rang again, followed by the metallic rasp of harpoon cannons firing. Long needle-like missiles fired towards them, intent on pulling the little platform onto the ship's deck and harvesting the souls on board.

At that very moment the dowsing eye froze, pointing into the darkness.

'At last,' whispered Torbalan. With his last vestige of strength he scratched a line onto his map.

The platform jerked into life and a long pipeline snaked towards them at high speed. It hit the platform violently, knocking it to one side just as a volley of needle harpoons whistled past them, missing their target by inches. As Jack slid to the edge of the platform, he felt the pipe take hold of them and they moved abruptly away from the Weavers' ship.

Another volley of harpoons shrieked through the mist, but dropped short of the accelerating platform and disappeared into the muddy waters below. The wailing cries lessened and drifted into nothing, and Jack felt his strength returning. Torbalan was already on his feet and working away on his map, as if nothing had happened.

'I found him,' he said excitedly. 'I've found a Limner.'

Eloise and Davey sat up, each with a look of despair on their tear-filled faces. Jack was sure he looked exactly the same and took no joy in their escape – he felt only the pain of the lost souls they had left behind . . .

# 15

## MONTY'S DEAL

The little platform sped onwards through Oblivion until, after several hours, it began to slow down. They were cold and wet from flying through the mist for so long, and the wind had chilled them further. As they jolted to a stop they were flushed with warmer air that lifted their trodden spirits.

Torbalan smiled at Jack, Davey and Eloise. 'Nothing's impossible, eh?' He winked at them and, with a scribble on his map, the platform began to rise rapidly. The air chilled again, and the mist darkened and blurred. There was a crack like thunder and the platform rattled to a halt. Jack opened his eyes and saw that the platform had walls and a ceiling again. But this was not the small cupboard under the stairs of the Hanging Tavern: they were in a well-stocked larder.

The room was tiny, but at least the ceiling was tall enough to stand upright. The shelves groaned under the weight of meats, bread, jars of home-made pickles and dusty bottles of wine. In front of them was a closed door.

'Last stop,' said Torbalan.

'We are at the Limner's?' asked Eloise.

Torbalan studied his map. 'As best as I can tell, yes.'

Jack tried the handle; it was unlocked and with trepidation he opened it and stepped out of the larder.

'Thank you all,' Torbalan said as he ushered Davey and Eloise out with an unconvincing smile. 'Do let me know if you require my services again.' He pulled the door shut behind them. Almost immediately a thunderous clap sounded and a plume of blue smoke poured out from beneath the door. The Boagyman had gone.

Jack found himself in a large kitchen, dark and deserted. A clock on the wall read two-thirty. Outside aeroplanes droned overhead, bombs exploded in the distance and sirens echoed through the empty streets. They had returned to London, 1940.

Silently they ventured out of the kitchen, Eloise in front with her hand gripping the hilt of her sword, Jack and Davey behind her. As they walked through a long corridor into a grand hallway Jack wondered who this house might belong to, what new strangers he might meet. A wide stairway curved gracefully upwards from the marble floor, its polished oak banisters reflecting blue moonlight. Flashes of anti-aircraft fire illuminated the hall in staccato bursts, lifting objects out of the gloom: a striking painting hung on the wall, a collection of fine vases nestled on a delicate mahogany table, a superbly crafted grandfather clock.

'Well,' said Davey, 'looks like no one's home, might as well help ourselves to that larder back there.'

'Someone *is* here,' Eloise said quietly.

'Your dead friend is quite correct,' a gravelly voice echoed out of the darkness. Eloise whipped round, her sword drawn, as she tried to find the voice's source.

'Please, put away your sword, there is no need for hostility.' The voice came from a reception room just off the entrance hall. The door was open and Eloise cautiously entered, with Jack and Davey following nervously behind.

Book-laden shelves interspersed with all manner of odd-looking antiques and collectables covered three walls of the little room. At its centre was a large reading chair. A white-haired old man in a purple velvet smoking jacket stared back at them, stroking his neatly trimmed beard.

'I presume you travelled here with a Boagyman?' he said as he put the book he had been reading onto a table next to the chair. 'I really must get a lock put onto my larder.'

'Are you a Limner?' said Eloise, her sword raised in front of her. 'You can see beyond the visible?'

Her question went unanswered. 'Really, I have no stomach for swordplay, put the weapon away.'

Eloise slowly placed her sword back in its scabbard.

'Thank you,' said the man. 'Now, shall we start afresh? My name is Montgomery Falconer, and this is my home. Everyone calls me Monty. You may call me Monty if you like.'

155

Jack stepped forward and said, 'Hello, Monty. The lady with the sword is Eloise, that's Davey and my name is Jack.' He held out his hand to Monty.

'No!' Eloise shouted and tried to pull Jack back, but he was already shaking the old man by the hand. Monty held his hand for the briefest of moments, yet time seemed to stretch out for ever. His hand was cool and slender; it reminded Jack of his nan's. But he felt something else as well – a burst of images inside his head. It was so fleeting that he could not make sense of what he had seen, like something had just stimulated long-forgotten memories, but he felt connected to places and events he had never seen, to a history that stretched back beyond his birth. It was like he was travelling along his own Sorrowline. He recoiled in surprise, breathless and shaking.

'I am sorry, Jack,' Monty said, his voice broken. 'I should not have touched you without first explaining. I had presumed your Paladin friend had already completed that small task, but no matter.' Monty rubbed his hand.

'Did you . . . did you read my mind?' Jack asked, still in a daze.

'He is a Limner,' Eloise said tersely. 'He senses through touching. He sees through his fingers.'

'Quite a romantic explanation, Eloise,' Monty said, regaining his composure, 'but true enough. By touching you I was briefly connected to everything you have ever touched. I could see the chain of events that has brought you here, even the events you yourself have never directly witnessed. Each life is a single strand in a much bigger web. I can see that web.'

'What does that mean?' asked Jack.

'It means I know what brought you here. You're looking for the Rose of Annwn.' Monty's face was unreadable, like an unchanging death mask. 'You're not the first, you know? Many have searched for it over the years, none have found it. But they all think *I* can help.' The Limner shrugged.

'Can you?' asked Davey.

'As I said, many have asked that of me. Until today I never knew where it was.'

'And now you do?' Jack leaned closer to Monty, listening intently.

'Now I do. The Rose has touched you, Jack. And now *you* have touched *me*. A Limner – at least, one worth his mustard – can see beyond mere light and shade. We see through the cracks of space and time to the infinite beyond. And, if we are very, very good, we can see things that no other man can see. And I am very, very good. Thanks to you I can now see the Rose. Strange that it was hidden from me for all this time, but now I understand why.' Monty smiled; he was enjoying this. 'I suppose what you're asking yourself,' he continued, 'is: am I going to help you find it, or am I going to scurry off to tell Rouland where it is.'

'We don't have much to offer you but—'

'That is not true, Jack. I saw a great many things when we shook hands. You are a Yard Boy, are you not?'

'So they tell me,' Jack replied doubtfully.

'And one of remarkable range, if I am correct. Then a deal can be done. I have little time for Rouland. He wishes nothing but control. I prefer the world with a little bit of chaos around the fringes; it makes for a much more enjoyable life. But Rouland has offered me much in the past to find the Rose, and I would have accepted his offer had I known how to fulfil my side of the bargain, something I was unable to do until this day. The Rose is a thing of great power, if the legends are to be believed. Rouland seeks that power so that he can rule Otherworld and all other realms, including our own. It's all whispered nonsense, of course, but Rouland believes it, says he's been there. Belief in a thing can be very dangerous.'

'But the Rose exists?'

'Oh, it exists all right,' Monty said. 'I no longer question the validity of the Rose. As for the folklore that surrounds it . . .' He waved his hand dismissively.

'Where will I find it?'

'First you must give me what *I* desire, then the location of the Rose is yours to do with as you see fit, and Rouland need never know.'

'What do you want?' Jack asked uneasily.

Monty grinned broadly. 'Straight to the point. Well done,

young Jack. What I desire is something only you can give me. I am a collector, you see.' Monty gestured to the many shelves, full of rare books and ornaments. 'When I was young I used my gift to find things, rare objects that had a value in the Second World. I have lived a comfortable life here in this house, and grown to love my collection more than you could know. But the problem with collecting beautiful things is that you are never satisfied. There is always one more beautiful thing to collect.'

Monty stood slowly, his old bones creaking under his slight weight. He hobbled over to his bookshelf and studied the titles, running his fingers along the spines.

'How far back can you go?' Monty asked. 'How far back in time will the Sorrowlines take you, Jack?'

'I don't know, I've—'

'He's the best I've ever seen,' Davey interrupted. 'If anyone can fetch you something Jack can.'

Monty laughed. 'You make an excellent salesman, Davey. I require a book: *On the Nature of the Concealed Realms* by Magnus Hafgan.'

Eloise's eyes widened. 'You want *that* book? Your price is too high.'

'Of course.' Monty chuckled. 'I forgot that you would know of it.'

'Rouland sought that book too. In it is a guide, a way back to Otherworld. That, combined with the Rose, would give him everything he desires.'

'Yes,' Monty soothed. 'It is a rather rare edition. In fact, there is but one copy, which was last recorded in the January of 1813.' He said the date slowly, letting the enormity of his request sink in.

Davey was aghast. '1813? No one's ever been that far back!'

'I know.' Monty smiled. 'Do you think I have not tried before? I have commissioned many a Yard Boy in the past, and none has ever succeeded. But I sense our young friend here is quite special.'

'What do you want with this book?' Eloise said tersely.

'I am a collector.' Monty gestured to the many shelves filled with books.

'You will give it to Rouland.'

'Perhaps.' Monty's lips stretched into a wire-like smile. 'But there is much to study in that book. Many secrets are hidden inside its pages, and I must know its true value before a sale can be made. It would take me years to properly digest its contents. Then, and only then, will I choose a worthy owner. You will find I am a patient man.'

'I'll do it,' said Jack impulsively.

Davey pulled at his arm. 'Jack, it's dangerous. You go back that far and you could get lost, or worse.'

Eloise nodded solemnly. 'Davey is right, Jack. The task is too dangerous.'

'Now, now,' Monty said, waving a cautionary finger in front of him, 'let's not fill the boy's head with horror stories.

It's a simple choice. You can either agree to my terms, bring me the book and I will tell you where to find the Rose, or we part as gentlemen. Perhaps a deal can be made with Rouland.'

Eloise drew her sword again, but Jack held up his hand. 'I said I'll do it.' He just knew he had to follow this link to his family, to find his place in the First World.

'Jack...' Davey's eyes pleaded with him.

'Where will I find it?' Jack asked, ignoring Davey's concerns.

'Right here on Wren Street,' Monty said. 'There is nothing random in my purchase of this property. This house used to belong to the last-known owner of the book, one Jane McBride. You'll find a church at the end of this street, on Grey's Inn Road: St Bartholomew's. There is a headstone, dated the thirteenth of January 1813: Timothy McBride, Jane's husband. After his death the book disappeared. That book should live on for ever. If you bring it to me I will ensure that it does.'

Eloise grabbed Jack's arm. 'This book,' she said, 'it is a dangerous thing. Perhaps it is better lost.'

Jack shook his head. 'It's our best chance to find the Rose.'

'Perhaps this is exactly what Rouland wants: the Rose *and* the book in his reach.'

The same thought had occurred to Jack. He knew the risks were high. 'I have to try, for my family.'

Eloise stepped towards Monty. 'I will remain here until Jack returns. No other deals will be made.'

Monty sighed as he dropped back into his reading chair. 'As you wish.'

Jack nodded and walked towards the entrance hall without another word. Davey ran after him. 'Jack, wait for me!'

Outside it was still dark and quiet. Davey caught up with Jack as he crossed the road.

'Are you mad?' Davey asked.

'I don't think so. What choice do I have?'

'No one ever went so far back. Fifty years is a good stretch, some manage sixty. Over a hundred? It's impossible.'

'I did over seventy getting here,' Jack said.

'You got lucky. You don't know the dangers. You've not even been trained.'

'So train me!'

'I'm not a Yard Boy.' Davey sighed. 'I don't have the same gift as you.'

'Your older self said you were. And he promised to train me.'

'I say lots of things, Jack.' There was a pathetic, self-loathing tone in Davey's voice.

'But you still know more than me,' Jack replied. 'You can help me get through.'

'It's madness.'

'You're right,' Jack admitted. 'But I'm going to try

anyway, so are you coming with me or are you going to wait with Eloise?'

Jack stared at Davey, waiting for an answer, hoping his fear wasn't showing. Davey didn't reply. Jack shrugged and turned to walk towards the little church nestled at the end of the street.

'Wait! I'm coming, I'm coming.'

# 16

## FOOL'S ERRAND

'Here it is,' Jack shouted. 'Timothy McBride, the thirteenth of January 1813.'

The church's graveyard was small and run-down, and there were only a few intact headstones still standing, so it hadn't taken long for Jack to find the right one. A large stone statue of an angel with its wings outstretched marked the grave.

He stopped and turned to Davey, a new question bursting to the front of his mind. 'Can I bring things through with me?'

'Did you arrive here naked?' Davey said.

Jack smiled to himself, relieved that he hadn't.

'You can bring things with you, but it's harder if they're bigger,' Davey explained. 'Remember that and you should be fine.'

'*Should?*' Jack replied, the mix of doubt and trepidation dancing in his stomach growing.

'Look, you wanted to do this, not me. So, are you going to find the Sorrowline or not?' Davey asked impatiently.

Jack put his hand to the old gravestone.

'Can you feel anything?' Davey asked.

'No, not yet.'

'I told you it was crazy. It's too long ago,' Davey said. 'The Sorrowline will have gone by now.'

Suddenly an image flashed into Jack's head: a horse pulling a laden cart. 'I've got something.'

'What? I don't believe it.' Davey put his own hand on the stone.

'It was really faint,' Jack said, 'but it's getting stronger now.'

'I can't feel anything.'

Jack opened his eyes and looked at Davey. 'Have you *ever* been a Yard Boy?'

'No,' Davey confessed. 'My old man was, so everyone thought I would be too, an' I got trained by a Journeyman, for a while. Showed me how to open up a Sorrowline, all the basics, but I never got the knack of it. I just don't have the gift like you.' He let his hand drop from the stone.

'Wait,' Jack said. 'It's fading again. Put your hand back.'

Davey did as Jack asked and closed his eyes.

Jack smiled. 'Yeah, it's there again.' He grabbed Davey's other hand and clasped it tightly.

Jack could feel it now, Davey's touch somehow amplifying his own. A stream of images washed over him – he saw the burial, and the accident that caused the death; the pain of broken bones pulsed through him.

'I felt that!' Davey said, laughing in spite of the dim pain.

Jack pushed and felt a way in. 'I've got it,' he whispered.

Unexpectedly his hand was in pain, as if being pulled apart. He tried to drag it out of Davey's, but it was too late, he was in the Sorrowline. He couldn't scream, he couldn't move, yet the pain grew. It felt as if his arm was stretching out, shredding, one fibre at a time. Inside the pain was a flood of images, more vivid than he had ever experienced on either of his two journeys through the Sorrowlines before.

He was a young boy crying over his dead mother, yet it was not his own . . .

His drunken father was holding him under the cold waters of the Thames, willing him to die, and he felt the horror of betrayal by someone beloved . . .

He was hitting back, and suddenly free and running barefoot through the dark streets of London . . .

He was alone in the rain, shivering and hungry . . .

He was befriended, then betrayed by a white-haired boy . . .

Two men were hitting him in the face, dragging him over cobbles, taking him deep underground . . .

He was thrown onto a strange ship, and then he was leaping off it, into the unknown . . .

He was back in London, sore and broken, with no one to help him . . .

The fear and loneliness numbed the pain, but it did not

subside. He wished it would all go away, he could bear it no longer...

He felt a rope around his neck, felt his own fear, his own regret, his own cowardice...

And then he saw his own face, looking back at him...

Jack was drowning in memories.

Just when he thought he could take no more he felt frozen ground beneath him, and soft flakes of snow falling on his face. His brain felt heavy, full of new memories, and a tremendous sense of loss and failure filled him with sadness. His arm still hurt, and when he tried to move it something was holding it down. He turned his head to see what was wrong: the unconscious body of Davey lay heavily over it. He pulled out his arm and rolled Davey onto his back checking quickly. Yes, he was still breathing.

Jack looked around the snow-covered graveyard. The large angel statue had gone. He stared back at Davey in disbelief: had his friend really travelled with him through the Sorrowline?

'Davey,' he whispered, 'wake up.' He tapped him gently about the face and Davey's eyes flickered open.

'Why are you slapping me?' Davey's voice was dry and rough.

Jack laughed. 'Do you know what just happened?'

Davey sat up with a start.

'We both came through the Sorrowline,' Jack explained. 'This is 1813.'

'Are you sure?'

'Yes, I think so. The headstone has gone, and look, it's snowing!'

'But what am *I* doing here?'

'You came through too, Davey. Together, we were strong enough to get us through. I suppose it runs in the family, after all.' Jack could hardly control his glee. He had not dared to admit how terrified he had been about coming to 1813, about what might happen, about doing it alone. He held out his hand to Davey and pulled him onto his feet. Davey was unsteady at first and, for a moment, Jack thought he might be sick, but after taking several deep, chilly breaths the colour began to return to Davey's face.

'We're really in 1813?'

'Yes,' Jack said. Somehow he just knew it.

'And I came through with you?'

'Yes. You're a Yard Boy too, Davey.'

'I . . . I suppose I am.' Davey's face broke into a smile, then a toothy grin. His eyebrows arched and then he laughed loudly. Abruptly Davey stopped, spinning round like a startled animal.

'What's wrong?' Jack asked.

Davey shivered. 'Dunno. Just felt like we were being watched.'

Jack studied the churchyard, but he couldn't see anyone else nearby. 'Come on,' he said cautiously. 'Let's get out of here.'

168

Davey nodded, and the two boys slowly retraced the steps they'd just taken in 1940 – out of the churchyard, back down the street and towards the grand townhouse that would one day belong to Montgomery Falconer.

The snow-covered street was busy with the clatter of hansom carriages and carts, their horses wary of the icy roads. Men busied about their day. Some stood talking and laughing, with thick plumes of icy breath drifting about their heads. Others stepped briskly on the white path, intent upon their business. Here and there were small children, playing happily, seemingly unaffected by the chill as they skipped through the drifting snow. Jack gazed at the contrasting differences in the city he had now known in 2013 and 1940. So much was still familiar, unchanged down the decades, yet other parts were unrecognisable. The wooden ramshackle streets with their narrow winding paths full of horses and carts made London feel like an historic theme park built in a farmer's field.

Little attention was paid to Jack and Davey, their dirty 1940s clothes did not seem so out of place here as they might have been in Jack's time.

'Do you suppose we'll get back all right?' Jack asked.

'Dunno,' said Davey. 'I didn't think we'd get here, be a miracle if we got back 'n' all.' He smiled still, but his eyes betrayed a faraway look of alarm.

Jack shuddered. 'We *have* to get back.' He had to save his mother's life.

Back in 1940, the row of houses had looked worn and weary, and bore the scars of ill-judged modifications. Now, so much further in the past, the houses were smart and new, their clean outlines softened by the growing blanket of snow.

As they approached the McBrides' house Jack hesitated. 'What are we going to do? We can't just knock on the door and ask her for the book.'

Davey thought for a moment, then announced, 'Leave this to me; this is my area of expertise.'

Jack observed the puffed-up confidence of Davey, and a sudden realisation came over him: the dark visions he had seen in the Sorrowline, the life lived on the street, the years of hardship, the tragedy of a broken youth: those were not all Timothy McBride's memories laid down inside the Sorrowline. Some had been dragged up from the hidden parts of Davey's mind. He looked at his friend and pitied him for what he'd been through.

Davey knocked confidently on the door of the large house. After a moment they heard someone in the grand entrance hall, then the door opened and a small man looked at them suspiciously. He was dressed in the tight-fitting uniform of a domestic servant, no doubt the McBrides' butler, Jack supposed.

'Good morning, sir,' Davey beamed.

'It's three in the afternoon,' the butler said drily.

'Is it?' Davey looked up into the grey sky. 'My apologies.

My master has sent me, sir. *Morrow and Vale Book-binders*, at your service. He has asked me to collect a book for repair.'

Jack was impressed at his quick thinking. Davey's broad accent was instantly tamed, reminding Jack of the older David he had met in 2008.

The butler squinted at Davey and Jack, and pulled out a pair of half-moon spectacles, which he propped on the end of his long nose. 'What is your master's name, boy?'

'Mr William Vale, sir. Morrow and Vale Bookbinders.'

'Never heard of him,' the butler hissed. 'Wait here.' He slammed the door firmly, leaving Jack to wonder if he would ever return.

Eventually the door opened again, and a tall elegant man stood in the doorway.

'What's all this about a book?' the man asked. 'I require no repairs.'

'I believe it was the lady of the house who placed the order,' Davey said quickly. 'It's called *On the Nature of the Concealed Realms*. If you could bring it we will be on our way, sir.'

At the mention of the book's title the man visibly tensed. 'My wife is unavailable,' he retorted. 'And I have no interest in that detestable book.'

'Wife?' Jack said, aghast.

'Yes,' the man said. 'What of it?'

'You're Timothy McBride,' Jack said, his stomach in knots. 'What's the date?'

'I beg your pardon?' Timothy McBride frowned.

'Today's date,' Jack demanded. 'Do you know what it is? Is this the thirteenth?'

'Young man, your manners are as polished as your grasp of time is accurate. Today is the twelfth.'

Jack reeled backwards, stumbling down the high steps.

'I will inform Mrs McBride,' Timothy McBride said curtly to Davey. 'She will contact your employer directly, if such an employer really does exist. Good day.'

The door closed firmly.

'What was all that about?' Davey said, pulling on Jack's shoulder. 'You blew it. You looked like a lunatic.'

'Something's wrong, Davey. This is the twelfth, not the thirteenth. We've arrived on the wrong day.'

'We overshot, that's all,' Davey said quickly. 'It happens. Travelling down a Sorrowline, it's not like taking a train to a station. The further back you go, the end-point gets ... sort of ... fuzzy. It fades away. Vague, like. We've arrived on the twelfth instead of the thirteenth: so what?'

'So what?' Jack said incredulously. 'Timothy's not dead. He doesn't die until tomorrow. That was him, that was Timothy.'

'And?' Davey said casually.

'He's going to die tomorrow!' Jack cried. 'Don't you see?

172

If we can warn him then maybe he won't die.'

Davey shook his head firmly. 'No you don't! You can't start messing with that sort of stuff. It's interfering with the natural order of things.'

'We've just travelled back in time over a hundred years to fetch a book. How is any of this natural?'

Davey shrugged uncomfortably.

'He's gonna die in an accident with a horse and cart,' Jack continued. 'The memories were in the Sorrowline, we both felt it happen. If we can warn him, if we can change things then...then...'

'Then what?' Davey said angrily.

*I can save my mother!* Jack wanted to scream. Instead he turned away.

'Jack, it's already happened. This is all history.'

'But...what's the point?'

'What d'you mean?'

'If we can't change things, if we can't make things better, then what's the point in being a Yard Boy?'

'Things happen for a reason. It's not our place to question—'

'Not our place?' Jack interrupted angrily. 'If it's not our place then whose is it?'

'I dunno,' Davey said awkwardly. 'Who's to say what the right thing to do is? If Timothy doesn't die then someone else might. Who are you gonna pick, Jack? Who?'

Jack fumbled for an answer.

'It's too big a thing for us to guess at,' Davey continued. He stopped and a sympathetic frown crossed his face. 'However much you want to, you can't help your mum. Forget about changing stuff, before you do more harm than good.'

Davey's reasoning only made Jack more determined. An image of his mother clouded his thoughts and he looked up at the big house, straight into the eyes of Timothy McBride at one of the frostbitten windows. An overriding compulsion took him and he ran back up the steps and rapped on the door.

'Jack!' Davey shouted, but the younger boy would not be stopped. He knocked again, impatient for an answer.

The butler opened the door slowly.

'I must speak to Mr McBride!' Jack shouted. 'His life is in danger.'

'Be off, lad,' the butler said, pushing him away from the door.

'Please, I have to tell him. He's going to die tomorrow.'

'I should call the parish constable. Be off, I say, before I do.' The butler had almost closed the door on Jack when a calm voice ordered him to stop. Timothy walked to the door, past the sighing butler, who was reluctant to remove himself from the doorway.

'Thank you, Wainwright,' Timothy said with a polite nod. The butler stepped aside, retreating into the gloom of the entrance hall. 'Well, out with it, boy,' Timothy said, inspecting Jack with a stern resolution. 'What have you to say?'

'I know this will sound crazy,' Jack spluttered, 'but stay at home tomorrow. Don't go out. Cancel whatever it is you're doing.' He could hear the desperation in his voice and wondered if Timothy could too.

'Tomorrow? Impossible!' Timothy replied impassively. 'I have a luncheon appointment.'

'If you go out tomorrow, you'll be hit by a carriage, and...and die.'

Timothy considered Jack's words for a moment, and then his thin lips smiled. 'How utterly preposterous. Are you a gypsy? I'm afraid I don't go in for such mystic mumbo-jumbo, and I am certainly not giving you any money, if that's what you want.'

Timothy began to close the large door. Jack put his hand out to stop him. 'Please. What can I do to convince you?'

Timothy smiled, but the warmth had gone from his face. 'You already have, young man, you already have. Now please remove yourself from my doorstep. Good day.'

Jack hesitated, then stepped back, letting his hand drop from the door. He felt like an executioner condemning an innocent man to death, and as the door slowly closed Jack knew what it was like to be utterly helpless. Wearily he stepped back down to the street.

Davey put his hand onto Jack's shoulder. 'Well, what did you think he'd say?'

'I don't know. I had to try.'

'That makes you one of the good'uns, Jack. At least you tried. More than I would have done.'

'Maybe we could watch him tomorrow,' Jack suggested. 'We could keep him out of danger. Or—'

'Jack, you're not thinking this through,' Davey said as he grabbed his shoulders. 'If he don't die there won't *be* a Sorrowline and we'd have no way back to 1940. We'd be trapped here for ever. He *has* to die. Don't you see?'

Jack looked back up at the big house, smoke rising from its chimneys, and tears fell from his eyes. Tears for Timothy McBride, but most of all for his mother. Her death replayed again and again in his mind's eye. He was desperate to avert it, yet realisation was slowly dawning. Davey was right; he hadn't thought through the consequences of his actions.

'Come on,' Davey said. 'Let's find another way in.'

The snow fell about the two boys. Soon, Jack knew, the road and path would become one under a thick white gown.

Davey walked ahead, his figure rapidly fading into the blue-grey haze. The fresh footprints were already filling up with new snow as Jack turned away from the house.

There was no alternative but to stay in 1813 until Timothy McBride was dead.

# 17

## EFFECT AND CAUSE

Davey and Jack walked the narrow streets around the McBrides' grand residence, looking for a weakness, the best way in. As the feeble light was defeated by the grey clouds Davey rested in the doorway of a noisy pub. The warmth of its interior beckoned, yet both boys resisted its siren call. They stood in the cold facing the rear of the house; a high wall separated it from them.

'What do we do?' Jack asked.

'We get over that wall,' Davey said with the flash of a hope-filled smile.

'How? It must be twice my height.'

Davey nodded silently to a withered tree planted close to the wall, its twisted branches almost reaching the brickwork. 'It'll be easier than the Carlton!' At that he sprinted over the road and began to pull himself up the gnarled trunk. He grinned devilishly at Jack, goading him to follow.

Jack trudged over the road. The tree grew ominously with every step he took towards it.

'Come on!' Davey teased. He was already high up in the branches, away from the gas light. Jack did not fare as well. The surface was slippery and, terrified he would plunge to the ground, he lost his footing several times. A branch groaned, then snapped under his weight. Somehow he held on and scrambled quickly to Davey's vantage point.

With a breathless grunt Davey leaped forward, away from the relative safety of the old tree, towards the wall. His grubby fingers clawed at the bricks, like a desperate cat, and he managed to get a hold. His leg swung up, and as Davey pulled himself into a squatting position, Jack could see the relief in the other boy's face.

Jack pushed away from the trunk himself, half leaping, half running towards the wall. His arms stretched out in front of him, desperate to grab something. Then, in a blur of motion, he was sprawled next to Davey on the top of the wall. His shirt had been yanked up almost to his neck, a rough handful of material hidden in Davey's fist.

'You can let go now,' Jack said eventually, once his heart had stopped pounding so hard. 'I think I made it.'

Davey laughed with relief and released the crumpled shirt.

The other side of the wall was a murky dark space so Davey lit a match and let it drop into the void. Its pathetic light picked out the shapes of snow-capped shrubs and bushes before the chill twilight consumed it. Davey hung from the wall and dropped into the shadows with a heavy thud.

'Quickly,' he hissed, 'before someone sees you.'

Jack nodded, silently wishing that there was no vicious dog – or person – down there waiting, as he threw his legs over the wall and flung himself into the unknown.

He landed on top of a thorny bush, which tore at his trousers, pricking at the cold skin beneath. He rolled with the fall, coming to rest on his back on the frosted lawn. Davey's grinning face loomed over him. 'All right?'

'Still here,' Jack replied, pulling himself up.

At the other end of the large lawn was the McBrides' opulent house, hidden in the gloom of the late afternoon.

Davey led the way, his path hugging the line of the trees, towards the patio doors. Dark curtains covered the glass, but the faintest halo of light gilded their edges. Davey raised a tentative hand to the door. As he pressed down on the handle, to Jack's surprise it turned and opened. He had a moment's pang about what would happen to them if they were caught breaking and entering, but then followed Davey through the door, closing it with a sharp click behind them. They huddled together as they quickly surveyed the room. They were in a parlour. In the daylight hours of summertime, with the curtains flung open, it would have been a gloriously uplifting space, but in the gloom of winter it gave way to terrible geometric shadows that conjured up phantom assassins.

Davey scuttled towards a half-opened doorway that presumably led further into the house, pausing on his haunches as he listened intently. Jack slid up next to him and saw the disturbed look on his friend's face.

'What is it?'

'Voices,' Davey said in a hushed tone that told Jack to be silent. Jack heard nothing.

'Now,' Davey said, and he slid through the door. Jack ran after him, into the long corridor that led to the grand entrance they had seen from the street.

Davey turned again and, for the second time, Jack found himself in the reading room of this house, one hundred and twenty-seven years *before* the first occasion. Despite a low fire burning in the hearth, the room was in darkness, but Jack could already tell that its layout was uncannily similar to before.

'We're looking for a book, right?' Davey said, nodding to the small library that lined the room's many shelves.

Jack nodded. 'We'll need some more light.'

Davey saw a lamp sitting on an oak table that followed the line of the large bay window. He pulled out a box of matches and lit the wick. Jack wondered what else Davey kept stowed away in those deep pockets. As the lamp flickered into life, both boys jolted.

They were not alone.

A young woman, whose complexion blended in with the ghostly palette of the frozen world outside, sat behind the table. Her hair was a rich copper and pulled tightly away from her porcelain face. Jack suppressed a shudder. How had they not seen her before?

She stood and walked towards Jack and Davey, apparently completely at ease with their presence here.

'Please, sit. Do join me for tea,' said the woman.

Jack looked to Davey, expecting him to bolt for the door. Instead, he nodded calmly to Jack and sat on one of the matching chairs in front of the table. Nervously Jack also sat down.

The woman rang a small bell and a maid appeared. Refreshments were ordered and, after a brief spell, the maid returned with a silver trolley, placing it carefully to the side of her mistress's desk. A heavy-looking fruit cake sat atop the trolley next to an overweight teapot with steam lazily rising from its spout.

'My husband has told me quite a tale,' the woman said at last. 'He is upstairs completing paperwork, and will not be down until Wainwright calls us to supper. We are quite alone.' Her hushed tone seemed both reassuring and threatening. Jack stole a glance at Davey. He looked relaxed, but Jack had already learned to see beyond his bullish veneer: his eyes betrayed the look of a trapped animal. Jack felt the same.

'You ... you're Jane McBride?' Jack said.

She smiled and began to pour from the teapot into three delicate china cups. 'Timothy has told me of a young man,' she nodded to Jack who was already warming his fingers on the teacup, 'a young man who has warned him of his imminent death, a death that will happen tomorrow, under the wheels of a horse and cart.'

Jane's gaze was piercing. Jack cleared his throat. 'It's true, I'm sorry. I know it sounds impossible, but you have to trust me.'

Davey shot him a cautionary glance.

'And how would you know such a thing?' Jane asked. 'Timothy thinks you're of gypsy stock, but I can see you are not. Perhaps this is some highly amusing jape conjured up by two urchins intent upon stealing from those more fortunate, or perchance you are insane and deserve to be locked away.' Her eyebrows lifted as she glared at the pair. White embers drifted from the fire and danced high into the air, circling around the room.

'We're not mad,' Jack assured her.

'And then there is the matter of your presence here. I could have you hanged.' Her smile was like ice.

A terrible alarm gripped Jack. This wasn't working out. Every fibre in his body told him he should flee, yet his legs seemed to disagree. His eyes looked to the fireplace. The fire was growing in strength, its flames tinged with an emerald green, which pushed the embers ever higher.

'Simple thieves,' Jane continued. 'Why would you be anything other than that? And yet, your clothes are strange, your manner is not quite as it should be. So, another option presents itself to me: you are from the future.' She put down the teapot and waited patiently for Jack to say something. When there was no reply, she smiled and picked up a large knife from the trolley. Jack couldn't help noticing its sharp blade glinting in the firelight. 'Cake?' she asked.

Neither boy answered and she put aside the knife.

'Yes,' she said, 'you are here for something precious.'

'I don't know what you mean,' Davey lied, putting down his empty tea cup. His voice sounded laboured, slurred.

'Really?' Jane's smile disappeared. 'How very interesting.' She held up a slim book from within a concealed pocket on her bodice. She turned it over lovingly in her hands, its ancient leather surface catching the light.

'You came for a book,' she said angrily. '*This* book.' The golden words on the cover came into focus in front of Jack's eyes: *On the Nature of the Concealed Realms.*

Jack gave a silent cheer at the sight of their goal, so close at hand. He fought the urge to reach out and take it.

Jane returned the book to its pocket. 'Perhaps my master can reveal the truth.'

'Don't be botherin' Mr McBride,' Davey mumbled.

Jack recoiled: something was wrong with Davey. It was time to leave, he knew it. He made to pull himself out of the chair but his legs felt as if they were being dragged through tar.

'This's been a misunderstandin', tha'sall. C'mon, Jack.' Davey made to stand up, but his legs buckled, and he fell back into his chair. His sallow face reflected the haunting green glow emanating from the fireplace.

'I am not talking about my feckless husband, or any other Second Worlder,' Jane replied. 'He has no notion of the real structure of the Earth. I have only one true master, the one who will bring us all to salvation.'

The hairs on Jack's neck stood on end. He knew the name she was about to utter, and it terrified him.

'Master Rouland will be happy to deal with two stray Yard Boys on a fool's errand.'

They were trapped! But Jack's senses were dulled. He tried again to stand, failing as Davey had. His legs and arms were heavy. He let himself sink into the chair, its sides enveloping him as darkness drifted over his eyes.

It was the heart of the night when Jack awoke to a slap round the face. He was still in the reading room, but Mrs McBride had gone and the fire had died away to a few glowing embers. Davey was standing over him.

'Shhh,' Davey whispered. He moved away to creep behind the door. 'That witch drugged us.'

'The tea?' Jack guessed.

'Maybe. Hundreds of ways she could have done it,' Davey whispered. 'I've been listening. She's in the hall, talking to some people.'

Jack joined him and peered through the crack in the

door at the candlelit entrance hall beyond. He could see and hear Jane McBride, arguing with her husband.

'This does not concern you,' she said, her voice clipped and hard. 'Once this night is done Rouland will rule all, and I will be at his side. And you' – she viewed her husband with open contempt – 'you shall be forgotten. I will feed you to the Dustmen.'

'Jane, please,' Timothy pleaded, 'I don't understand what any of this means. You are ill, I fear. You have not been yourself this last six months. I have supported your passions, yet you have gone against me, perhaps even against God. It is not too late to repent.' Timothy moved closer to his wife but she pushed him away with a ruthless strength, and he fell backwards onto the cold tiles.

'Repent?' she scoffed. 'I have nothing to repent for. My soul is clean and pure. Look inside yourself first.'

'That blasphemous book is the source of your dis-temper.' Timothy pulled himself to his feet, waving a trembling finger at his wife. 'It has corrupted your mind.'

Jane's hand pulled the book from the pocket of her dress. 'You do not comprehend Hafgan's legacy – you never could,' Jane laughed. 'Go to bed, Timothy, and when you wake all of this will be forgotten.'

Davey put his mouth close to Jack's ear. 'Let's make a run for it.'

'But what about the book?' Jack said, now certain that he had to keep it from Rouland.

185

In a piece of perfect timing Davey pulled the door wide open and, in a single move, he burst out of the reading room, straight into Jane. His assault took her by surprise and she fell to the marble floor with a heavy thud, her cold eyes rolling back into her head. Timothy watched in shock as Jack bolted for the front door – Davey had already flung it open and leaped down the steps into the night.

Jack sprinted into the empty street, terrified and shivering. Somewhere far away a bell began to toll out the hour. As the clock reached its twelfth chime – midnight! – he heard Timothy McBride shouting, chasing them along the street. The boys ran across the lane, narrowly missing a lone horse and cart. The horse reared up, startled by the commotion and galloped forward. As Jack and Davey watched, Timothy skidded round the corner, losing his footing on the icy path, and fell under the feet of the speeding animal, its hooves smashing into him.

Jack heard the screams. He could not look back, but kept running, with tears streaming down his cheeks.

They stopped several streets away. Jack held onto a wall to steady himself while Davey nervously paced up and down, biting on his fingernails. A whistle broke through the air and the commotion of raised voices rattled overhead.

'We caused it, Davey,' Jack said at last. 'We caused his death.'

'We didn't kill him,' Davey said.

'I know, but we did cause it to happen. If we'd not come back here he'd still be alive.'

'We came on his Sorrowline; we couldn't have come if he wasn't already dead.' Davey shook his head. 'It's stupid to blame ourselves. If you want to blame anyone, blame Rouland – he got us into this mess in the first place.'

Jack shivered. The night was freezing cold. 'But it was all for nothing,' he said, his jaw chattering from a mix of freezing air and adrenaline. 'We didn't even get the book.'

Davey allowed the glimmer of a smile to appear on his face as he put his hand into his pocket. He pulled out a small object and handed it to Jack, who looked down at it in disbelief. *On the Nature of the Concealed Realms* rested in his numb hands.

'How?' he gasped.

'I took it when I pushed into her,' Davey said. 'I'm a bit of a dab hand at collecting things.'

Jack smiled admiringly, then pushed the small book deep into his trouser pocket.

'Let's go home,' Davey said.

They kept to the shadows, avoiding the late-night stragglers who populated the dark streets.

'He didn't stand a chance, poor soul,' said a chubby woman to her friend.

'I 'eard the driver was as drunk as a lord,' her companion replied.

'He'll 'ang for that.'

'They says it weren't his fault. They says two funny-lookin' urchins led him to it.'

Jack shuddered, skulking out of sight behind a wall.

The women passed by, deep in their conversation.

'We should get out of here,' Jack whispered to Davey, 'before it's too late.'

It took them almost half an hour to return to the tiny church, and by then Jack's teeth were chattering uncontrollably. His toes were painfully cold and the chilly air passed straight through his shirt, stinging his chest.

'This is it,' Davey said, pointing to a scrub of snow-covered earth.

'It all looks different, covered in snow. You sure?'

'Positive,' Davey said reassuringly.

'What do I do?'

'What do you mean?'

'I've never gone forward before.'

'It's the same as travelling downstream: just feel your way in,' Davey said. 'Once you've travelled down a Sorrowline it stays open for you.'

'But there's no headstone yet.'

'The Sorrowline is still there.'

Jack knelt down in the snow with his arms outstretched in front of him and closed his eyes. He felt nothing.

'It's not here,' Jack said.

'Try harder,' Davey said unsympathetically. Jack could

feel the pressure on him growing.

'You try too.' Jack pulled at Davey's arm.

Davey shrugged and crouched next to him, placing one hand on his shoulder, the other outstretched, mimicking Jack's pose.

Jack smiled. Even with his eyes closed he felt the warmth from Davey's hand coming through his thin shirt. He recalled a day, several years ago, when he had been playing with his father in the park. It had snowed the night before and, even though the covering was slight and already melting, Jack had pestered his father into taking him out to play. They had struggled to make even a few small snowballs, but Jack had loved every minute. It was one of the few times after his mum died that he and his father had laughed together, their cares temporarily forgotten in the slush. When they returned home, wet and tired, they had sat together in the big armchair near the window drinking hot chocolate and watching the sun melt the snow into dirty water. His father had wrapped an arm around Jack's neck, resting his warm hand on his shoulder, just as Davey was doing now. Jack wallowed in the memory.

Suddenly he felt the Sorrowline. He reached out with his mind and—

'Oy!'

A gruff voice broke Jack's attention. He turned to see a stout man with a wide moustache waddling through the snow towards him, another taller man in an old-fashioned police uniform – a parish constable, they were called, Jack remembered from his history lessons – just behind him. The man pointed, shouting at Jack and Davey, and the constable broke into a run.

'Let's get out of here!' Jack said to Davey.

'Too late to run! You have to find the Sorrowline.'

'There's no time,' Jack said desperately as he forced himself to refocus.

'Rouland!' Davey gasped.

Jack opened his eyes again. There, calmly walking up the steps through the church gate, was Rouland with Jane McBride. His clothes were of this period, but as simple and elegant as he had appeared when Jack met him in 1940. Opulent, understated grandeur. His chiselled face appeared timeless, like a statue, with penetrating eyes that could carve a man's soul in two.

'How can he be here, in 1813?' Jack said. 'Has he followed us?'

'No, he was already here. He's been around for centuries. He hasn't met you yet.'

'He looks the same.'

'Sorrowline!' Davey snapped. 'Concentrate!'

'But if he sees me here, he'll remember me in 1940.'

'Then get us out of here!'

The advancing constable was almost upon them. Jack closed his eyes and blew out slowly, pushing all the distractions from his mind. He felt a rough hand on his shoulder, and then it was gone. He had caught the end of the Sorrowline and was already enduring all of its potent emotion as he raced along it into the future. He felt the now-familiar giddy rush of alien memories, the laments of others, and then he was facedown on dry soil once again.

He opened his eyes and saw the old carved angel statue looming over him. Anti-aircraft blimps dotted the sky overhead. He had made it back to 1940. He laughed at how close they had been to capture and rolled onto his side to give Davey a relieved smile, but the grin soon dropped from his face. His head spun round quickly and he was on his feet in a flash. He scrambled round the back of the angel statue to check, but he already knew the truth: Davey had been left behind in 1813.

# 18

## SOUP AND SORROWLINES

Jack entered Montgomery Falconer's reading room wearily. Monty sat in his armchair while Eloise stood resolutely near the door, her hand caressing the hilt of her sword. Time had passed since Jack's journey with Davey to 1813, but Eloise looked as though she hadn't moved an inch. Outside the sun had risen and the world had woken up, yet the room seemed to be in suspended animation.

'Back so soon?' Monty said as he watched Jack from over the top of his reading glasses. Then, as he saw Jack's dirty shirt, his wet feet, and his defeated expression, a frown grew over his old face.

'How long have I been gone?' Jack asked breathlessly.

Monty huffed as he opened up his fob watch, screwing up his face to see it. 'Ten hours, give or take.'

'What happened?' Eloise asked.

Jack sat by the fire, rubbing his cold feet with his numb hands. 'We got back, we made it through.'

'We?' Monty asked.

'Me and Davey, we both went back to 1813.'

'Impossible!' Monty scoffed.

Jack ignored him. 'We came back to this house; we met Jane and Timothy McBride. He was still alive, we'd gone back a day further and—'

'You have the book?' Monty's eyes widened and he leaned forward, listening intently.

'Jane was working for Rouland; she was going to take us to him. We escaped but we were chased, we saw Timothy die . . . ' Jack's voice faded away. He watched the flames in the fireplace, dancing and flickering.

'But you have the book?' Monty was on the edge of his seat. He seemed not to care for the details of Jack's story.

Jack's hand touched his trousers; he could feel the book in his pocket. 'Davey has the book,' Jack lied, hoping the old man didn't suspect. He felt a sudden need to protect this mysterious book. He had to safeguard it, at least until Davey was safe again. He kept his distance, making sure Monty couldn't touch him and discover the book's hiding place.

Monty slumped back in his chair.

'Where *is* Davey?' Eloise asked.

'He must be in 1813. He didn't come back through with me. We were being chased, and I thought he'd made it into the Sorrowline too, but when I opened my eyes I was alone.'

'I recall such a story,' Monty said at last. 'Many years

ago, Rouland told me of two Yard Boys, from upstream, who came to London and stole something very valuable to him.'

Eloise nodded grimly. 'The book is important to Rouland.'

Jack wanted to ask his new friend more, to know what Rouland wanted with it, but he hesitated, not wanting to talk more in front of Monty.

'The book is *vital* to Rouland,' Monty cut in, his stare piercing through Jack. 'I know this because Rouland engaged me on several occasions to try to find it again.' Monty's gaze drifted out of the window. 'I failed him on every occasion. The book was lost to time.'

'You never told us Jane McBride was one of Rouland's people! We could have been caught,' Jack said.

'Rouland has people everywhere, you already know that. But Jane is an interesting case. Not many Second Worlders have learned the secrets of the First World and become such an important part of it, but Jane managed such a feat.'

'What happened to the Yard Boys, in the story Rouland told you?'

'Well, I'm not quite sure,' Monty mused. 'If I remember correctly Rouland said that the two boys – presumably you and your friend – were chased but made good their escape before they could be apprehended.'

'That means Davey's still alive!' Jack said, relieved.

'How do you know?' Eloise asked.

'Rouland didn't capture Davey, so he must have got away *after* I left.'

Monty sighed and said, 'That is not the only alternative, I fear. You have not long been a Yard Boy, have you, Jack?'

'No.'

'And so you do not yet know the consequences. There can be a heavy price to pay for travelling the Sorrowlines.'

'What sort of price?' Jack asked.

'I'm afraid not everyone who enters a Sorrowline makes it out again in one piece. Some return but are not themselves, others are never seen again, they are consumed. When compared to the other possibilities death can be the preferred fate.'

'He's still alive,' Jack said firmly.

Monty waved a hand nonchalantly. 'If you insist.'

'I do, and I'm going back for him.'

Eloise gasped. 'Back where? To 1813?'

'Yes. I'm gonna bring him back.'

Monty's face broke into a condescending grin. 'Have you any idea what you are suggesting? Sorrowlines are not mere roads, to be traversed back and forth on a whim. They are delicate strands, woven out of loss and regret. If you travel along the same one too often it will break. And two people in one Sorrowline? I would imagine you have already caused irrevocable damage. Perhaps that is the reason why Davey did not make it back with you.' Monty sighed heavily.

'I can't just leave him. I have to try,' Jack said desperately.

Monty threw his hands up. 'You, young man, are as stubborn as my late wife, and probably as foolish. So be it. After all, it is perhaps the only hope of my possessing the book. But I will not allow you to go in this state. First you must rest, eat and be properly dressed.'

'He needs me!' Jack shouted.

'Pah!' Monty scoffed. 'Davey is a single moment suspended in time. That moment will wait for all eternity if need be. You are no good to me, or him, if you are exhausted, or hungry, yes?'

Jack nodded. He feared if he closed his eyes he would be lost to sleep in seconds.

'Then rest first.' Monty stood slowly, his old bones complaining. 'A hot meal, dry clothes, then on to adventure! Or death,' he added more quietly.

The smell of hot vegetable soup and fresh bread jolted Jack out of his slumber. He had been dreaming of his mother, but he couldn't quite grasp what had been happening. As he rubbed his eyes the images faded away, refusing to return.

Eloise still kept guard at the reading-room doorway, like a lethal statue, not ready to trust Monty. A tray waited for Jack by the fire. Aromatic steam wafted from the soup, and fresh thickly-cut vegetables floated in the rich liquid, inviting him to devour them. He took a large silver spoon from the tray and picked up a heavy collection of tempting vegetables. Impatient, he burned his lips and tongue as the soup warmed him from within, but he instantly felt awake and refreshed.

'Better?' Monty asked as he entered the room.

'Yes, thank you. Much better.' Jack broke off a handful of bread and dipped it into the soup.

'I have brought you boots, I think they will fit,' Monty replied. 'There are socks also, and a woollen jumper, a jacket, scarf and hat. They may be a bit on the large side' – he patted his belly – 'but they will keep you warm. It was cold in January 1813, was it not?'

'Yes,' Jack said, 'it was snowing hard.'

'I thought so,' Monty said excitedly. 'As you can see I enjoy reading on a great many subjects, and I recall that the temperatures of the time were somewhat severe.' He stood, casually flicking along a shelf of books. 'I do so envy you and your ability, Jack. To be able to step into history and live it, not just read about it in a book,' he explained, echoing Jack's own thoughts. 'It must be exhilarating. But, alas, being a Yard Boy is a rare and special thing. It is a gift that runs in the blood of but a few families. I could never hope to learn such a skill, no more so than a sparrow could teach me to fly.'

'What about the risks?'

'I am sure it is worth the risks.'

Jack looked at the clothes. 'You don't really care what happens to me, do you? You only care about the book.'

Monty chuckled. 'My boy, I am not your enemy.'

'Just as long as I do what you want.'

'Our interests converge,' Monty said sternly.

'For how long?'

Monty picked up the empty soup bowl. 'You should dress.'

When Jack was dressed in the new clothes – the precious book still safely in his trouser pocket – Monty returned with a scroll of paper, which he spread out on the table.

'I have been giving your situation some thought,' he said.

'What situation?'

'The Sorrowlines, dear chap, the Sorrowlines. You have already travelled downstream a great distance. The Sorrowline may be unstable. There may be another option.' He jabbed at the paper.

'What is that?' Jack said.

'A map! A map of the graves in the churchyard. Graves, locations, dates. Another Sorrowline might be safer, if we can find one.

The map showed rows of rectangular plots. Each contained a name, a date and a reference number.

'A-ha!' Monty exclaimed after several moments of study. 'This might just do!' He pointed to one of the plots marked on the right-hand side of the map. 'The third of January 1813, a young girl of only five years.'

'The third?' Jack repeated. 'That's...' He tried to calculate the days in his head.

'Ten days,' Monty said instantly. 'A whole ten days on your own in 1813. It is a daunting challenge, yes?'

Jack rubbed his chin, thinking quickly. This would be the biggest challenge of his life.

'The winter will be harsh, you will have to find food and shelter, somewhere to stay, somewhere to wait it out until the thirteenth. I would advise against you attempting to take anything with you through the Sorrowline. Your trip is perilous enough without complicating matters. You will have to be resourceful.' Monty grinned.

Jack hesitated. He opened his mouth, certain the task was too great. And then he remembered the memories Davey had unintentionally shared, of a harsh upbringing where he had endured much worse than Jack would have to. And from those memories he gained a new insight, a new resolve that pushed him on into the unknown of the past.

'All right,' he said, before he could change his mind, 'I'll do it.'

Monty's eyebrows arched upwards. 'Really? You would put your friendship before your safety, young Jack?'

Jack nodded resolutely.

'You are very generous with your life,' Monty continued, a puzzled tone in his low voice. 'You defy Rouland, when you know it is futile, and you risk everything for a stranded friend.'

'Wouldn't you?'

'No, I would not. You and I are not alike, not at all.' Monty faltered, his face awash with bewilderment. 'So young, with so much to lose, and me, so very old, with nothing that cannot be bought and sold. You confuse me, young Jack.'

Jack stood to leave. At the same moment Monty barred his way, his uncertainties apparently forgotten. 'If you get back,' he said firmly, 'if you actually do it, and you find Davey, take the book from him.' He half smiled. 'Just in case.'

Disgusted, Jack stepped past the old man and walked towards the hall. As he approached Eloise he smiled feebly. He was sure his own doubts must be evident on his face, like a child crying for help. He looked away quickly, hoping she had not seen. Her firm hand took his arm. Strong, powerful.

'I will be here when you return,' she said. 'You *will* return.' Her words were like a commandment. He nodded, understanding, and she let her hand fall away.

Jack left the house, and 1940, behind again.

# 19

## THE GRAVEDIGGER

Somewhere far away a clock struck midnight, and Jack knew that the thirteenth had finally arrived.

He crouched close to the church, shivering. The snow was falling heavily, just as Jack remembered, and the stones of the graveyard all wore white toupees that made their hard grey surfaces resemble jet.

He was tired and hungry, and his weary mind replayed the events since he had returned to 1813, the images gritty and visceral. It had been far harder than he had ever imagined.

The journey into the Sorrowline had been simple enough, once he had found the entry point. The more Jack travelled the more he was getting used to the feeling and knew what to reach for. Even older, more faded Sorrowlines like this one were opening up for him without a struggle.

Once inside things had been much different. The sensations had been troubling, somehow disturbing to Jack. There was something painfully unrefined about one so young, a girl of only five – the outpouring of sorrow was different, laced with anger and regret. Jack had felt every instant of the girl's decline. The first pangs of disease, the hope for recovery tempered with the realisation of the inevitable, and then the rapid fall into death.

There had been little pain, yet he had arrived in 1813 crippled with sorrow. He had opened his eyes, and heard his own cry, like an orphaned animal calling out in grief. It was unfortunate that he had arrived just before the Sunday service. The terrified churchgoers, dressed in their finest, witnessed his cry and feared he might be possessed. Eventually one of the women approached him with a mix of concern and fright. He scrambled to his feet and ran away into the winding streets, still reeling from the sensations he had endured.

On his previous journey to 1813 with Davey, he had witnessed only a tiny fraction of the great city, shrouded in night and snow. But as he weaved aimlessly through the narrow lanes bathed by a feeble winter sun, he saw its vast majesty. Thick smoke hung over the rooftops like an ominous blanket, hemming London in, depriving it of light and soaking up all colour from the world, leaving only shades of brown and grey. The stench was unbelievable, a noxious mix of raw effluent, rotting vegetables and butchered meat.

He saw horses everywhere, their dung mixed with straw and ash into a lumpy carpet that covered the edge of the roads, capped in places by the first flurry of snowfall.

Jack kept to the back streets, hiding amongst the boxes and barrels, the rubbish and dirt, the flotsam and jetsam, until the horror within him subsided, like a slow tide drifting lazily out to sea. He knew nothing of this time, and found himself appalled at the gritty reality of it all, the cheapness of life.

He had wandered like this for most of Sunday, not eating or sleeping, not yet desperate enough to steal food. He was already exhausted and hungry. If he was to be of any use to Davey he knew he had to find both food and shelter.

He spent that first night in a neglected pigsty in the back yard of a large house. He shared the floor with two unhappy sows who snorted and grunted until they wearily accepted his presence in their home. Even with the heat from the animals it was intolerably cold, the wind rattling through holes and cracks on every side, and he did not sleep at all. At first light he returned to the streets and vowed not to spend another night like that again. The bitter loneliness had been almost unbearable, and only the dark hope of somehow saving his mother had kept him going.

He saw other boys about his age, cleaning the streets of manure. He considered asking for a job, but when he saw one of the boys being beaten by his master he thought again.

Without realising it he found himself once again outside St Bartholomew's. He watched an old man, bearded and solemn, as he walked gingerly through the graveyard with a spade over his shoulder. The man stopped and turned to view Jack staring at him.

'Can you dig?' he shouted.

'Yes, I think so,' Jack said, trying to recall if he ever had.

'Follow me.' The old man walked back into the churchyard without another word.

Jack discovered his name was Sexton Clay, and he was the church groundsman. His old limbs were tired of digging the frozen earth and he was happy to have the help of a young boy. In return Sexton agreed to provide food and shelter in his tiny house opposite the church.

Jack told him he was an orphan, but Sexton asked few questions, seeming to trust him on sight, and Jack was content enough to have a silent companion as he wandered the churchyard. The old man appeared to be at least seventy years old; his thin frame rattled when he coughed – which was often – but his leathery face conveyed an inner strength.

That first day was the hardest Jack had ever worked. Together they dug a new grave in the frozen January ground, and by time the sun disappeared his hands were covered in blisters and his back ached.

They walked back to Sexton's home, and Jack's guard lowered completely; he felt no threat at all from the genial old man. They shared a simple meal of bread, ham and cheese, and after an hour in front of Sexton's fire Jack fell asleep. He spent the night in the chair, not stirring until the morning when Sexton brought him eggs and tea.

And so it had continued, his days filled with difficult, back-breaking work that ripped at his hands and tore at his muscles, his long nights spent in front of Sexton's fire, eating and sleeping. In his few private moments he took the chance to study the book he and Davey had stolen from Jane McBride. The yellowed pages were covered in a language he did not understand. Handwritten rune-like symbols ran in vertical lines filling each page. Jack was sure there was a code to it, but he was unable to decipher it. Here and there were scrawled notes in English. Some were number sequences, or equations, others marked lines of text with comments like *important* or *marvellous proof*. The last page was different, filled with a grid of text and numbers he could understand, but mixed up into a long sentence of gibberish. It reminded Jack of the word-search books his nan enjoyed completing.

Then on the eighth, as they watched the flames together in silence, Sexton asked, 'Where are you from, Jack?'

'London,' Jack said lazily.

'*When* exactly?'

Jack looked up into Sexton's dark eyes, frozen in sudden fear.

'You a Yard Boy?' Sexton said, stroking his wiry beard with a gnarled hand.

At first Jack hesitated, his fingers gripping the arms of the chair tightly – was this another trap he'd found himself in? Then, in a moment of rare abandon, he said, 'Yes.' He shifted uncomfortably as he waited for the old man's response.

Sexton raised his hairy eyebrows and nodded. His head turned away from Jack, back to the fire, and he settled into his chair, as if the bizarre conversation was a normal everyday occurrence.

Jack leaned forward, unsure which of the dozen questions burning his mind to ask first. 'How? How did you know?'

'We've met,' Sexton said, without looking away from the flames. 'We *will* meet, anyway. Thought I knew you. Couldn't place it till tonight.'

'We've met?' Jack asked in amazement. 'When?'

'Long while ago. Hard to remember.'

Jack knew that the Sorrowlines could easily twist the normal arrow of time into knots. Here was a man who Jack must one day meet again, but from Sexton's chair it was his distant past.

'What are you?'

'Yard Boy, like you,' Sexton replied. 'Used to be, long time ago.'

'Do you still have the power?'

Finally Sexton looked up from the fire, his brow furrowed into a dozen wrinkled troughs. 'Still? No.'

'When did you lose it?'

'Was a teenager. Thoughts of girls come into your head, something else goes out.' Sexton sighed regretfully. His cracked lips tightened over his teeth. 'No more questions. Tired.'

In spite of Jack's persistent questioning Sexton remained closed, his few answers giving no further clues to his past. He talked freely about his beloved wife, about how they had met and married, how he had lived a blissfully normal existence in the Second World, about how much he missed her since her early death almost twenty years ago, but he would not entertain any further discussions about his youth in the First World.

Of his previous encounter with Jack he would say no more and retreated to the sanctuary of his bed where unwanted questions could not penetrate.

As the twelfth finally arrived Jack felt a trembling anticipation. The day was bitterly cold and he spent it clearing the church paths of frozen ice. In the afternoon he watched for the arrival of himself and Davey with tempered curiosity. Sure enough, two figures appeared on the ground without ceremony. Jack had expected a flash, or a peal of thunder, and was somewhat disappointed by the silent arrival. Hidden by the wall he watched as he and Davey recovered and walked away from the church.

'That you?'

Jack jumped at the sudden voice over his shoulder. Sexton leaned against his spade, watching the new arrivals with mild interest.

'Yes,' Jack offered, 'and my friend, Davey.'

Sexton nodded. 'Remember you saying before.'

'How long ago is "before"?'

Sexton turned away and observed the falling snow. 'Getting colder.' He walked away in silence.

That evening, after another unsuccessful interrogation of Sexton, Jack was dozing in his chair by the fire when he awoke to the sound of voices coming from the doorway. Sexton was arguing with an unseen visitor.

'I don't know anything,' Sexton said with a bitter hiss.

'Two Yard Boys,' a hidden voice said, 'here, somewhere close by. You must know! You must have felt it.' The voice was male and flowed like silk over a sharpened knife. Jack instantly knew its identity.

Jack quietly pulled on his shoes as he strained to listen to the conversation. He had to get out of here before he put Sexton in any more danger.

'Fifty years since I travelled,' Sexton replied. 'Know nothing.'

'You are full of lies,' whispered Rouland.

'No lies,' Sexton said.

'There are always lies.'

There was a sudden noise, like the crackle of lightning.

Jack peered into the room. A glowing spark connected Rouland's outstretched hand with Sexton's chest.

'Please,' Sexton gasped.

'You will not rest with your wife's bones, safe underground,' Rouland shouted over the growing noise. 'Burn, instead!'

Sexton fell to the floor, his body in spasm. Rouland's hand remained in the open doorway, outstretched and pointing. The room seemed frozen, with neither Rouland nor Jack moving. Only Sexton gave away the passing of time as his body twisted and pulsated. His legs and arms shook rapidly, until eventually they slowed and dropped to the floor.

Rouland waited until Sexton's body was quite still, then he took hold of the handle and slowly closed the door behind him. Jack watched his silhouette pass the window before his horror released him and he dashed over to Sexton. The life had already gone from the old man's white face. An intense heat grew about the old man's body, as if a fire raged within. Then the lifeless body dissolved to a grey ash, and all evidence of Sexton Clay's life vanished.

Jack had never seen anything like it. Dizzy, nauseous, unable to think, he ran from Sexton's house, into the thin, angry streets nearby. He hid in the shadows of anonymous doorways, fearful that Rouland might return to Sexton's home at any moment.

He was weary and tired. He had lived another life this

week, a life that had left him older and full of anger. Why did Sexton have to die? It made no sense to him. He doubted if it ever would. His stomach was weighed down with guilt. So many people in his life had died. Was it because of him? Was it his fault?

As midnight approached he returned to the small churchyard and found a hiding place close to the spot where he knew he and Davey would soon come.

An hour had passed since the midnight bells tolled. Jack heard the rising tide of commotion from the nearby streets as word of Timothy's terrible accident went out. And then, finally, he saw two boys approaching at speed. Everything happened in a blur. He saw himself search for the Sorrowline as the parish constable approached. Rouland appeared again with Jane McBride. The first Jack found his Sorrowline and disappeared. Davey was left alone and confused, scrambling out of reach of the perplexed constable.

This was his moment.

Jack leaped from his hiding place and grabbed Davey roughly by the arm.

'I'll explain later,' he said as he pulled Davey through the snow to the other side of the churchyard, to the grave of the young girl, to the Sorrowline that would take them back to 1940.

The constable recovered and gave chase.

'We're going into this Sorrowline here,' Jack explained

quickly. 'We're going in together.'

'Upstream? That's impossible.'

The constable was suddenly over them, his hands telescoping towards them.

'No time.' Jack grabbed Davey with both arms and pulled him close to his chest. He could already feel the Sorrowline calling out to him. He closed his eyes and fell backwards.

'No,' Davey cried out in terror, his voice distorting as the two boys disappeared. 'You'll kill me!'

# 20

## TRANSFORMATION

Even before he opened his eyes Jack knew he was not alone. He had Davey with him. He smiled to himself feeling the warm glow of satisfaction inside. Then he remembered the last words Davey had shouted as they disappeared down the Sorrowline – 'You'll kill me!' – and a chill apprehension took over.

Davey wasn't moving, his weight pressing down onto Jack. He rolled him off, feeling his chest for movement. Nothing. He wasn't breathing and his face was pallid and grey. Jack's mind froze in panic. What was he supposed to do? He'd done first aid at school, but he hadn't paid attention.

'Davey?' Jack shook him frantically, slapping him about the face, desperate, screaming, 'Breathe!'

Nothing. He put his mouth to Davey's, and blew. Nothing. He blew again, his salty tears dropping from his face and splashing off Davey's bloodless skin. He hammered on his friend's chest, willing him to live.

Nothing.

Jack pushed on Davey's upper body again, blowing into his mouth, breath after desperate breath.

And finally Davey gasped, a long difficult inhalation that made him convulse and cough. He rolled onto his side, spitting and retching, and his eyes flickered open, wild and unfocused.

'What . . . what did you do?' he asked between short breaths.

'You got stuck.' Jack couldn't hide his pride. 'I came back down another Sorrowline. I brought you along it with me.'

Davey's head dropped into his hands. 'You dragged me back along a Sorrowline, one I didn't enter first. That's not possible.' Davey stabbed his finger at Jack, and then sighed wearily. 'Well,' he continued, 'it's not supposed to be possible. Yard Boys can't travel *up* a Sorrowline, unless they've already travelled *down* it.'

Jack raised his eyebrows. 'Well, you're here, aren't you?'

Davey pulled himself up onto his feet, looking dizzy and uncertain, and began to stumble away from the graveyard. He stopped at the entrance, steadying himself against the stone wall. It was the middle of the night and the streets were once again slumbering, save for a black cat that arched its back against Davey's leg, purring softly. 'Where are we? What year?'

Jack sucked in the air and closed his eyes. It was just

as before, just as Old David had said. *You ride through a Sorrowline, you just know the date, you feel the date.*

'We're back in 1940. The twenty-fifth of September,' Jack said with conviction.

'OK.' Davey nodded. 'Tell me again what happened?' He pushed the cat firmly with his foot. It hissed its dissatisfaction at him as it skulked away.

'Do you remember being in the graveyard?' Jack asked.

'Yes, of course,' Davey snapped, rubbing his head.

'We tried to get the Sorrowline back to 1940. I made it in and you got stuck behind.'

Davey nodded slowly. 'I remember now. You disappeared. That fella nearly grabbed me. Then I saw you again.'

'I came back here, but Monty said it was dangerous to travel down the same Sorrowline again, and—'

'He's right!' Davey interrupted. 'You shouldn't have come back for me.'

'That's why I found another Sorrowline,' Jack said. 'The one we just used. It brought me back to 1813 ten days before you. I've been working as a gravedigger for the last week, waiting for you.'

'You should have left me,' Davey said quietly.

'I wasn't going to do that.' Jack was struggling to see what Davey's problem was.

'I'm not a Yard Boy, Jack,' Davey sighed. 'I never really was. I don't think I travelled with you, I think you carried me.' Davey's face was stern, a mix of sadness and awe. 'Jack, you've done something no other living Yard Boy has ever done, and you don't even realise it. There's no other way to explain it. You dragged me back to 1940, just like you carried the book.' Davey gazed squarely at Jack and said, 'I don't know any other Yard Boy like you. In fact' – and his voice rose in excitement – 'you're more than a Yard Boy. You're gonna be a *Timesmith*!'

'A Timesmith?'

'Maybe, yeah. I've never known anyone who can do the things you do. There hasn't been a Timesmith in years.'

Jack scratched at the path with his heel, his mind far away. 'I can't be, I'm hardly even a Yard Boy. I think I'm just lucky.'

Davey shivered, avoiding Jack's stare. 'It might not be snowing here, but I'm still freezing.'

Jack put the awkward discussion out of his mind. He couldn't be a Timesmith; he was just a normal boy, despite everything that was going on.


As Jack approached the front door of Monty's townhouse he noticed it was ajar, a sliver of the dark interior barely visible beyond. Jack slowed as he moved up the old steps, Davey at his shoulder. Splintered wood jutted out where once a lock had been.

'Davey,' Jack whispered, his hand held out in warning.

Davey saw it too. He pulled at Jack's arm and stepped up to the open door.

The ominous silence fractured as Davey pushed open the creaking door. The hairs on Jack's neck bristled as he followed his friend into the reading room. The darkness robbed it of its detail, leaving vague shapes for his mind to fill.

Davey stopped abruptly. For a moment he was still, blocking Jack's view, then he moved forward and Jack gazed at the prone body of Montgomery Falconer lying on the floor. The signs of a struggle were all around but Jack had not noticed them until now: Monty's reading chair lay on its side, books were strewn over the floor, and a glistening spray of blood disfigured the expensive wallpaper above the fading fire.

'Is he alive?' Jack asked, his voice only just audible.

Davey knelt over the Limner, turning him over and lifting his limp head onto his lap. 'He's barely breathing.'

Monty's eyes opened, wide at first, and then they fell back to heavy slits as he fought to keep his vision.

'Don't worry, we'll fetch a doctor. You'll be fine,' Davey said.

'Rouland,' Monty said dimly. 'He was hunting for you.' His dull eyes stared directly at Jack.

'Where's Eloise?' Jack asked.

'Gone,' Monty coughed. 'Rouland must have her now, I suppose. You have the book?'

Jack pulled it from his trouser pocket and showed it to

Monty. He smiled feebly until a liquid cough brought pain back to his face.

'It is the greatest weapon you could have against Rouland. You and the book, like you and him, are inextricably linked. It will provide the answers you need, young Jack, when you most need them. I would have liked to have studied it myself. It is no good to me now, of course. Rouland would take it from me eventually, and I am not a defiant man.' Monty's eyes seemed to be filled with self-pity. His body arched upwards, struck with a merciless pain. 'I did not think I would have the strength to resist him. But you make an excellent teacher, young Jack. Your example gave me food for thought. You shamed me.' Monty pulled his hand up to his chest, a framed photograph tightly in his grip. In it Monty – younger, happier – posed with a dark-haired woman. 'My wife, Clara. She was proud, like you. I had forgotten that for so long.' Monty smiled again, a defiant tone roused in his voice. 'She would have been ashamed, you see. I have been a coward since her death, but not tonight, at the end. And, after all, endings are all that really matter.'

'Monty,' Jack said, 'the Rose. What about the Rose? Do you know where we can find it?'

Monty ran his tongue over his dry lips. 'He asked the same, he has the same fire within. You are the answer to his question.' He coughed as his body began to shake. 'The Rose is real. Ask your mother.'

Jack pulled his hand away sharply. 'What does this have to do with my mother?'

Monty's mouth broke into a crooked smile, his voice barely a whisper. 'Everything, Jack Morrow, everything.' A spot of darkness grew in the centre of his chest, his face contorted in pain and his arms and legs spasmed. Jack recoiled in horror; he had seen this death before.

'Davey, get back.'

There was a moment of smouldering heat as Monty's chest turned to ash and dust. The transformation spread, consuming his frail body in seconds.

'Rouland did that,' Davey whispered angrily.

A solemn mutual hush overcame the two boys as they stared at the pile of ashes on the floor. The earthly remains circled in the draught, and then unexpectedly lifted upwards, forming a ribbon of dust that grew as it turned. The colour drained from Jack's face.

'Dustmen!'

Jack and Davey pushed for the door and ran towards the street. Behind him Jack heard the dread tone of a Dustman's growing pains. Davey began to sprint back along the street.

'Where are we going?' Jack cried out.

'The church.'

Behind them the Dustman crawled out of the door. As it touched the frame the wood blackened, aged and became brittle charcoal. It half leaped, half flew along the street, hunting by feral senses that defied human definitions.

Davey ran up the path to the church and hit the door with the full force of his body, bouncing off it like a rag doll. Jack caught up and lifted Davey off the cold ground. Behind them the Dustman cried out again as it crossed the entrance to the graveyard and bounded up the little path towards them.

Jack leaned against the old wooden door, his heart pounding.

Beside him Davey hammered desperately on the entrance. 'C'mon! Open! Open!'

The thing loomed over them, exultant. It raised its arm and Jack closed his eyes, expecting the worst. Then, suddenly, he was falling backwards. He landed on the hard floor of the church, rolling into Davey. He looked up as a pale young man slammed the door in the face of the Dustman.

# 21

## MESSAGE FROM THE PAST

The dim shelter of the church was eerily peaceful. Outside, the remorseful wailing of the Dustman continued as it reeled and thrashed with a child-like frustration.

'It cannot enter here.' The man smiled. 'Not even a Dustman could break that rule.'

Jack turned from the door and saw the young vicar who had rescued him. The dark garb of his office contrasted with his albino-white hair. The starkness aged his otherwise youthful appearance, and his red eyes were filled with wisdom beyond his years.

'Who are you?' Jack asked.

But before the man could answer, Jack's eyes made out the familiar shape of Davey to his right.

His friend's voice was tense. 'I know you: Warnock!'

The man's face flashed with anger, quickly succeeded by recognition. 'Davey? Is that you?'

Suddenly Davey pushed the vicar to the ground, his knee clamped down on his neck. 'Bet you never thought you'd see me again.'

'Davey!' Jack shouted, seeing the anger on the other boy's face. 'What are you doing?'

'Evening the score!'

'Please,' Warnock gasped, 'I was . . . different back then. Just a boy.'

'You sold me,' Davey hissed as his weight pushed down on Warnock's throat.

'Stop it, Davey!' Jack shouted.

Fury erupted onto Davey's reddened features. 'Give me one good reason why I shouldn't just kill you now.'

'Because,' Warnock whispered between stolen breaths, 'you are not a killer.'

Jack put his hand onto Davey's shoulder and, as if a spell had been broken, he released his grip on the vicar. Warnock rolled onto his side, coughing and rasping.

Jack saw Davey's pained rage subside and asked, 'Who is he?'

'This,' Davey said with contempt, 'is Warnock. He sold me, like an animal, to a realm-ship captain. He left me for dead, for just a few coins.'

'It is true,' Warnock said quietly. 'I betrayed you, I sold you. I presumed you would be dead in a matter of weeks. My heart sings to see you alive, Davey.'

'And you don't even deny it?' Davey shouted. Jack had never seen him so confused, so utterly lost. He remembered the shared memories when they had travelled together in the Sorrowline, and he thought he understood the depth of his grandfather's feelings here. Davey, who did not give out his trust lightly, had trusted this man and he had betrayed him.

'I had nothing,' Davey continued. 'Then I met him.'

'Yes, I remember it well,' Warnock said as he stood up. 'I found a hungry young boy, alone on the streets. I took you in, fed you, gained your trust. Then, when you were stronger, I sold you. Your face has lived in my nightmares each night since then.'

'I could have died!'

'I know. A part of me, the worst part, did die that night.' Warnock's red eyes filled with tears. 'I have prayed for forgiveness ever since. My prayers have led me here.' He gestured to his garb.

'I ain't got no forgiveness for you!'

The heavy vibration of a distant explosion and the whine of an air-raid siren filled their ears.

'Germans,' Warnock shivered. 'It seems there is more than one demon abroad tonight. At least the Dustman will not remain here for much longer. We must shelter from the air raid. Please, this way.'

Davey hesitated, his eyes looking to the door.

Jack took his arm. 'C'mon. We can't go outside, can we?'

'I don't trust him, Jack. I *can't* trust him.'

Warnock gestured into the church towards an anonymous door set back behind the altar. He made his way nimbly to it and held it open for Davey and Jack to enter. The door led to a steep staircase, which took them down into the crypt. It was a low space, full of old chairs stacked neatly along one wall.

'I think it is no coincidence that you should find me tonight, Davey,' Warnock said. 'It seems the First World has caught up with me here. You were not the only souls seeking sanctuary tonight.'

In the middle of the floor was a long shape covered with a blanket. As Warnock approached he bowed his head in reverence and his lips moved as he uttered a silent prayer.

'One of the accursed Paladin came here not long ago. She was badly injured. She is with God now.'

'No!' A grim foreboding ate away inside Jack as he knelt down beside the veiled head.

'You know her?' Warnock asked.

'You'd better pray we don't,' Davey replied.

Jack pulled away the blanket to expose the bruised and bloodied face of Eloise underneath. Her chest bore witness to a frenzied attack, a large open wound exposing a motionless heart sitting within her cracked ribs. Jack's stomach lurched, his head felt dizzy, and he stepped away, seeking out the cold wall to steady him.

'The sword!' Davey raged. 'Where's her sword?'

'What?' Jack said, half-dazed.

'Her sword, it can heal her! We have to find it.'

'She was only just alive when she came inside,' Warnock stuttered. 'She did not have a sword.'

'It can't be far. Find it!'

Remembering what had happened when Eloise had been reunited with a sword in the junction chamber, Jack followed Davey back up to the church and began to frantically scan the room for Eloise's weapon. He saw a trail of white blood marking the stone floor and he followed it through the church until he saw something glint in the shadows.

'Here!' Jack shouted, pulling the heavy sword up with both hands and dragging it back down the stairs and into the crypt.

'Give it to her, quick!' Davey urged.

Jack dropped to his knees and gently placed the hilt of the weapon into Eloise's cold hand. Almost immediately her fingers twitched and she gripped the sword tightly. The muscles in her arm flexed and Jack saw her exposed heart begin to beat again, feebly at first but then with vigour as the sword blade began to glow an incandescent green, the dried blood coating its surface boiling away to leave the metal spotless.

'Eloise?' Davey whispered. 'Can you hear me?'

There was a loud crack as the bones in Eloise's chest moved into place, the torn flesh knitting back together at an incredible speed. Finally, her chest expanded and she drew in a long breath of air. Her eyes flickered back to life and she let out a hoarse scream of terror, groping blindly about until her hand found Jack's.

'It's all right,' Jack said – none of this was really all right – and placed his other hand on her shoulder. 'You're safe now.'

She gazed up at Jack, her eyes milky and unfocused. 'I was falling, into blackness.'

Davey knelt closer. 'What happened to you?'

Eloise's face contorted into a deep frown as she forced the fragments of her painful memories to realign. 'We waited, as we planned,' she said, her voice tiny. 'For ten days we waited for your return. Then, last night... Rouland came. I fought my Paladin sisters. I lost. I escaped here.' A flash of fear appeared on Eloise's face. 'Rouland: he had a Grimnire with him.'

'What's that?' Jack asked.

'Big thing in a cloak,' Davey replied flatly.

'The Grimnire are masters of destiny,' Eloise said, scowling with pain. 'They live between realms... and govern over them. They are angels to some... demons to others.'

Davey frowned. 'What does he want with a Grimnire? They don't usually take sides.'

'He is planning a journey,' Eloise replied without emotion. 'He read something in Montgomery's thoughts before he killed him, something which pleased him greatly.'

'Where's he going?'

'I do not know,' Eloise said. Her eyes closed as she grimaced from the pain of her body's rapid healing. 'But if Rouland is in league with a Grimnire then there is nothing to hold back his ambition.'

Warnock stepped forward, his sharp features caught in the light hanging from the ceiling. Eloise saw him and her eyes narrowed. 'Who is this?'

'My name is Warnock,' the vicar said softly.

'Ignore him,' Davey said. 'He's nothing.'

Eloise turned to Jack and said, 'Did you find the book?'

'Yes,' Jack replied. As he pulled the stolen book from his trouser pocket it fell open on the last page. The confusing grid of handwritten letters and numbers appeared in front of him, neatly spaced, all perfectly in line.

'You are impressive, Jack,' Eloise said respectfully. 'What is the grid?'

'I don't know,' Jack replied, sitting on the stairs. 'I've hardly had a chance to look at it.'

Eloise knelt down next to Jack and stared in wonder at the matrix of letters and numbers. 'I think it may be a cipher, a coded message. They were common years ago in the First World, to pass secret messages between rival houses. I have not seen one for a long time.'

'I studied them, in an earlier life,' Warnock said apologetically. 'Code-breaking could sometimes be profitable.'

Davey scowled. 'This doesn't involve you. Keep out of it.'

'Usually,' Warnock continued, 'the key to the code is

knowing the first letter of the message. Sometimes it was written in a slightly different way—'

'We don't need your help!'

'A letter above the line, perhaps, or just below. Or the letter might be slanted, or marked with a dot. Older ciphers were—'

Suddenly Davey shot towards Warnock again.

'Davey!' Eloise shouted feebly. 'Let him speak.'

Jack watched Davey stop and scowl at the vicar. He stood for a moment in front of Warnock before joining Jack on the stairs.

'What's it mean?' Davey said from over his shoulder. 'I'm not too good with books,' he added quietly in Jack's ear.

'I don't know either.' Jack began to run his finger over the line of letters, carefully looking for something that might make sense.

'They all look the same,' Eloise noted. 'None are slanted, or marked.'

As Jack got to the end of the first line he felt something which caught his attention. To be sure he ran his finger over the line several times in each direction.

'What you doing?' Davey enquired.

There. Jack smiled. It was subtle, easily missed, but he was certain he'd found something. His finger rested on a letter.

Eloise leaned in closer. 'What have you found, Jack?'

'Monty said the book would provide answers when I most needed them,' Jack replied, bursting with excitement. 'I think he was right.' He took Davey's finger and pushed it onto the page. 'Can you feel it?' Jack continued. 'The letter, it's raised up.'

Davey laughed, his finger gliding over the page. 'Yeah! You're right! I can feel it.'

'What is the letter?' Eloise asked, her calm voice hinting at impatience.

'J. It's the letter "J",' Davey said, his finger racing ahead to the next line.

Jack felt a tingle pass up his spine. He stared afresh at the letters in the grid as Davey's finger stopped over one of the letters.

'The "A", it's raised as well,' Davey laughed.

Jack's eyes rushed excitedly across the page. His hand jumped to the next line down. He already knew which letter would be next. Even so his stomach jolted when he felt the raised curve. 'It's a "C".' His finger slid forward. He closed his eyes until he felt the next raised text. He opened his eyes and gasped.

'K,' Eloise said. 'J, A, C, K.'

The room dissolved away as Jack's attention focused onto this tiny book with his name inexplicably hidden in it. His finger traced its way over the lines until he found an 'M', then an 'O'. The rest of his surname suddenly screamed out of the page.

'Jack Morrow,' Davey gasped.

'Who is Jack Morrow?' Warnock asked sheepishly.

'I am,' Jack said, his mind dizzy. There was his name, *Jack Morrow*, hidden in a book stolen from 1813. He passed the book to Eloise, drained by this new revelation. 'Here, you do it.'

Eloise traced the text as Jack had done. 'The letter "T" ... the letter "I" ... ' Eloise said in a hushed voice. The room was silent, all eyes focused on her hand drifting over the page. The letters came more quickly now, until a new word was made.

'*Timesmith*.' Davey announced. He looked at Jack. 'I said so, didn't I?'

Jack sighed heavily, bracing himself for something he knew was even bigger than he could have possibly imagined. 'How can this be in a book that's over one hundred years old?'

'This book has many secrets,' Eloise said, without looking up. 'Many have died to read its contents. But you succeeded, and are named within. You should heed its message.'

'What message?' Jack said, baffled.

Eloise smiled stonily. 'There is more here. Numbers. A six ... and another. Then a two ... zero ... zero ... eight.'

'A code for something else?' Warnock offered.

'No,' Jack said, a sickening feeling clawing up his body from his feet. He knew those numbers instantly. 'It's a date.'

'A date?' Davey said, pacing the floor. 'Six, six. The sixth of June?'

Jack nodded grimly.

'2008,' Eloise said slowly. 'The sixth of June 2008. You know this date?'

Jack nodded uncomfortably as he tried to keep his emotions in check. 'That's the date my mum died.'

The room fell into an uncomfortable stillness. Jack fought with his conflicting thoughts, unable to fully comprehend what this all meant.

'Is that it?' Davey said.

'Yes,' Eloise nodded. 'The code ends there.' She winced in discomfort, lifting her sword onto her lap. The light of its healing glow spilled over the book.

Jack gasped. The green pulsing light had illuminated some of the letters, each one responding to the glow and reflecting the light back.

'What is it?' Davey said, returning to the stairs.

'Another code,' Eloise said, 'hidden in the grid.'

'The first letter is "R",' Jack saw.

'It is the same "R" that was raised up, that spelt out Morrow,' Eloise noted.

Jack hardly heard this, his eyes already jumping ahead, joining the glowing letters together into a word. '*Rouland.*'

Davey pointed to three glowing letters that remained at the bottom of the page. 'What about those? "CJM"?'

A tear splashed onto the page. Jack wiped his eyes. 'It's my mother's initials: Catherine Jean Morrow.' His frustration and anger boiled up inside him. 'But what does that mean?'

Eloise gently closed the book. 'I think Rouland is connected to your mother's death, in 2008.'

'How? Why?' Davey was angry.

'He seeks the Rose.'

'Monty, he said he knew where the Rose was,' Jack said grimly. 'He knew when he touched me. When I asked him about it he said, "Ask your mother".'

'And if Rouland found that out before he killed him, he would do anything to hunt her down,' Eloise replied. 'Even travel upstream.'

'But he's not a Timesmith. He can't travel to the future,' Davey said.

'He has made a deal with a Grimnire,' Eloise said. 'A Grimnire can take him upstream.'

'He's going upstream,' Jack replied, 'to the year 2008. He's going to kill my mum and get the Rose.'

There was a low rumble as a distant explosion rattled the church.

'But how can you be sure?' Warnock pried.

'I think he is right,' Eloise replied.

Jack opened the book and stared again at the page, so familiar and yet so strange. He was convinced now, however unlikely it seemed, certain that this was a message intended

231

for his eyes, a warning to point him in the right direction. 'Rouland means to kill my mother, and I have to stop him,' he said firmly. 'He's going upstream, to 2008, and so am I.'

'You wouldn't stand a chance on your own,' Davey said firmly.

'I have to go.'

Eloise sat up, holding onto her sword for balance. 'I will protect you.'

Jack shook his head. 'Eloise, you're hurt. You need time to rest.'

'I will *have* time. I am OnceDead. I cannot age. I cannot die. I will wait for you here. When you arrive in 2008 you will find me and I will protect you. Then together we will destroy Rouland, and I will have my peace.'

Jack understood. To him the Sorrowline journey would take mere moments, but Eloise would wait in real time, for more than sixty years, never ageing, until she caught up with Jack again.

'If you stay here Rouland or his Paladin are gonna find you again,' Davey said to Eloise.

'Not if you entomb me. Bury me deep in the ground. You will have to incapacitate me, of course; otherwise I will be found.'

'How do we incapacitate you?' Jack asked, dreading the answer.

'Take my sword, strike me through the heart. You will restore me with it upstream.' Eloise showed no emotion,

232

no fear whatsoever. Jack couldn't believe how resolute, how brave she was.

'You want us to kill you and hope your sword fixes you again in . . .' Davey paused briefly, his lips counting, 'sixty-eight years' time?'

'Yes.'

'This is ridiculous!' Davey nervously ran his fingers through his thick brown hair and walked to the end of the small crypt. 'You don't have to do this. You can hide. You can fight.'

'Rouland thinks me dead,' Eloise observed. 'We can use that to our advantage.'

'And who's to say you'll come back to life in sixty-eight years' time?' Davey replied. 'Jack might put the sword in your hand and nothing happens. Nothing! Then what?'

'We have little choice. If Rouland is going upstream, and Jack is going there too, then he will need protection or everything is lost.'

Warnock took a step forward. 'I can watch over her. I am a young man and, God willing, I may survive another sixty years or so.'

'You?' Davey said with contempt. 'Why would you help?'

'Davey,' Warnock sighed. 'What happened between us, it has stayed with me ever since. I thought I'd killed you. I have prayed for the chance to make it up to you somehow. Now the good Lord has seen fit to bring you to me again. This is my chance, Davey. I know I can never make amends for what I did to you, but perhaps by doing this I might be able to live with myself again.'

Davey's anger seemed to subside, giving way to pity. 'I won't ever forgive you, you know that?'

'I know.' Warnock smiled heavily. 'But I have to try.'

Davey nodded and looked at Eloise, then Jack. 'This is madness, it'll never work. But if Jack's going then I'm going too.' He grinned devilishly at Jack. 'You can carry me like you did before.'

'But what about the dangers?'

Davey raised an eyebrow. 'I'm your bloody grandfather and you'll do as you're told, young lad!' He managed half a smile. 'I'm family, after all, so this concerns me, don't it? Someday I'm gonna have a daughter, and if she's in danger then I should be there.'

Jack hesitated. Yet something deep inside his mind was telling him to do as Davey suggested. He tried to fight against it, but the compulsion seemed to gain momentum with each passing second. With a heavy resignation he held out his hand. Davey gazed down at it, then shook it firmly.

Outside, the noise from the night-time bombardment had grown louder and there was a great rumble as a nearby building took a direct hit. Its death-cry vibrated through the crypt like the low howl of a mournful beast.

Eloise raised herself to her feet, her miraculous return to health now completed. She held up her sword to Davey.

'I am ready.'

# 22

## BACK TO WHITECHAPEL

Warnock took them deeper, to a long-forgotten chamber, once a wealthy family's tomb, which contained several heavy stone sarcophagi, their contents now nothing more than bone and dust.

Eloise climbed into one of the tombs, into the dirt, as Jack, Davey and Warnock stood over her. Jack tried to hide the turmoil of emotions he felt inside when Eloise nodded her readiness and Davey raised the heavy sword over his head.

'I'm sorry,' he whispered as unbidden tears streamed down his ruddy cheeks. He thrust downwards with an almighty effort. The blade hit home and pierced Eloise's heart. Her face contorted into a silent scream as her hands grabbed at the sword, its edge cutting into her palms. Then an unearthly glow bled out of her body and fed the sword. Warnock shouted the Lord's Prayer repeatedly, but his efforts to drown out Davey's pitiful cries were in vain. Jack turned away, unable to watch any more.

The sword's glow faded as the last of Eloise's life-force drained from her beautiful eyes. Her heart stopped.

'She is suspended,' Warnock said bitterly. 'Trapped somewhere between this world and the next.'

Davey withdrew the sword and wiped its blade on his sleeve. He wore Eloise's scabbard around his waist and he returned the sword safely into it. 'Jack,' he said, as he swabbed his face dry, 'I need your help.' He stood over the heavy stone lid. Together they lifted it into place and Eloise's tortured face disappeared. 'This had better work,' Davey muttered, his voice trembling with regret.

Warnock nodded. 'I will not fail you, Davey.'

Outside the bombing had stopped and a portentous silence veiled the city. The church had lost two of its stained-glass windows, but otherwise had survived almost unscathed. The surrounding streets had fared worse; Monty's house had taken a direct hit, and had been reduced to a pile of brick and wood. The Limner's demise would be chalked up as just one more statistic in a bloody war.

Dawn was still a few hours away. They had a long walk ahead of them, back to Whitechapel Cemetery where Jack's adventure had begun.

Two boys – grandfather and grandson – walked solemnly through the ruined streets of London. The city, scarred and torn by the constant nightly bombardment, bore witness to the random lottery of war. Stinking rubble was all that remained of some streets, while others seemed untouched. Winners and losers in a fatal game of chance.

They saw a few dazed survivors walking through the dirt, their skin and clothes painted grey, like mute zombies lumbering through a post-apocalyptic landscape. Some roads had been cleared of rubble; a semblance of order was maintained as market traders set up their stalls and vans attempted to deliver their goods. Oxford Street bustled with life. People chirped greetings to passing soldiers in blind defiance to the carnage only streets away. Above it all, visible through the smoke and fire, stood the perpetual outline of St Paul's Cathedral, an impassive witness through the centuries.

They rested near Aldgate and drank from a fountain. Jack washed his grubby face, drying it on the sleeve of his dirty shirt before they continued their grim passage. 'Could we not travel by junction chamber?' Jack was exhausted.

'I'm out of coins,' Davey said cheerfully, 'and I don't want to draw attention to myself by trying to get hold of some more.'

So the boys kept going on foot, the streets becoming smaller and darker as they approached Whitechapel until they were in a maze of alleys, many of which Jack did not recognise. Here the city was alive still, its heart beating, unrepentant, shaking its fist at the fire that rained from the sky, night after night. Smells and colours bombarded

Jack's tired senses. The aroma of cooking meat wafted from a row of market stalls, tempting his empty stomach. As if in reply to Jack's idle thought, Davey handed him a hot bacon sandwich.

'Where did you—?'

'Don't ask.' Davey flashed a wide smile. Jack grinned in reply. They walked together through the busy market-place, eating their stolen food, content in the silent rapport between them.

Finally they came to Vallance Road and Whitechapel Cemetery.

Davey entered first, turning to Jack after he had surveyed the graveyard. 'I think we're alone. Let's get this over with.'

Jack led them to the far corner of the churchyard, where he had arrived in 1940. He stood on the disturbed soil, letting his hands feel for the Sorrowline that had brought him here.

Memories of his family came into his mind; somehow they were all linked to this place. Whitechapel Cemetery was special; Jack knew that from the stories his nan had told him. It was unique, in fact: the last cemetery in the centre of London. His mother had campaigned to keep it open, her social spirit repaid with a small scrub of land, and a headstone. Now, he realised, there was more to it than that. His mother was a First Worlder, like him. Yet she had lived in a council flat, away from the strange majesty of the secret world Jack had started to uncover. He wondered why.

He had been only seven years old when she had died. Jack's father would never talk about it, but he had gleaned some details from his nan before the dementia had stolen her memories from her. His mother had been attacked in the family flat, left to die alone, her killer never found. In Jack's mind, that killer now had a face: Rouland's.

But even the image of his mother was slowly dying, like the afterglow of a fire, leaving nothing for Jack to hold onto, apart from this eerie place and his growing hatred for Rouland.

His memories of her were like a patchwork. Some of them were true recollections, some borrowed from over-heard conversations, old photographs and videos. Others were idealised fairy tales, stories that he told himself to make life more bearable. Over the years it was hard to tell what was real any more.

Then he felt something – a connection, slim but tangible. The cool Sorrowline was there, full of pain and laughter and memory. He beckoned Davey to move closer to him, then he held onto his young grandfather, wrapping one arm round him tightly so that their heads rested on each other's shoulders, his other hand touching the plot of soil. The graveyard faded from his mind, his world became an ever-shrinking circle of awareness and everything faded into grey until only he, Davey and the plot remained.

He let out a long shallow breath, and then they were gone, together inside the Sorrowline, travelling upwards, their speed increasing with every passing second.

The flood of emotions came in waves, at times it threatened to drag him into a chasm of despair, and then, just as he felt he could bear no more, the emotions drifted away, leaving a numb emptiness that pressed onto every inch of his skin.

His mind drifted. They were racing back up to 2008, back to the day his mother died. The date was burned for ever into his memories: the 6th of June 2008, a storm-filled summer's night. He would arrive there again, unable to do anything to save his mother. She would already be dead. Anger and frustration coursed through his being, and then, at the centre of his lamentation, was a word – something that Davey had said to him earlier, a suggestion of a deeper ability within Jack. It was a word he'd seen hidden in the code.

*Timesmith.*

The word ran through his mind like a needle of ice. Opportunities revealed themselves to him. The Sorrowline was not a simple tunnel, with a beginning and an end. It was a network, like the roots of a tree, intertwined, linked, a universe of connections.

And there it was. The Sorrowline spoke to him.

*What do you want?* The words were a question forming around him.

*I want to save my mother*, Jack replied in his mind without hesitation. He didn't care about the consequences of changing the future. To hell with the future! If he could put his family back together again he would, and nothing would stop him. Nothing.

Something brushed up against his skin, not a physical thing, but a notion. An idea. A suggestion. He could take the Sorrowline and arrive sooner, before his mother's death. It was possible, he knew it. All he had to do was ask, and the Sorrowline would submit. The question formed in his brain – as feelings and emotions.

*Two days. Give me two days to find her. I can save her. Two days to find the Rose and keep it from Rouland.* Yes, he thought, that should be enough.

Instantly Jack felt a change. The Sorrowline buckled and collapsed inwards, and he was propelled in a new direction, along a new Sorrowline. The smell of fresh flowers raced into his nostrils, followed by a new wave of inconsolable emotion, tension and primal fury. The unbearable torture was blissfully brief.

Jack and Davey landed on the dirt, their mouths contorted in breathless screams. Jack squinted as he opened his eyes; the sinking sun was dazzling in the cloudless sky. Intuitively he knew it was the evening of the 4th of June. The Sorrowline had granted his wish. He had two days to save his mother.

He turned to look at Davey. Their bloodshot eyes met and both boys burst into a fit of triumphant laughter.

'You did it, didn't you? This is 2008?' Davey said, shaking his head. He circled around in awe, taking in the beautiful tableau of glass and steel buildings painted a burnt orange by the setting sun. He stopped to face Jack, and tears pooled in his eyes; he brushed them away as casually as he could.

'You OK?' Jack asked. He knew the feeling – of arriving in the same place but so many years apart, the familiar and the new thrown uncomfortably together.

'Yeah.' Davey smiled. 'Don't suppose we have time to have a look around? Maybe a few bars? I could use a stiff drink.' He raised his eyebrows and smiled weakly.

'Come on,' Jack said. 'Let's find my mother, before it's too late.'

Davey held up his hands. 'Aren't you forgetting something?' He gestured to the sword at his belt. 'What about Eloise?'

Jack recalled with a shiver. How could he have forgotten?

'Yes, of course. I'm sorry. But hide that sword – tuck it under your coat.' Eloise had given her life – what remained of it – for them and now he'd forgotten her? He nodded in shame and followed Davey out of the cemetery.

At first Davey kept up a punishing pace towards St Bartholomew's church – to Eloise. But as they got closer into the centre of London the sights became unrecognisable to him. The congested roads full of taxis, the drunken office workers retreating home, the wail of sirens, had all conspired to overwhelm Davey's senses. Jack took the lead, moving quickly, not giving passers-by the chance to do more than glance at them before they rushed past. The busy streets trapped the hot evening air, making it thick and stale. By the time they reached Gray's Inn Road Jack's back was wet and his feet ached.

'I need a drink,' he said, exhausted.

'Me too,' Davey agreed, but showed no signs of slowing down. 'It's not far now.'

As they turned the final corner Jack expected to see the little church, old and tired, a welcome relic in the urban sprawl of tomorrow. What they saw made them both stop instantly.

In front of them stood a huge office block of glass and steel, some twenty storeys high, its interior lit up against the starry night sky. The little church was nowhere to be seen.

# 23

## CODE LAZARUS

'What's happened?' Davey's voice trembled. 'Did we take a wrong turn?'

'No, we're in the right place,' Jack replied, despair welling up inside him. 'Isn't it obvious? The church has been demolished, and that office has been built on top.'

'No!' Davey gasped.

The building was sleek and modern, its interior space on show through the vast armour of glass that hung from its skeletal framework. The exterior was a symphony of simplicity, adorned only with a wide sign that read *Calthorpe Associates*. The illuminated letters shone down on them, a bitter echo of the beautiful stained glass that had once been there.

'There's still a chance she's OK. She might still be under there,' Jack said, desperate to believe it was true.

'And how are we supposed to get to her?'

Jack considered the options, of which there were few. 'We could break in, get into the basement and see if the crypt is still down there,' he proposed.

Davey looked doubtful. 'That's the best you can come up with?'

Jack shrugged.

Davey began to walk towards the brightly lit reception, his grip on Eloise's concealed sword tighter than ever. As Jack and Davey approached the wide glass doors opened automatically with a gentle hiss. Davey halted, immediately alert.

'It's all right.' Jack couldn't help grinning. 'The doors are automatic. They open by themselves when you walk up to them.'

He pulled Davey back a step, and the doors dutifully closed again. 'See?'

They stepped forward again, and Davey laughed as the doors opened once more.

'Ridiculous,' he said.

A long curved desk dominated the reception area, behind which were several sculpted chairs. The desk was lit from below, the layers of plastic and glass fracturing the light into a rainbow of shifting colours. Another sign with the same logo as outside covered the far wall, its faceted surface hypnotised with constantly changing hues.

At this time of night the reception area was home only to a lone security guard, a giant of a man who hardly fitted into his clothes. As Jack and Davey approached he sat up in his chair, putting down a dishevelled crossword book.

He tugged at his regulation blue shirt and matching tie, and straightened his identity badge.

''Ow do, lads,' the man said, his voice baritone deep and gruff.

'Hello.' Despite the challenge ahead, Jack felt more confident now he was back in a time he knew well. 'Can you tell me what happened to the church that used to be here?'

The man's friendly manner instantly changed, his eyes darting from Jack to Davey. 'Demolished, long time ago. Hit by a bomb in the war.' As he spoke he reached for his phone and dialled an extension. 'Just a mo', lads.'

Jack glanced uneasily to Davey.

The guard spoke quietly into the phone, 'Hello, sir. Sorry t' bother you, but I think I've got a Code Lazarus.' The guard scanned Jack and Davey. There was a brief pause, then, 'That's 'em all right.'

An unconvincing smile fixed itself like a mask onto his chubby face as he placed the phone down. 'Wait here, lads,' the guard said in his jolliest voice. 'Someone's comin' to help.'

Jack forced a polite smile and stepped away from the desk.

'What do we do?' Davey asked nervously.

'I don't know,' Jack replied. 'Should we run?'

'What about Eloise? We're no good to her if we get caught.'

'I don't like this one bit,' Jack whispered. 'What's Code Lazarus?'

'How should I know?' Davey said gruffly. He glanced back to the guard, who was watching one of the monitors concealed under his desk.

An echoing ping broke their concentration. The polished metal doors of the main elevator opened and an old man stepped out. He wore a thick dressing gown and slippers, and walked unsteadily with a cane. The old man shuffled towards Jack and Davey, a beaming smile growing over his white face, then he stopped directly in front of Jack and tears filled his blood-red eyes.

'It's really you, it really is.' The feeble voice trembled.

Jack gazed in disbelief at the old man in front of him; his chiselled albino features were covered with wrinkles and liver spots, but his face was still recognisable.

'Warnock?'

Warnock grabbed Jack and hugged him with a newfound vigour, his cane falling to the floor with a clatter. 'I've waited so long.'

He pulled Davey towards him, unable to control his joy. Jack saw them meet each other's eyes – deep with unspoken emotion.

'I don't believe it,' Davey half laughed.

Warnock chuckled. 'Well, who else would it be? I made a promise, didn't I?'

* * *

Warnock poured tea from an antique service as Jack studied the London skyline from the windows of the penthouse suite. The architecture was still open plan, glass and steel, but Warnock had softened it with a collection of fine furniture and antiques.

Davey stared, open-mouthed, at his surroundings, at the view and, most of all, at Warnock's wrinkled face. 'Have you run out of stone and wood in the future? Why's everything made of glass?'

Warnock chuckled. 'You will adjust, in time.'

Davey sat down next to the him. 'You're so old.'

'Old and weak and tired, yes. And you are so very young, my friend. It is good to see you again.'

'What happened to the church?'

'Not long after you left, the church took a direct hit,' Warnock explained. He shuddered as he recalled the relentless onslaught of the Blitz. 'I was in the crypt at the time, which withstood the worst of that terrible night. Eloise's tomb was untouched, but I had to move her for safe-keeping. After the church was demolished God and I parted company, and I went into business. I have had some measure of success over the last sixty years, some-thing that has allowed me to outstay my welcome on this Earth, and to keep my promise to you, Davey. When the opportunity arose I purchased this scrap of land so that I might watch out for your return. I knew the date of your arrival was almost upon us so I had the guards inform me if ever two boys matching your description enquired about the church.'

'And Eloise?' Davey asked.

'Safe. She has been returned to this very building, her casket intact. I see you have her sword.'

Davey nodded, his hand on the weapon.

'Then drink up, and I shall take you to her.'

They descended in what Warnock told them was his personal elevator all the way down to the sub-basement, Davey gasping again at the speed and technology. The doors opened and they entered an empty space of concrete walls.

Warnock stepped forward and placed his hand on a discreetly hidden scanner in the corner of the room. A cool blue light washed over his bony hand and, with a click, the far wall began to move, rolling slowly to the right to reveal a second chamber of similar size to the first. At the centre stood an old stone sarcophagus raised up on a low plinth. Warnock smiled and invited his guests to enter.

'Is that her?' Jack asked, his face tight.

'It is,' Warnock said reverently.

Davey was already pacing around the tomb, checking it for damage. Jack joined him and together, with a struggle, they lifted the heavy lid from the sarcophagus and lowered it to the floor.

Inside lay Eloise, unchanged since the day they had

sealed her within. The open wound in her chest stared back at them accusingly, and a fresh wave of guilt and nausea swept over Jack. Davey unsheathed the sword and placed it into Eloise's stiff hand.

A pensive moment passed, none daring to utter a word, yet the sword remained inert. As the empty silence grew Jack's anticipation turned to fear.

'It hasn't worked,' Davey wept, his hands trembling. 'She's dead.'

Jack had never seen Davey so upset. He felt it too, struggling to hold himself together.

'No!' Warnock gasped. 'Have I waited in vain for all these years?' The old man looked his true age for the first time and Jack suddenly feared he might collapse right there.

Then, suddenly, the lights overhead flickered and died and the small room disappeared into blackness. A tiny ember of light, almost imperceptible at first, illuminated the interior of the sarcophagus as the sword began to glow, its energy reawakened and pulsing into Eloise's hand. The light grew stronger until it blazed orange like the autumn sun. Arcs of electricity cascaded over the length of the sword and sparks and flashes danced upwards, over the ceiling like fireflies. Then, as the light threatened to blind Jack, it unexpectedly died away to nothing and they were once again in darkness. The lights above reluctantly fizzed back to life and Jack leaned forward and peered into the sarcophagus.

Eloise remained unmoving, though her chest had healed, and the sword lay dormant by her side. Then her eyes opened.

'I was falling,' she said at last, her voice dry and brittle. 'I was falling through blackness again.'

She sat up with slow deliberate movements, her body stiff after its long repose. She lifted a hand to her face, letting the fingers flex and stretch, the bones cracking and popping as they remembered their function.

She studied Davey's face, as if he was a stranger. Eventually a weak smile lifted one side of her mouth. 'You are Davey.' She turned to face Jack. 'And I know you too ...Jack.' Finally she peered at the ancient features of Warnock.

'Eloise,' he said. 'It's me, Warnock, your guardian these long years.'

'You have grown old,' she said at last. 'The plan worked?'

'Yes,' Jack said, 'it worked. Welcome to 2008.'

They returned to the penthouse where, over the next three hours, Eloise recovered slowly. Jack dozed lightly, eager to leave as soon as possible but Warnock insisted they rest and eat. As the first rays of morning light crept over the city his thoughts returned to his mother.

*Tomorrow. Tomorrow she dies.*

'Davey,' he said, waking his friend. 'We should go.'

251

They looked over to Eloise. As if anticipating Jack's urgency she stood stiffly and nodded. 'I am ready,' she said.

Warnock raised his cane and said, 'Perhaps I can help one last time. I'm afraid my fighting days are long behind me; my only battle left now is with the Almighty – and I suspect He shall win in the end – but at least I can provide you with transport. My car is yours. My driver is on standby and he will take you wherever you need to go.'

'No carriage. We will go on foot,' Eloise announced abruptly. 'I have rested long enough.'

'Suits me,' Davey said.

Warnock sank back into his soft chair. 'As you wish.'

Jack realised the huge sacrifice the man had made to dedicate his life to the care of Eloise. She knelt next to him and kissed him tenderly on the forehead. 'Thank you, kind sir. Your vigil is over, but I will never forget your devotion. I am in your debt.'

Warnock's eyes glazed with tears and he looked away, focusing on the dawn skyline outside. His voice faltered. 'Go now, before you make a fool of an old man.'

Eloise stood, her hand caressing the life-giving sword that now hung from her slender waist. Jack and Davey walked with her to the elevator.

As the doors opened Davey turned back to Warnock. 'What you did to me,' he said at last, 'selling me like that, I can't forget it, not ever. But this' – he gestured to Eloise

– 'this was a good job. A bloody good job. I reckon this probably makes us even.'

Warnock smiled feebly as tears broke over his aged face. He gripped Davey in a clumsy embrace. 'Thank you,' he managed before he turned away.

Jack and Davey got into the lift and the doors closed, leaving Warnock to his solitude.

With the dawn light chasing the long shadows away they travelled cautiously back to Whitechapel. The city was waking up and the streets were already full of cars and buses.

'The city has grown,' Eloise said flatly.

'Grown?' Davey replied. 'This ain't London, it don't even smell right. And all these glass towers, they look like they'd blow away in the wind! Give me bricks and mortar any day of the week.'

As they approached Whitechapel Jack led the way to a block of orange brick flats. It was like he had walked into a memory. He was back at the home he had grown up in. He had been very young when they lived here, but it all came flooding back to him, like opening an old photo album. This was his life before it had fallen apart, before the day his mother had died.

Tomorrow.

A day that he was going to change.

Jack stepped through the entrance, towards a waiting

figure. Davey and Eloise followed Jack into the courtyard, and the gates closed behind them with a clang that echoed off the brick walls. Jack's legs went weak and his voice disappeared deep inside him.

The woman tilted her beautiful face to one side, her dark hair falling over her shoulders, and she smiled at Jack. There was nothing to fear here, nothing at all, yet he felt an ill sensation, a deep foreboding that made him believe that the world was off kilter. Surely he was dreaming.

The woman stepped forward and held out her hand to Jack. He took it without hesitation, consumed in her warmth and the beauty of nostalgia. She was exactly as he remembered her, like a frozen moment of time.

'Hello, Jo-Jo,' said his mother.

# 24

## HOMECOMING

Jack's hands shook. His mother had poured him some juice and placed it on the table in front of him, but he had not dared to pick it up for fear of spilling its contents.

The room was just as he remembered it. The smells and colours ignited waves of early recollections in him. This place had sunk into his subconscious, buried by terrible memories. Now a wave of happier instances had been unlocked and Jack wallowed in the good times. Here he was, standing in that past, studying the fine details he had forgotten: the dead plant on the shelf, the framed pictures of forgotten holidays, the worn carpet that was Jack's first playground. It was all here, larger than life, screaming out its mundane Second World credentials. And at the centre was his mother, his dead mother: Catherine Morrow.

Smiling benevolently she turned and spoke to Davey and Eloise, who waited by the door. 'Please, can I have a moment alone with Jack?'

Eloise nodded and retreated into the corridor outside the flat. Davey stood for a moment, looking uncomfortable.

He opened his mouth to say something, but before he could Catherine began to close the door.

Jack was alone with his mother. He had imagined this moment since the first realisation of his ability, and he had known exactly what he would say. Yet now that the moment was upon him – that his dead mother stood in front of him, alive and well – every planned thought escaped him. This woman was like a stranger to him, a face out of a picture. He reached out his shaking hand to pick up his drink, and then retreated again.

'It's so very good to see you, Jack,' Catherine said softly. 'You're going to be a big lad. You get that from your dad.' She sighed heavily. 'I wonder what he would say about all this. Jack, he doesn't know, he doesn't know the things that we do. He's Second World through and through.'

Jack wondered if he should tell his mother that Dad was now in prison, but somehow it seemed irrelevant amongst everything else he wanted to tell her. Finally he summoned his voice from its hiding place deep within him. 'Mum,' he said unevenly, 'you're in danger.'

'Jack, I'm fine.'

'No, Mum, you're not,' Jack retorted. 'You have to pack a bag, now, and get out of here.'

'Why?' Her green eyes studied Jack keenly. 'Because I'm going to die?'

Jack dropped his head, unexpectedly overwhelmed.

'I'm sorry,' she said. 'I didn't mean to upset you. This must be very hard for you.' She picked up a packet of cigarettes from the top of the television and opened the small balcony door. 'This is hard for me as well.' She lit a cigarette, blowing out grey smoke which she wafted away with her other hand. 'Filthy habit, I know. I got it from my old man.'

Finally Jack asked, 'What do you know about the First World?'

'Too much,' she sighed.

'And you know your life is in danger?'

Catherine smiled as rings of smoke drifted out of the open door. 'It has been since I stole the Rose.'

Jack steadied himself. *She stole it?* 'Then you do know about the Rose. What is it, Mum? What is the Rose of Annwn?'

Catherine smiled. 'Don't you know yet?' She watched him, waiting. 'Jack, *I am* the Rose. It lives inside me.'

The answer made no sense to him. 'How?'

Catherine rolled her eyes. 'That's a long story.'

Jack tried to suppress his frustration. He was tired of vague half-truths. 'Mum, don't you think I deserve to know?'

'Yes, you do. If anyone deserves the truth it's you, Jack.'

'So tell me how you stole it. Tell me how *you* can be the Rose.'

A muffled moan rattled through the room. Catherine looked up and laughed.

'That's you, Jack, younger you: Jo-Jo.' There was the old nickname again, the name that had died with his mother. It stung like a needle to hear it spoken by those lips.

'Mum?' A small voice called from the bedroom.

Catherine stubbed out her cigarette. 'He's awake early. I'd better see to him. He has nightmares, you remember?'

She left the room, leaving Jack to wallow in his frustrations.

Nightmares. Jack had forgotten about the nightmares. How could he have forgotten them? Jo-Jo would be seven years old, Jack recalled, his nights tormented by vivid dreams of strange places. A trickle of images returned to him of those disturbed nights. He had thought he remembered this time so well, but he saw now how much had been left forgotten in the past.

He walked over to the open balcony door, his mind drifting. How could his mother *be* the Rose? He leaned against the cool metal railing and let his eyes drift over the view. There was a man in the courtyard, and he was looking back at him. Jack stood up straight, the hairs on his neck prickling. He couldn't make out who the man was, his features hidden under the shadow of a dead tree, but as if in reply to Jack's gaze the watcher stepped further into the shadows. Jack felt uneasy, exposed. He moved away from the railing and closed the door.

'He's resting for now.'

Jack wheeled round to see that his mother had returned to the room. She peered at him, pride filling her eyes. He had missed her so much.

'So, you're a Yard Boy. How did you discover your talent?'

'By accident,' Jack said. Did she know? he wondered. Did she know that he had used *her* grave for his very first journey through the Sorrowlines, albeit unwittingly? His discomfort grew, and he looked away.

'Tell me, where have you been to?'

'The Blitz, 1813 and here.'

'1813?' She whistled.

The growing clamour for answers grew inside him, until he could stand it no more. 'Mum, what am I? What are you? What is this all about?'

Catherine sat down on the battered leather sofa, and she beckoned Jack to join her. 'My family have been First Worlders for generations,' she said. 'We're one of the old Houses, the noble families, on my mother's side – not that you'd know by looking at us.' She nodded towards the door, towards Davey somewhere on the other side. 'I was born into that world. I grew up knowing all about Yard Boys, and Journeymen, and Grimnire. But it's a dying world; the families fight more and more amongst themselves, and as many of us wanted a more peaceful life, we came here, to the Second World. I never planned on staying more than a few months. But then I met your dad.' She smiled, a faraway look in her eyes as she played with the pendant that hung from a chain around her neck. 'Plans changed.'

Jack wondered if his father might appear at any minute.

'He's at work,' Catherine said, 'and he knows nothing of the First World. I kept it secret, to protect him, to protect you.' A heavy smile crossed her cheeks. 'Jack, I'm an Operator. You know what that is, don't you?'

Jack recalled Castilan using the term. It seemed so long ago now. 'You can read minds?'

'That's the first thing you master. But it's not the last. An Operator is someone who can do things with their minds.'

'What sort of things?'

Catherine looked up to the dead plant sitting on the shelf, and it instantly lifted up and drifted through the air towards Jack. It neared his face, then disappeared – a wave of charged static tickled his skin – and then reappeared back above the shelf in an instant, wobbling back down into place.

Catherine relaxed; she had been holding her breath. 'There are a bunch of fancy scientific words for what I can do: telepathy, psychokinesis, precognition, clairvoyance, but they don't really tell you how much fun it can be.'

In between her fingers Jack saw tiny sparks, like dwarf lightning. He couldn't believe what he was seeing. The sparks collected together to form a ball of electricity that writhed to be set free. 'There is energy everywhere, even in the air between my fingers. An Operator knows how to move that energy.' She was smiling, enjoying sharing her hidden secrets with him.

'It's hereditary, so maybe you'll be able to do it too, one day.'

Jack grinned.

'Don't be too keen; I say it as a warning. Operators have their uses, but it's the sort of power that can corrupt. I can read your mind; I could even plant a thought into your head, and you'd think it was your own. A skilled Operator can make someone commit murder, or jump off a cliff. They can be very dangerous. It can change someone for ever.'

Catherine stood and rubbed her arms, as if a sudden chill had robbed her of warmth.

'When I met your dad, when we fell in love and got married, I vowed never to use my skills again. It was a joy not to know what he was going to say, to ignore the impulse to turn him to my way of thinking. I revelled in the normality of our life together. Then we had you.' She turned and looked directly at him, her eyes filling with heavy tears. 'At first everything was fine, but then you were sick. Very sick.'

'I remember,' Jack said softly. The memories of futile hospital visits, of doctors with needles, of painful tests, were still vivid.

'I knew nothing in the Second World could ever hope to save you,' Catherine mused. 'But there was a chance in the First. I couldn't lose you, Jack, I couldn't. I found something, something that could save you.'

'The Rose,' Jack said.

'Yes, the Rose.'

'How did you steal it?'

'Our House has many allies, or at least we used to. I returned to the First World, called in every favour I could, all to find the Rose. You don't want to know the things I did to find it. Terrible things. I did what I had to do, what any mother would have done, and now there is a price to pay. The Rose, it's a living energy. It has restorative powers. I used its power to heal you. The Rose's scent is on you.'

'Rouland wants the Rose,' Jack said urgently. 'I think he's coming here to find it.'

'I know. The Rose amplifies my own abilities. I can sense what's ahead.'

'I can help you, Mum, you can come with me.' Jack spoke quickly. 'I can take you back through a Sorrowline, somewhere safe.'

Catherine shook her head firmly. 'It's too late, Jack. Nowhere is safe for me, but you still have a chance.

Agents of Rouland are coming now, coming to find me.'

She nodded towards the balcony, clearly aware of the figure Jack had seen earlier, the man keeping watch outside. 'You must go now, Jack.'

'No!' Jack's anger erupted. 'I've not come this far, and been through everything I've been through just to turn round and leave you. I won't lose you twice, Mum! Davey and Eloise can help too, we're not alone.'

Catherine turned from the balcony, staring Jack down. 'Davey is not to be trusted.'

'But he's your—'

'I know exactly who he is, Jack! He's an Operator, like me. Hell, he taught me how to do it. He'll manipulate everyone around him, and it will corrupt him completely.'

'But Davey's my friend.'

'Then think again, Jack.' Catherine looked to the door. 'They're coming.'

She closed her eyes, as if she was concentrating intently upon something. When her eyes flickered open again Jack saw the animal terror within them. She ran from the room and returned moments later with the seven-year-old Jo-Jo. The child's eyes were groggy, confused and tired.

'Mum,' he said, looking up innocently, 'can I have some breakfast?' Then he saw Jack. 'Who's he?'

'This is Jack.'

Jo-Jo cocked his head. 'My name's Jack too. Mum calls me Jo-Jo.'

Jack found he couldn't speak for the emotion inside him.

'You're going on a journey with Jack,' Catherine said quickly. 'Don't be scared.' She turned to face Jack. 'We don't have long. Take Jo-Jo, hide him.'

Jack took his younger self's hand in his. How could this be *happening*? It was only the 5th of June. His mum had *one more day*, didn't she? Before he could protest further the room shook with a thunderous racket and Catherine pulled Jack and Jo-Jo into the hall, to the small cupboard which opened by itself. A bluish mist tumbled out from within and the thin sickly figure of a Boagyman crawled out. At the same moment the front door opened and Davey and Eloise burst through.

'There are Paladin everywhere!' Davey screamed.

Catherine pushed Jack and Jo-Jo into the small cupboard.

'Mum! Get in!' Jack screamed. He was pinned to the back of the cupboard, unable to get up. He saw his mother, her fists clenched, somehow pushing Eloise, Davey and the Boagyman into the cupboard without touching them. He felt the rage of static all around him. He squinted through the bodies and saw his mother, her hair floating upwards, arcs of lightning tracing over her body. Books and toys began to rise up into the air and circle around Catherine's head as the front door shattered into a thousand shards and two Paladin broke through.

Catherine moved her hands up and the two knights fell to the floor in a twisted heap. Then a figure loomed into view, old and full of malice. His hands also sparked with raw energy as he floated towards Catherine.

Jack screamed as the air was sucked out of his mouth. The cupboard door slammed shut and they were instantly falling into the chill darkness. One image was burned into Jack's retina, an image that threatened to topple him from consciousness. He had seen the face of his mother's attacker, and, with a shocking realisation, he had known it instantly. They had met once before, on Jack's first exit from a Sorrowline.

Jack's grandfather, full of hate, electricity sparking from his hands, loomed into view. And Old David was laughing as he attacked his own daughter.

# 25

## INTO OBLIVION

He fell in silence; the only sound Jack heard was his own breathless panting. Then even that faded away, leaving only the rhythm of his blood raging through his veins. Everything was happening at arm's length, as if he was at the end of a dark tunnel, observing with a cool detached indifference.

Davey was desperately yelling something, but Jack could not hear his voice. With slow deliberate movements he let go of Jo-Jo's hand. Jack looked up, and Davey filled his vision. A rage grew inside him, a rage that seemed to press outwards from his skull, tightening his skin and suffocating any last rational thoughts. He was like an animal now, inconsolable and feral. His muscles tightened and he leaped forward, his hands at Davey's face. He screamed, fists flying, his knees pushing into his chest. He felt the bone crack inside Davey's nose as his fist pounded into it. An explosion of blood spread over his face, painting it red. His fingers found Davey's throat and he squeezed with a violent might.

Then something yanked him backwards: Eloise. She pinned him down onto the platform floor.

'I'll kill him!' Jack screamed. 'I'll kill him now, then none of this can happen.'

Eloise held him in place, an expression of confusion on her white face. 'What is wrong with you?'

Davey sat up clumsily, and Jack saw the bruised and bloodied face of his grandfather.

*I did that*, he thought.

'What the hell's the matter with you, Jack?' Davey asked, spitting blood from his swelling lip.

'You killed her. It was always you,' Jack answered with fury.

'I didn't do nothing.'

'You will! That was *you*, *old* you. You attacked my mum, your own daughter. How could you?'

Davey's mouth opened, about to yell something back, then the slow insipid realisation of Jack's statement hit home.

Eloise stared, shocked. 'He was Davey?'

'Jack, that can't have been me, can't have!' Davey stammered, 'I can't do what he was doing. He was an—'

'An Operator?' Jack shouted.

'Yes.' Davey's response was quiet and hollow. The wind rattled accusingly about them. 'But I can't do that,' he protested. 'I'm no Operator, I can't do nothing.'

'Not yet, but you will be. And it'll corrupt you and you'll

267

kill my mum,' Jack cried. He looked up at Eloise, her hands still pinning him down. 'Let me free, let me end this now!'

'And if you kill Davey now, how will your mother be born?' Eloise asked quietly. 'How will *you* be born?'

The thumping rhythm inside Jack's head slowed and subsided. His vision pulled everything towards him, and the tunnel came to an end. His terrible rage became a flood of tears, as he understood how pathetically helpless he was.

Then a new dangerous thought entered his mind: what if Davey was already an Operator, naturally gifted and worming his way into Jack's mind, planting soothing notions to calm his anger, pretending to be his friend? How could he judge if he could not even trust his own thoughts? He turned to Eloise, his face pleading for help. 'He's an Operator; he's messing with our minds!'

'Jack.' Her voice was even and level. 'If Davey was an Operator, I would know. True, I do sense some latent talent, but it is undiscovered, untrained and incapable of malice. Perhaps one day he may become an Operator, but it is but one of a thousand possible paths that he may choose to walk. Fate and destiny are less than rigid. The future is never certain.'

'It is!' Jack cried. 'I've been there. I've seen it. I've lived it.' He pulled his legs into his chest and huddled on the side of the platform, watching Davey with an intense doubt.

Davey shook his head. 'Jack, I can't apologise for

something I ain't done. I'm not that old man! You have to take me for what I am right now, here, with you. Come on, Jack, I'm on your side!'

Davey's large eyes were full of hurt. And yet his mother's warning rang in Jack's ears. He turned his face away, staring into the void.

Jo-Jo had watched and listened, like someone half awake. Finally he spoke. 'Where's my mum, Jack?'

'Don't worry.' Jack smiled rigidly. 'She'll be OK.'

'Where are we going?'

'I don't know.' Jack looked down at the child and questioned why he could not remember these events happening to him. Perhaps things were different for Jo-Jo, unfolding in new and unexpected ways. Perhaps things could be changed, after all. He pitied the child, knowing what was to come in his life. The desperate emptiness left behind by the loss of his mother would be there always, like a dark immovable stain.

The Boagyman – his name badge read *Bubak* – sniffed indignantly, eyeing his passengers with suspicion. His appearance was similar to Torbalan's, but Bubak's hair was a fiery red.

'You not be a bother?' Bubak spoke slowly, stumbling over the words. 'No more fighty fighty?'

Jack looked up at Davey, then back to Bubak and shook his head.

'Good-o.' Bubak smiled toothlessly. 'Journey is long.

Better journey with no fighty fighty.'

'Where are you taking us?' Eloise enquired.

'Safe place.' Bubak winked. 'Ealdwyc, far away: the lady's instructions.'

They travelled forward along a tangled web of pipes, Bubak stooped over his map, working to take them to safety. Suddenly they were hit from the side with such force that the platform shifted up, pushing Davey over the side. Jack saw Davey's fingers reaching for something to hold onto as his body fell over the edge. Without thinking, Jack lunged to grab Davey's hand, his quarrel forgotten. The pain was almost unbearable, his shoulder protesting the burden. He heaved desperately, determined to pull Davey back to safety. He shifted his weight and jerked his body upwards but Davey did not move. He twisted to get a better grip, and Davey slipped further down, threatening to pull Jack over as well.

'Let me go,' Davey pleaded.

Below them, wading out of the mist was the massive bulk of a ship. Harpoons impaled the bottom of the platform, their ropes pulling them closer and closer to the vessel.

The platform jerked again, throwing Davey back onto its gyrating surface. Jack fell backwards, breathless. His eyes darted over the platform. Where was Jo-Jo?

'I have the child.'

Jack turned to see Jo-Jo gripped tightly under Eloise's arm, his face gasping with terror.

'Weavers?' Bubak cried out doubtfully. 'Never this high up. Never!'

A pitiful bell rung out and the soul-sapping cry of the Weavers followed it. Jack felt his spirits sink. As the mist cleared, the deck of the vessel came into view.

'What do we do?' Jack shouted to Davey, but he had already fallen to his knees.

'Weavers!' Bubak shouted out. 'Begone! These folk are mine: Boagyman Bubak.'

Out of the fog came an echoing melodic voice, raw like glass on glass. 'We take your passengers.'

'This is Boagyman's province. Go back to Endless Sea! No Weavers! No weaving.'

There was a terrible pause, then, 'We seek no souls this hour. We hunt for another. He claims them. He wills it. We submit to him. You submit to Weavers.'

*Rouland*, Jack realised. They're talking about *Rouland*. Even here in this strange realm Rouland could reach out and find them.

'Not nice!' Bubak whimpered as the wailing took hold of him. 'Not nice at all.'

The high-pitched lament rattled Jack's skull until he could bear the pain no longer and darkness circled the edge of his vision. His head dropped heavily onto the platform and he slipped into unconsciousness.

\* \* \*

'Jack, wake up.'

He could hear the voice, but nothing worked. His eyes refused to open, and his head felt like it was filled with lead. Someone shook him roughly, and the voice spoke again.

'Jack, please.'

Who was it? He could hardly tell. The voice seemed distorted, deep and vibrating, as if he was hearing it from the inside of a hollow metal tank. He took a deep breath and tried to clear his head. His ears popped, and air rushed in painfully. With a mighty effort he finally opened his eyes. He was in a tiny room, Davey in front of him with Jo-Jo, who was looking around nervously, biting at a fingernail. Eloise was also there, solemn and contemplative. A faint green glow illuminated them all from below, emanating from Eloise's sword grasped tightly in her fist. Bubak was nowhere to be seen.

As Jack's eyes adjusted to the low light he could see the walls were made of chiselled stone. The low ceiling pushed down on them, forcing Eloise to stoop. In front of them was a locked door.

'Jack, are you all right?' The voice belonged to Davey.

'What happened?'

'I dunno. We all passed out. Thought we were as good as dead. Those Weavers are big trouble.'

'We are *still* in trouble,' Eloise said grimly. 'The Weavers have delivered us to this place for a reason. And our

272

journey here must have been long: night has fallen.'

Jack's stomach knotted into a ball. It would soon be the 6th, he realised. The day he had dreaded.

'I don't wanna be here,' Jo-Jo pleaded.

'It's going to be all right, Jo-Jo,' Jack soothed. 'We'll get you home soon.' He stood up and smiled at Jo-Jo, forcing his own doubts and fears to subside for the sake of the child.

'Well, let's find out where we are, shall we?' Davey smiled and invited Eloise to break the door.

She raised her sword as far as she could and jabbed forcefully at the door lock. It splintered under the assault and the door swung open, illuminating their miniature prison. Outside was a long hallway with several doors on either side. They stepped over the broken splinters of wood and cautiously surveyed the scene.

Jo-Jo gripped Jack's hand. 'Can we go home?'

'It's going to be all right,' Jack repeated, adding a grin. The child looked up at his future self and seemed reassured.

'I think he likes you,' said Davey with a half-hearted smile of his own.

Jack did not respond, cautious of Davey in a way he hadn't been before.

Eloise walked ahead, listening at each door in turn, gently trying the handles. She pointed to a door on the right. 'This way.'

The door led to a spiral staircase made of finely worked stone with a curved metal handrail. The air became cooler as they ascended and their guarded steps echoed loudly up the stairwell. They arrived at a landing with another door facing them. Eloise turned the handle and, with a low click, the door opened.

Jack could not quite comprehend what he was seeing. He stepped through the door, with Eloise and Davey in front of him, into a huge hall. They stood at one side of a vast space full of chairs arranged neatly into rows. The chequered tiles on the floor led his eyes into the middle of the chamber and up one of its many immense stone columns, past intricately crafted stained-glass windows – their colours diminished by the night sky outside – to an arched ceiling high above. The carved stone had a radiant quality that exuded shades of orange and brown light.

Jack walked along the length of the hall, towards a massive circular space that extended to the left and right. Beyond this there was an elaborate altar, which shone out in the soft light. Here the roof scaled new heights, ending in a beautifully ornate dome which took Jack's breath away. Slowly he remembered; he had been here before. It was on a school trip to study the greatest cathedral in London. He had taken little notice at the time, enjoying the excursion more than the history around him. Now he wished he had listened.

'This is St Paul's Cathedral,' he said at last.

'I know.' Davey's voice, full of trepidation, echoed around the vast chamber.

'Rouland is here,' said Eloise in a whisper. 'We must leave.'

She turned towards the entrance, and Jack and Davey followed, Jack pulling at the confused Jo-Jo. They ran the length of the nave, their footsteps a discordant chorus that bounced off the revered walls and headed for the large double doors that led to freedom. Abruptly Eloise stopped, her feet sliding over the tiles.

'What's wrong?' Jack halted behind her and peered over her shoulder.

Two women dressed in dark, ancient armour barred their way.

'The Paladin,' Davey groaned heavily. 'Not again.'

Jack wheeled round. More Paladin stood at the edges of the cathedral. Each drew their sword, the rasp of metal mechanical and cold. Eloise held out her sword, bracing herself for the inevitable deadly assault. Far away, Jack heard the sound of hard shoes on the tiles, slow deliberate footfalls that pounded out like the drum of a soldier. The footsteps grew louder and Jack looked back towards the altar. A lone figure walked out of the dim shadows, his steps confident and deliberately measured. The man was tall, elegant and carried himself with a self-assurance that drew Jack to him. He knew at once who it must be.

Rouland stepped into the orange light, beautiful and chilling, exotic and menacing, intoxicating and lethal. He was immaculate in his suit of dark armour he had worn on Jack's first encounter with him deep under London. He smiled a sinister smile, the orange light making his perfect skin look as if it reflected the dawn rays of Hell itself.

'Good evening, Jack, it's been a very long time.'

# 26

## FINAL JOURNEY

'You have led me on quite a journey, Jack Morrow.' Rouland smiled. 'For a while you have been that rarest of things to me: something new and unpredictable.'

As Rouland talked, his Paladin slowly advanced, tightening their trap. Eloise swung her sword in a wide circle, daring one of them to come too close.

Rouland raised his hand. 'Please, there is no need for violence here.' The Paladin halted, but Eloise remained on guard.

Rouland turned his attention back to Jack. 'That smell, Jack, that intoxicating smell. It is so much stronger now. You have found the Rose?'

'No.'

'We are past games and lies, Jack. I have come here, at no small cost to myself, I might add, and I *will* have the Rose.' Behind Rouland Jack saw an eerie shape moving, a thin figure standing almost ten metres tall. Its dark robes were adorned with crows' wings, overlaid in an intricate pattern. It wore chains of bone, and a large ticking clock face swung around its chest. A hood, out of which grey smoke belched, concealed the wearer's head. It seemed to have too many hands – at least four that Jack could see – all thin and skeletal but with heavy rings of gold and amber covering each digit. In one of its hands it carried a long ceremonial scythe. The ivory blade was encrusted with glittering jewels, and the pitted wooden staff was adorned with carvings from a primordial language that whispered secrets from a forgotten age.

The creature checked the time on its clock face and, with a flurry of its heavy robe, disappeared again into the shadows leaving a trail of grey smoke in its wake.

Jack shuddered and reached out for Jo-Jo. The younger boy was sobbing quietly, terrified.

'Where is the Rose?' Rouland shouted as a wild torment consumed him and his beautiful face contorted with anger.

'Leave him alone!' Davey stepped in front of Jack and Jo-Jo.

'Davey! Davey-boy. Have you finally chosen a side?' Rouland mocked. 'But that always was your problem, wasn't it? You never could stick to your principles, always jumping from one to the other, as the mood took you. You are like a wind, Davey, blown in so many directions. And your mind; such a malleable thing. Your older self, he could hardly resist my dominion over him. I think he was actually glad to serve me. No more being so alone, so secretly afraid of life. I took it all away from you, Davey. I gave you a purpose again, after all these years.'

'You're lying,' Davey hissed.

'Why lie? I have no reason to. The day will come when you will turn to me, willingly. It is a comfort, is it not? A reassurance, to know your own destiny.'

'Shut up!' Davey screamed.

Rouland's hypnotic gaze shifted back to Jack. 'Does he know?' he asked. 'Have you told him what he will become?'

'I've seen the future,' Jack spat.

Rouland smiled again, enjoying the sport of their conversation. 'So you know it cannot be changed. And still you tried. Tried and failed to change events that were to be. And so you will *always* fail. The future is not for you to choose. Others police that rich realm.' He looked briefly towards the cloaked creature, which had floated out of the shadows again as it listened to Rouland's speech.

'Your destiny is set, as is mine. Yours is to deliver the Rose to me, mine is to wield its power over this world, and all realms from here to the depths of Oblivion, to the frozen wastes of Niflheim, and on to the shores of my beautiful Otherworld where my throne shall rest.'

'Well, good luck with that,' Davey scoffed, puffing out his chest in defiance.

'You mock me? You *dare* to mock me?'

'You're an easy target.' Davey smiled recklessly.

Rouland looked over his shoulder at the dark hooded creature with smoke spilling from its cowl. 'You would be wise not to anger me, Davey. My life is long, and my memory its equal. The day will come when you will call on me, and I will remember your words tonight.'

'I doubt that,' Davey said, his voice sounding uncertain.

Then, as if for the very first time, Rouland's gaze fell upon Eloise. He studied her for a brief moment and a flicker of shock danced over his eyes.

'Eloise?' he said finally. 'I had hoped never to see you again, yet now that you stand before me I realise that I have missed you.'

Eloise took a step closer. 'I have missed you too, master. Every moment of my imprisonment I prayed that I might look upon your beauty again.'

The hairs on Jack's neck stood on end, suddenly uncertain what sort of influence Rouland might hold over Eloise. He fought to control the adrenaline-fuelled tremble in his hands, steadying them on Jo-Jo's shoulders. He couldn't believe what Eloise was saying – his allies seemed to be falling away, one by one. He looked to Davey by his side, resolute and defiant, ready to fight for him, and his heart lifted, in spite of his many doubts.

Rouland smiled at Eloise, like a father teaching a wayward daughter. 'You have learned the folly of your actions then, child?'

'My folly was great, master. I have had many long years to contemplate my actions and I see now that I was misguided.' Eloise's face was unreadable, her voice unwavering. 'I know now the error of my ways.'

Rouland filled with a superior pride and straightened his back to look down on Eloise.

'My folly was not to strike you down sooner.' She raised her sword in front of her, and the Paladin raised theirs in reply.

Jack finally began to breathe again, just as the dread fear of the inevitable battle rushed through him.

Rouland raised a steadying hand to his Paladin. Seemingly distracted, he peered up to the vast ceiling. 'It cannot be,' he said, circling like a tiger, sensing something approaching. He turned to face Jack, a threatening laugh falling from his lips. 'The Rose, Jack. It is *here.*'

Rouland looked up again, a childlike wonder filling his dark eyes. Without warning Davey sprinted towards Rouland. His body coiled and he leaped into the air, crossing the wide space between them with one impressive bound. Somehow he was on top of Rouland, tackling him to the ground. For a moment everything seemed to have frozen. Nothing moved, and then the Paladin were everywhere. Eloise fought three at once, her suppressed rage let loose upon them.

Jack, Jo-Jo still silent at his side, watched in stunned disbelief as Rouland recovered and lifted himself off the ground, his hand about Davey's throat. With a twist of his arm Davey was airborne, flying sideways through the nave. He hit one of the stone columns and landed in a crumpled heap.

The Paladin circled closer and closer, bombarding Eloise with their overwhelming numbers. She fought on, and two Paladin dropped to the ground. She raised herself up onto the pews and suddenly the swordfight was mobile, rushing through the cathedral. Eloise led the Paladin away from Jack, and a space opened up in their perimeter. Jack looked back to Davey: somehow he was still alive, his face twisted in pain and concentration, his eyes seeming to shout out one word to Jack.

*RUN!*

Jo-Jo responded first, running away from the battle. 'Let's go, Jack!'

Jack ran towards one of the doors on the side of the nave, Jo-Jo blindly leading the way as behind them he heard the noise of sword hitting sword. He dared not stop. He reached the door; it was unlocked, and he and Jo-Jo slipped inside. Ahead was another spiral staircase.

'Up there,' he said to Jo-Jo, then Jack followed his younger self up the steps and was at the first floor before the Paladin burst through below him. He didn't stop to look, running faster and faster, higher and higher.

'I'm scared,' Jo-Jo shouted as he reached the top of the stairwell.

'Me too,' said Jack. He held out his hand to the younger boy. 'But we'll be OK, I promise.'

Jo-Jo took his hand.

The dark shapes of the Paladin circled up towards them, like a flock of birds closing in for the kill. In front of them was a door and Jack prayed it would be open – he didn't care where it led to. He pushed it, but it didn't move. Despair grew as the Paladin flocked closer and closer and he grabbed the handle again, tugging with all his might. It creaked open stiffly, just enough for them to get through. He turned and pulled the door shut behind them, running again along a new corridor, no thought to where he was going, other than getting Jo-Jo to safety. Almost immediately he heard the Paladin fumbling with the door, dragging it open and advancing. Ahead the corridor turned to the left. Jack turned with it and stopped at a door set back slightly. He opened it and entered, pushing the door tightly shut behind himself and Jo-Jo.

They were in a tiny room full of old boxes and books. Jack let go of Jo-Jo's hand and began to stack anything he could find in front of the door. He stepped back, inspecting his hurried work.

'What do we do now?' Jo-Jo asked.

'I don't know.'

Hearing voices approaching from the corridor, Jack spun round, his desperation growing with every second. In the corner, hidden behind three large wooden crates, was a rusty metal ladder, attached to the wall and rising vertically up through a small opening in the ceiling.

'Quick!' he shouted to Jo-Jo, pushing him up the ladder. Jack followed him up to a small metal platform, and as he stepped onto it he saw a tiny bolted hatch in front of them. He quickly undid the bolts and pulled open the hatch. The muggy night air hit his face, fast and howling, and he scrambled through the opening, but Jo-Jo remained behind.

'We can't stay in there,' Jack said, trying to keep the urgent terror out of his voice. 'This way. C'mon.'

Trustingly, Jo-Jo pulled himself through the hatch, outside, onto the roof of the cathedral. The dark sky brooded with a maelstrom of clouds, eager to shed their water. The wind clipped at their legs, pulling their clothes into sharp edges. Ahead of them Jack saw the peaked roof of the nave. A narrow gantry ran along its side. He closed the hatch as best as he could and stepped out onto it.

'Take my hand,' he said to Jo-Jo.

The child shook his head, his eyes wide with fright. 'Don't want to. I'm scared.'

'It's OK,' Jack said. 'I'll hold onto you.' He held out his hand, waiting for his younger self to make up his mind and Jo-Jo hesitated, but then grabbed hold.

The sky lit up with an almighty flash of white light, closely followed by a deafening peal of thunder. Jack gripped the railing, cowering automatically. Jo-Jo recoiled, crying out loudly. His little fingers tore at Jack's trousers.

Jack's eyes adjusted to the night again. He looked ahead and saw he was not alone on the gantry. His heart sank. David was there. Old David. Electricity boiled from his hand.

'What now, Jack? You're out of places to run,' David said.

'What happened to you?' Jack shouted over the growing storm clouds.

'Rouland!' David screamed. 'Rouland showed me the way, Jack.' The ball of electricity in David's hand grew larger and larger.

'But you're supposed to be my grandfather!' Jack shouted back. 'You killed your own daughter!'

'Not quite,' a voice cried out.

Jo-Jo gasped, 'Mum!'

Jack looked up in awe: there was his mother, still alive but badly injured. She floated in the air above St Paul's, electricity arcing from the clouds into her body. Her eyes were on fire and she glowed all over. For a moment Jack thought she was an angel.

'What's wrong with my mum?' Jo-Jo asked doubtfully. 'She doesn't look right.'

'You!' David screamed at Catherine. 'Why won't you just die?'

'Keep back, Jack, Jo-Jo!' his mother warned, her voice

like a tamed thunderclap. 'His mind's not his own. Rouland has him under his control.'

Suddenly David let loose with ball after ball of violent energy, his spite and resentment overflowing. 'No one controls me!'

Catherine fell in-between Jack and Jo-Jo, and David, her body absorbing the arcs of electricity. The lightning coursed through her and pooled in her palms. She held out her hands, trembling with hesitation. 'I tried to save you, Dad, I really did.'

'I don't need your pity,' David cried as he unfurled another volley of energy at his daughter. Catherine retaliated, letting the collected energy pour out of her towards him. The rooftop became flooded with a yellow light until all detail was gone. As the intense glow faded, and the smoke blew away, Jack saw David. His body was smouldering from the blast of electricity as he floated off the gantry, but using the arcing lightning to pull himself back up, he propelled himself towards Catherine.

'Mum!' Jo-Jo cried out again, tears marking his troubled face. Jack wrapped his arms around him, shielding him from the light.

The roof was lit up with flash after flash as Catherine and David disappeared inside a blaze of white lightning bolts. Sparks rained down, onto Jack and Jo-Jo.

Jack realised he was crying too, he and Jo-Jo frozen like two portraits. His mother was fighting for him, and she was hurt. He wanted to help her, to protect her, but all he could do was watch.

Then her voice spoke to him, inside his mind: *Get back, Jack.*

Jack covered Jo-Jo as best he could, and ran back towards the little hatch. At that very moment the hatch blew off, tumbling down to the ground far below. The silhouette of a Paladin emerged from the smoking hole, followed swiftly by another, and another. Jack froze.

The first Paladin scrambled upright and raced towards him and Jo-Jo. As she approached she opened her helmet and Jack saw that it was Captain de Vienne leading her sisters. A mechanical apparatus sat where her severed hand had once been. In it was slotted a new sword which rotated noisily. She screamed defiantly as she aimed the spinning blade at Jack.

A giant burst of electricity hit the rooftop in front of Captain de Vienne and her Paladin sisters, knocking them aside with brutal force. Two of the Paladin fell off the gantry, over the low sidewall, and hit the ground far below with a loud clatter. Captain de Vienne staggered backwards, clinging onto the rooftop with her one remaining hand. Her sword spun loudly, gouging long troughs into the masonry. She looked up at her attacker: Catherine, hanging in the air from ropes of electricity. Another volley of energy swelled out of Catherine's hand and engulfed Captain de Vienne's body in flames. The Paladin fell, screaming.

Jack looked up: David swayed in the air, dark and malevolent. One arm hung uselessly from his side. He raised his other hand and a ball of energy flew with merciless speed towards Jack and Jo-Jo. There was no time to move – it hit them both, throwing them backwards into the air. Jack felt as if time stood still, that single instant allowing itself to unravel. The sick sensation of vertigo spilled over him. And then he was falling, his grip loosened, and Jo-Jo was gone. Catherine's maternal scream faded away as he fell, leaving only the deafening sound of air rushing past his ears. He glimpsed the outer walls of the cathedral passing by. Then, abruptly, everything was still.

He couldn't turn his head. He felt soil on his cheek, in his nostrils, mixing with blood and snot. He lay there unable to hear, his face scorched, his hair smouldering. A hand appeared above his face and he looked up through the blood and smoke to see Eloise and Davey – young Davey, *his* Davey – above him. Jack raised his twisted hands up and saw that they were empty. He tried to cry out but his throat no longer worked. Somewhere nearby he knew that his younger self also lay bleeding.

He was going to die twice tonight, he thought.

In the sky above he saw Catherine turn and, with a wild rage, the rage of a mother protecting her child, she turned to face her father. Old David had landed on the roof and limped along its sloped surface. Catherine screamed, and an incredible energy poured out of her fingertips. It smashed into David, knocking him back onto the gantry. She rode the needles of electricity and dropped from the sky, down to the two broken bodies of her son that lay bleeding on the ground.

Jack saw her tear-filled face, but he could not hear her words. The world seemed to be closing in on him from all sides. The edges of his mind were going black, odd thoughts jumping out in random order. He laughed; he did not know why, though he didn't feel pain any more – he felt nothing at all, only the cold approach of blackness. It was at his toes now, clawing up his legs with an efficient indifference. All about him faces came and went; Davey was shouting, Eloise raised her sword, attacking a Paladin. His mother was out of sight. He so wanted to turn his head and see her. He could feel he was leaving, taking the first step along his own Sorrowline, laying its path so that others might follow it, and he wanted to say goodbye to her before it was too late. But nothing worked any more, his body was a useless broken rag, spent and crushed. His eyes became heavy. Why could he not reach out and tell them how much he loved them?

Davey, with his naive optimism, he forgave him his cowardice. He loved him but would never tell him now.

And Eloise, his brave protector who had given without question; she sought absolution for the crimes of her past, absolution that Jack would never now be able to give her.

Finally he thought of his mother, a woman he barely knew, a woman with infinite secrets. He forgave her for not being there for those long lonely years, he forgave her for dying. He let go of his anger, and his love for her overflowed within him.

He loved them all, and could never tell them.

He felt the call of the future, an endless tunnel. He could not resist any more, he did not wish to. A tranquil warmth washed over him and he let his eyes close.

Jack stopped fighting.

# 27

## THE GIFT

Jack was falling. Falling through the darkness.

*Jack.*

Was that a voice?

*Hold on, Jack, hold on.*

He could hear the words, but they were distant, like his own abstract thoughts echoing back off the wall of sorrow that surrounded him. He was a child again, with a clarity that took his breath away. He was seven years old, and everything hurt.

*Keep fighting.*

He was seven, his fingers hurt, and they made a funny clicking noise when he tried to move them. He wanted his mum.

Jack looked into the memory, like it was a tangible thing. He saw his mother kneeling next to him on the ground, her beautiful face over his, so close that her hair stroked his cheek and her breath warmed his eyes. He searched through his nerves, feeling for his toes. He was smaller, just a child. He laughed, then a creeping pain filled his lungs and his vision blurred into a red mess.

*It's all right, Jo-Jo. I'll save you.*

Who was talking? He couldn't tell. The images came in pieces, disjointed and with fragments of time missing in between them.

He saw his mother place her hands on his chest, she pushed down and his broken ribs cried out for mercy. Why are you hurting me?

*Don't worry, it'll soon be over.*

The pressure in his chest grew, and he tried to scream, his vision decaying. Then a subtle warmth flooded his lungs, like a hot bath on a winter's night. The pain was still there, but it was bearable now. His mother's face came back into focus and he realised it was her voice he had heard.

*The power of the Rose is healing you.*

The warmth was spreading through his chest. He felt one of his ribs crack, and a shard of white-hot pain overwhelmed him. The wave of pain subsided and he could feel his rib was better. Another wave of pain hit him, followed by another, as each broken bone righted itself.

His lungs emptied of blood, and the night air flooded in. The warmth spread to his crumpled legs, he heard cracking and popping and knew that a new wave of pain was on its way. He closed his eyes.

*Never forget, I love you, Jo-Jo.*

He opened his eyes again, his head spun. His consciousness shifted. He was no longer seven; he was twelve again, with broken limbs crying out to him. He had never felt anything like this; it was so terrible he wished for death.

*No, Jack. Don't wish for that. You have much to do. You must fight on.*

I don't want to fight, he thought, I'm tired. I hurt. Let me go.

*No.*

His mother appeared in front of him again, weary, an exhausted, haunted look in her eyes.

*I have nothing left to give you, except one thing. I'm giving it to you, Jack. You are the Rose now. Use it well, and it will sustain you. Abuse it, and you'll be consumed by it.*

The warmth hit his shoulders, followed by a terrible red shock wave. His neck cracked, so loud that his ears screamed and his vision broke into a thousand colours, each one a needle of fire. His face went ice cold, then red hot. He felt the sweat trickle down his hairline. The warmth did not stop, coursing over his skull, and then plunging within.

*Fight for me, Jack. Fight for me. I love you.*

The pressure grew inside his head, pushing down on every side of his brain until it felt like the size of a pea. He opened his eyes and saw his mother engulfed in ethereal ribbons of energy, pulsing and changing. The pain disappeared as he watched this beautiful display. He smelt the fresh scent of flowers, pure like nothing on Earth. The ribbons danced to their own rhythm, forming shapes around his mother. One shape stood out, repeated on every scale down to the microscopic, like a fractal reflection of the universe.

The shape was a rose.

Jack watched in wonder, knowing he would never see anything as beautiful again. But it was more than a vision; it was a sensory invasion. Music filled his ears, the music of Otherworld. This was the living energy of the Rose of Annwn, set free from its host.

The tendrils of colour changed direction and charged at him. They filled his vision, changing him in ways that would take him a lifetime to understand. He closed his eyes.

Jack was falling. Falling through the darkness.

And then he stopped.

He began to rise, slowly at first, and then faster and faster, until the darkness was rushing past him at such a speed that it turned a blinding white.

Abruptly the whiteness faded away leaving him uncomfortably alone. He could hear voices around him again, could feel the ground under his body. He smelt sulphur in the air, tasted rust on his tongue. Finally he opened his eyes and he saw the giant façade of St Paul's Cathedral rising up into the electric sky.

Tentatively he reached out to find his fingers and toes.

All seemed normal. He looked up to the rooftop. Why was he not already dead? Then a kaleidoscopic flood of images returned to him, of his mother and her gift of the Rose. He sat up quickly and looked about him.

He saw Davey and Eloise, tending to Jo-Jo. He knew his younger self was unharmed now, also repaired by the power of the Rose.

A wave of nausea overtook him. His mother, the living host, had given up the Rose so that it could save him.

*He* was the Rose now.

Jack stood cautiously, expecting his legs to collapse at any moment. He took a trembling step forward, then another and another. Davey looked up and ran to his side, putting his arm round him for support.

'Am I alive?' Jack asked.

'Yes, you are. But . . .' Davey's voice tailed off.

Then Jack saw a body lying on the ground a few metres away.

'Mum?'

He scrambled to her side, turning her over so he could see her face. She was still beautiful, like an angel, but all life had left her body. Jack held her close to his chest and cried out. He had never been able to say goodbye before, never really been able to grieve properly for the mother he did not know. He was too young to understand the first time round. Now he knew what he was losing. She had given her life to save her son.

*Fight for me*; that was what she had asked of him in return. His breathing slowed and he wiped his eyes. A new fire burned in his chest. He laid his mother down on the ground and closed her eyes, kissing her softly on her cheek.

He stood up straight and true, feeling taller and older than he had ever felt. He was more than a boy now, the Rose of Annwn burned inside him, and through it so did the hopes of Otherworld.

Jo-Jo stirred and knelt next to Jack, his small hands touching his dead mother. He couldn't leave her like this, abandoned in the dirt. At that moment he sensed something next to him. He turned to see an imposing hooded figure standing beside him resolutely, its four sinuous arms hidden within its dark cape. It glided respectfully over his mother's body and, with a gentle turn of its cape, she disappeared into it. This giant figure of blackness exuded reverence and respect, its hooded face bowed in dignified prayer.

The dark creature stood for a moment, and then looked skywards. Jack followed its gaze. As he watched the tumultuous sky he felt a warm drop of water splash onto his face, like a tear from heaven. He looked back down to the ground; the creature and his mother had gone. There, in the earth, something glinted. Jack knelt down and saw his mother's wedding ring, half buried in the dirt. It was a simple band of gold with a diamond at its centre. He rubbed it on his sleeve, cleaning the blood and grime from its surface, and dropped it into his trouser pocket. Then he saw something else, a familiar rectangle, soiled and burnt. He picked it up and dusted it down until the letters on the cover were visible again.

*On the Nature of the Concealed Realms* by Magus Hafgan. It must have fallen from his pocket when he fell off the cathedral, Jack supposed. He opened the pages, and his eyes fell on the mysterious grid of letters again.

The clouds above opened and a torrent of summer rain began to fall, wiping away the ash and blood of the night's battle. Droplets of water bounced off the tattered pages of the book, soaking into the discoloured paper. He was about to shelter it in his pocket when he saw something revealed in the water. A handwritten line at the very bottom of the page emerged from the dark circles of moisture. Slowly, letter by letter, a string of words emerged from the page.

*The sword is mightier than the heart. Nelson.*

Jack stared in disbelief, puzzled by this new revelation. Then the letters began to blur, dissolving into the moisture until they were gone. Jack put the book back into his pocket.

For a time Jack stood in the downpour as he thought about the cryptic text, his arms outstretched, the water washing away his grief and pain.

He felt reborn.

Not far away was the sword from a fallen Paladin. He reached to pick it up; the weight felt good.

'Jack.' Davey stood by his side. 'Rouland is still inside. He has more Paladin, and there are Dustmen coming. We have to get away now, while we can.'

Nearby a circle of dirt was beginning to move upwards into the wet air. Further away, in the shadow of the cathedral, he heard the curdling scream of another new-born Dustman.

Then, as if out of nowhere, he saw the silhouette of a man approaching from the shadows. The tatty, haggard, burnt figure of Old David approached, leaving a trail of pungent smoke behind him. He stared at his younger self, and at Eloise, remorse and regret written large over his charred features. His grim eyes found Jack's and he suddenly broke down. 'What have I done? What have I done?' He fell to his knees, a pitiful figure. 'Jack, I'm sorry. Kill me now before Rouland has me again.'

Anger boiled over inside Jack. He would delight in killing this man, for what he had done to his mother. Then he remembered Rouland, and he knew that David was as much a victim as the rest of them. He tamed his feral anger, pushing it deep down, and took a calming breath.

'Get up,' Jack said to David. 'I'm going to find Rouland. You still have a job to do.'

David looked up, confusion colouring his face.

'The Dustmen.' Jack pointed to the approaching spectre. 'You'll clear the path to the cathedral. And then you need to help me, when I first arrive in a few hours' time.'

'No,' David pleaded again. 'You have to kill me. The things I've done...'

'Stand up!' Jack demanded, his voice older, more authoritative than it had ever been before. 'You have to fight, David. And you have to help me. I'll be alone, and confused, and scared. I won't know what to do. You have to send me back to 1940, back to Davey. You understand?'

The old man nodded, wiping tears into his dirty cheeks. He stood clumsily, his bones clicking and creaking. He pulled his ragged coat to one side and took out a weapon of metal and ivory that Jack had seen before. Without a word he released the weapon on the closest of the advancing Dustmen and blew its body apart. The other Dustmen seemed to register the threat and converged on the noise. With a nod to Jack, David limped away into the darkness, firing his chronohorn as the Dustmen gave chase.

Suddenly the path to St Paul's was clear. There, on the grand steps, stood the strange elongated figure in a cloak of crows' wings. It beckoned Jack towards him.

Jack took Jo-Jo's hand and, with Davey and Eloise, returned to the ominous cathedral.

# 28

## MIND WAR

The cathedral was eerily still. Torrential rain ran down the stained-glass windows, casting rippling pools of light into the dim interior. The vast space soaked up the noise of the storm, numbing it into a faint memory.

'Why are we here?' Davey asked, afraid and confused. 'We could run.'

'And we'll always be running,' Jack replied. 'Rouland's responsible for my mum.' He felt older now, stronger, more in control than he had ever before.

'It is time.' Eloise nodded.

As they reached the bottom of the staircase Jack saw the strange cloaked figure again. Davey saw it too.

'A Grimnire,' Eloise informed them.

The Grimnire beckoned again. It glided serenely down a staircase that led to the crypt.

Jack frowned. 'The Grimnire brought Rouland here. So why is it helping us?'

'Grimnire are servants of none,' Eloise explained. 'It has brought Rouland here for its own purposes. There are greater schemes at play than Rouland's.'

Jo-Jo squeezed Jack's hand tightly. 'Where are we going, Jack?'

'It's OK.' Jack grimaced, hardly hiding his own doubts. 'We're following that thing.'

As they travelled down the stairs the light grew dimmer, casting feeble shadows onto the old walls. The Grimnire cast no such shadow, and its robe did not touch the ground.

They turned a corner into the large crypt, and suddenly the Grimnire was gone. Ahead, in the centre of the room, stood another figure, timeless and immaculate, his eyes closed in meditation. As they entered, Rouland's dark eyes snapped open, and his icy gaze impaled them.

'Please, Jack, let me convey my condolences,' he sighed. 'I know the pain of your loss.' Rouland's eyebrows arched in a sympathetic expression.

Jack felt the weight of the sword in his hand. His fingers tightened their grip.

'You killed her,' he said coolly.

Rouland shook his head. 'No. I came here personally to protect you and your mother from the Rose. It is a mighty power, Jack. It is not for the untrained. You will give it to me now.'

Eloise raced forward, her sword drawn. There was a blur of green light and a thunderous clap. When Jack opened his eyes again Eloise was spread out on the ceiling of the crypt, her limbs pinned in place by some invisible force. Pale blood trickled from the corners of her eyes and dropped onto the floor.

Rouland stood with one arm outstretched towards Eloise, keeping her contained. He looked down and observed her sword sticking out of his chest, feeding off his energy. He staggered back a step as he yanked at the sword with his free hand, pulling it out of his sternum, which cracked painfully. He exhaled, and then stood upright again, his composure returned.

He looked at the sword, turning it over in his hand before letting go of the handle. The sword floated in front of him, dancing softly in the air. Then, with a flick of his wrist, it flew upwards and impaled Eloise through her chest, forcing itself into the stone ceiling. As the sword fed she writhed against its power, desperately trying to pull her hands free.

'Very good, Eloise, I taught you something after all.' Rouland coughed. 'Another inch to the left and you might have hit my heart – you might have even succeeded. But, as ever, you failed. Miserably.'

Davey, as if shaken from a dream, screamed at Rouland, lunging wildly towards him. Before he could get close enough Rouland concentrated, his dark eyes like two black lines, and Davey found himself pinned to the wall. Rouland smiled as he studied Davey's struggling form, held in place by the secret powers of his terrible mind.

Jack shook his head. 'Let them go, Rouland. I have the Rose now.'

Rouland's eyes widened. 'Yes, I can see that. You are setting my senses on fire.' He closed his eyes. 'You do not have your mother's ability to hide it from me. You are shining like a beacon through time and space, calling all who seek it to you. You need protecting from the things that will come for you, things you cannot yet imagine.'

Jack curled his nose up in disgust. 'You're offering *me* protection?'

'I am the only one who can, Jack. There are many who would have the Rose. Things of darkness and malice. They can finally see the Rose, the gift that your mother has protected so well for all of these years. You cannot keep it safe. Only I can.'

His words flowed over Jack's anger like warm honey. He felt intoxicated by his persuasion. Jo-Jo cowered behind Jack's body, terrified. *It's going to be OK*, Jack soothed, and the boy's fingers relaxed.

Behind Rouland appeared the Grimnire again, stooping over a large sarcophagus, with one long arm outstretched, pointing to Rouland. As Jack watched, the Grimnire's body faded away but its arm remained for a moment as the pointed finger swung from Rouland to the sarcophagus, then that too disappeared.

The wound in Rouland's chest was deep and bloodless, beads of sweat pooled on his smooth forehead, and Jack perceived a subtle tremble in his breathing. His soothing mask of platitudes fell away, revealing only anger.

'Give me the Rose! Or your friends die, now!' A ball of white electric energy began to grow in the palm of Rouland's hand, lightning sparking up his arm. A low clatter of armour echoed through the crypt. The Paladin appeared all around them, their swords already drawn.

Jack turned back to look at Jo-Jo. *Don't worry. It's going to be OK.*

Eloise was blinking blood from her eyes. Davey was gasping, his eyes rolled back as the air was pushed slowly out of his lungs. And Rouland was smugly observing his enemies. He was patient, unflinching.

It would end here, Jack thought, in the crypt of St Paul's Cathedral. He knew he would rather die than give up the gift of the Rose, and a rapturous joy overcame him, a strange relief that he could not comprehend. He was out of options, nowhere to run, moments from death, yet he was no longer afraid to die. He had glimpsed what lay beyond and fear was not necessary.

Then he remembered the Grimnire, its pointed finger outstretched towards the sarcophagus behind Rouland, and in a flash of realisation he understood the message he'd read in the book.

*The sword is mightier than the heart. Nelson.*

Jack let go of Jo-Jo's hand. He smiled at Davey and

Eloise, and Eloise nodded resolutely as the life-force was sucked out of her.

Jack's eyes narrowed. 'I'm beginning to understand you, Rouland. The Rose is helping me. My mum was an Operator, and she thought I might have some of her gifts too. The Rose has shown me how to use those gifts.' For a moment he closed his eyes, focusing inwards. There, inside his mind he sensed the dark tendrils of another – Rouland – searching, prying, invading his thoughts and memories. Cold, uncomfortable fingers of hate burrowing into his soul. Jack opened his eyes again and smiled. 'I can feel you inside my mind.'

Rouland froze.

'Get out!' Jack shouted. He pushed at the invader inside his head and repelled it, forcing it away with the power of the Rose. Rouland reeled, pain flashing momentarily over his face.

Jack stepped forward. 'I can feel you trying to get back in, and I won't let you.'

The Rose circled through his thoughts. It was like a river of potential, offering up so much to him. The image of his mother, alive with electricity, popped into his head. As if in response to an unanswered question he felt his palm tingle. He looked down: electricity collected into Jack's empty hand until he was a mirror of Rouland. It was as if he'd known how to do this all his life. He wondered uneasily how much was instinct and how much was the

Rose, seeping into his every thought. He put the thought aside and let loose the unstable energy, its kinetic rage pounding into Rouland's body.

Rouland stumbled, steadying himself on the large sarcophagus that filled the centre of the room. There was a cough from Davey as his limbs were released. He fell to the floor in a ball of pain. Eloise, her hands finally freed, clawed at the sword feeding from her chest. With a gargantuan effort she pulled it out and she fell to the floor next to Davey.

Shock took hold of Rouland's face, then anger followed. He retaliated with all his might, throwing balls of energy at Jack. The force knocked him off his feet, but as the smoke cleared Jack stepped out to face Rouland again.

'You have no idea what I'm thinking any more, do you?' He took another step forward.

Rouland steadied himself. 'I do not need to read your limited mind to guess your next move, boy.'

'Really?' Jack whispered. 'Guess again.'

His grip on the sword tightened as he leaped forward with all the power he could find. He tackled Rouland around his neck, pushing him back towards the sarcophagus. As they fell Jack closed his eyes, feeling for something he hoped would be there. He smiled to himself; he had found what he was looking for. It was still there, after all this time, and it was letting him in.

Jack opened the Sorrowline and he fell into it, dragging Rouland with him.

# 29

## THE NELSON LINE

Euphoria overwhelmed Jack. Antiquated memories flooded over him in vivid waves of colour and noise. He saw great battles, felt panic paralyse him, smelled cannon fire and heard the confusion of warfare.

The tides of history flowed along this Sorrowline, revitalising the memories held here. Intertwined with the greater currents of history Jack felt the finer tributaries of personal loss; the grief of a wife, the secret sorrow of a mistress, the confusion of a daughter left behind. It was all here, ebbing and flowing.

Voices screamed out in his ears, terrified and anxious, calling out for their lost leader. A great procession of men held him aloft in their minds, chanting his name over and over again.

*Nelson.*

Vice Admiral Horatio Nelson, the hero of the Royal Navy who had fallen at the Battle of Trafalgar. Nelson was buried directly under the dome of St Paul's, in a great black sarcophagus. The same sarcophagus that Rouland had leaned against. The same sarcophagus that the Grimnire had pointed to. The same sarcophagus that had set Jack free.

He was travelling along Nelson's Sorrowline, back to October 1805, his arms wrapped around Rouland's neck.

They fell together for an age, and all the time Rouland screamed. He struggled against Jack's grip, wriggling to be free. His fear was palpable.

They fell through a new wave of emotion, more outpourings of strangers' grief. The blur of new images were full of patriotic fervour, the waves of emotion almost overpowering. Mixed in with these laments Jack sensed the edges of Rouland's mind, as he had with Davey, of his unnatural long life of memories. So much hate, so much pain. He saw a fleeting glimpse of his rise to power, his terrible experiments, and his quest for Otherworld, and he yearned to escape from this twisted mind. He retreated from it, sinking deeper into time, until he saw Rouland's earliest memory: he was washed ashore, half-dead, onto some forsaken coastline. And before that? Nothing. A wall of impenetrable blackness hid Rouland's earlier life from both of them. The blackness stung his mind and Jack recoiled, losing his grip on Rouland.

Then everything became white, and Jack knew he was nearing the end. The whiteness faded into absolute black, and his world fell silent.

Jack was on his back, sprawled awkwardly on the floor. The room was dark, cold and damp. A silent inhospitable place. He could not see Rouland. He listened for his breathing, but heard nothing. Jack fumbled towards the wall, feeling his way in the darkness. He heard a click, a door opened a crack and a feeble light illuminated the crypt. Jack stood upright against the wall as a lone man entered carrying a lantern that swung from his thin hand.

An uncertain voice cried out, 'Who's in here?'

The voice was not Rouland's.

'Hey!' the man cried out again, and Jack noticed something oddly familiar about his manner. His long face, bathed in the tepid light of the lantern, was less wrinkled than he remembered, his wiry beard more copper than white, but his features were unmistakable.

'Sexton?' Jack said as he stepped out of the shadows.

The old man jumped, waving his lantern to view Jack. 'Don't know you. How'd you know me? What you doing down here?' he asked gruffly.

Jack smiled, sure now that it was Sexton Clay, the gravedigger. He had seen this man die, at the hand of Rouland, in 1813. Now here he was, eight years younger, alive and well. The paradoxes of travelling back in time amazed and bemused Jack in equal measure.

'Sexton, my name is Jack Morrow. I'm a Yard Boy from upstream. We've met before . . . in the future. I came to 1813 with my friend, Davey. You helped me then, and I'm asking you to help again now.'

'Yard Boy?' Sexton looked uninterested. 'Whose line?'

'What?' Jack spluttered in confusion.

'Whose Sorrowline you on?'

'Vice Admiral Nelson's. He's died in battle. They're going to lay him to rest right there.' Jack pointed to where he knew the great black sarcophagus would one day be.

Sexton scratched his beard. 'Nelson? Dead?' He raised his thick eyebrows. 'Bloody typical.' He turned to leave, shuffling out of the crypt.

'Wait,' Jack said quietly. 'Another man came here with me. He wants to kill me, and my friends. I have to stop him.'

Sexton sighed heavily as he stopped to listen to Jack.

'I think he might be here somewhere. He's dressed in black armour. He's called Rouland.'

'Rouland?' Sexton gasped.

'Yes, have you seen him?'

'Not here.' Sexton turned away again, plodding slowly towards the stairs that led out of the crypt. 'I would know.'

A gust of wind blew past Jack, and he wheeled around to see Rouland, prone and vulnerable in the centre of the room.

Sexton gasped, 'Kill him now! Kill him while you can.'

This was Jack's chance. He still had the Paladin sword in his hand. It hummed softly, drawing his anger down through his fingers. As it did so its glowing radiance increased, responding to his emotions.

And yet he hesitated.

Rouland awoke, rising gracefully to his feet. At first he

seemed confused, studying his surroundings and process-ing the information. His fingers touched the open wound in his chest. He eyed Jack and smiled a long slow devil's smile.

'Did you drag me through a Sorrowline?' he asked incredulously.

Jack did not answer. His knuckles ached from his tight grip on the sword. His arm throbbed, as if the sword was crying out to be used. He held back as the tension inside him grew.

'The gall! How dare you touch me?' Rouland's contempt subsided, replaced by a reluctant admiration. 'I had heard stories of such a feat, but never for one second did I give them any credit.' He paced the crypt like a hungry tiger. 'And yet, here we are. Quite remarkable. The stuff of legends.' He put his hand onto one of the cold stone columns that supported the massive cathedral above, feeling its surface. 'I recall such a legend, an event, an anomaly from my own past. Two boys, who stole a book and disappeared *together* into the Sorrowlines. Together.'

Now it was Jack's turn to smile.

'That was you?' Rouland asked. He shook his head, a mixture of anger and frustration on his face. 'You had the book all this time? I must be getting old.'

Jack's hand touched his pocket; the book was still there.

Rouland's head shifted to Sexton, his gaze fixed and unavoidable. He studied him with an eagle-like scrutiny.

'I know you,' he said at last. 'Didn't I kill you once?'

Sexton said nothing.

Rouland looked again to Jack. 'What did you hope to achieve by dragging me back here? Did you think you might defeat me? Did you think you would stop me?'

'I have the Rose,' Jack said.

Rouland's eyes narrowed. 'Yes, you do. But now I know where it has been hiding all this time. You have brought me to the past, and shown me where to find the Rose. And now I know how to retrieve my precious book, I will be able to return to Otherworld triumphant. I will offer up this world so that I might rule the Other. You have given me a second chance, Jack, for which I am eternally grateful. Moreover, you may prevail long enough to see this world burn as sacrifice to my dominion. What a lucky child you will be to see such a thing.' Two balls of crackling energy began to grow in Rouland's palms.

Jack's hand trembled; the sword was calling out to him, its energy resonating up through his bones. He could barely hold it still.

'All these things will be thanks to you, Jack Morrow, Destroyer of Worlds.' Rouland's grin widened, his perfect teeth like a wolf's. 'Your mother would be proud.'

From deep inside Jack the Rose called out, showing him what to do. Time seemed to stop as Jack's mind broke through Rouland's defences, pulling each barrier down, one at a time. He could sense the signals travelling between the man's brain and his muscles. He could anticipate every move he might make.

Jack did not feel the movement. All at once he was flying through the air, the glowing sword dragging him forward. His face was upon Rouland's, their eyes only inches apart, Jack's scream mixing with Rouland's gasp.

Jack looked down and saw the sword embedded in Rouland chest up to the hilt, its glowing surface shimmering. The sword fed.

An expression flashed over Rouland's beautiful face, a look of disbelief.

Jack let go of the sword and Rouland staggered backwards, the blade dividing his dark heart in two.

*The sword is mightier than the heart.*

Incredulous, outraged, Rouland watched the sword, unable to halt its great feast, and he collapsed heavily onto the floor. There was a sudden tempest of sound and light, as if the accumulated sorrow and pain of Rouland's long life had been set free. Jack felt it all, and with it he felt the Rose sink deeper into him, subsiding into the dark unconscious parts of him.

The room fell into a heavy darkness as the air about them calmed.

'About bloody time.' Sexton's deep tones broke the terrible silence. Cautiously he stepped closer and kicked the motionless body. 'Need to hide this,' he said gruffly. 'Can you dig?'

# 30

## GRAND JUNCTION

Jack couldn't take his eyes off the body.

Sexton had left him alone in the dark space while he fetched a large canvas cloth to cover the grisly figure. Somehow, being left alone with Rouland's body was terrifying and Jack pulled his legs up into his chest, his back pushed up against the wall as the body made tiny involuntary noises that ignited every irrational fear hidden in the depths of his imagination. The minutes ticked by slowly.

Then the door opened and Sexton entered the room. Jack began to breathe again. Sexton threw the canvas over Rouland, covering the gaping chest wound, and the sword embedded in it. He gave two spades to Jack, and then grunted as he picked up Rouland's body.

He waddled through the passageways of the crypt to a hidden doorway that must be overlooked by all but those of the First World. Jack watched as he opened it, revealing a new staircase, leading further down into the earth below St Paul's. They followed the narrow stone steps until the stairwell widened and entered a huge vaulted space, vast enough to accommodate the cathedral above twice over. This sub-thedral was no mere forgotten cave. The ornate carvings, the gigantic columns, the superb stonemasonry told Jack that this was a place of great significance. The chamber was old but perfectly maintained. Marble stones mixed with elaborate mosaic patterns to create an impressive floor that stretched out into the distance, its grandeur undiminished by the fine orange mist that filled the air. Gas lamps hung about every column, adding volume to the mist. More swung from the very top of the chamber, picking out the magnificence of the architecture at its highest point.

Sexton kept to the shadows, moving quickly to one of the massive columns. He gestured for Jack to do the same. At first Jack thought they were alone, but as his eyes adjusted to the umber gloom he could see shapes moving deeper in the chamber. Ahead of them, amongst the huge columns, were dozens of raised circular enclosures, small pools about which people moved.

'Grand Junction,' Sexton explained.

Jack understood what he was looking at: this great space was the connecting point for hundreds, perhaps thousands of junction chambers, like the one at the Piccadilly Circus fountain. He saw two figures emerge from one of the pools, climbing out through a row of small steps set in the perimeter wall. The pair walked a short distance, entered another pool and disappeared.

'Be ready,' Sexton said in the same uninterested tone that Jack had grown accustomed to. They watched people come and go through the various junction chambers, waiting for the right moment. A lone figure crossed the vast floor and entered a pool to their right. The figure disappeared and the chamber was empty.

Sexton walked clumsily, Rouland in his arms, weaving between the columns as he edged closer and closer to one of the pools. He broke into a lopsided jog as he neared the pool wall and then dropped onto it, panting heavily, pushing Rouland's body into the water. It floated comically, the sword upright like the mast of a tiny boat.

Sexton climbed into the pool and nodded for Jack to join him. He pulled out a coin from his waistcoat pocket and threw it into the water. The water shimmered and glowed. Jack felt the ground below his feet disappear, and then he fell. The sensation was over in a matter of seconds and he found himself standing in a small room, plain and insignificant compared to the splendid elegance of the Grand Junction.

Rouland's body lay on the floor. Sexton stooped over it, checking that the sword remained in place. He picked up the body again, grunting and complaining, and shuffled towards a wooden door. Beyond was a damp staircase, so narrow that Sexton could not carry Rouland alone. Jack hoisted the spades onto the body and took Rouland's feet.

As they reached the top of the stairs Sexton opened another small door.

'Last stop. St Bartholomew's Church,' Sexton declared.

Jack laughed as they entered the yard of the little church. He had been here before – in 1940 *and* 1813.

Sexton took the body from Jack and paced over the grounds. He stopped under a twisted tree that had died long ago, dropped the body on the floor and took one of the spades.

'What are we doing here?' Jack asked.

'Burying him,' Sexton said.

'Why here?'

'Special place. Safe. Hidden.' He tapped the tree as if to signify some veiled meaning behind his words, then Sexton began to dig. Jack rolled up his sleeves and joined in. When they had finished, the hole was at least two metres deep. They pulled Rouland to the edge of the pit and dropped him in, taking care not to unhinge the sword in his chest. Sexton pulled out a long chain that hung about his neck; a large pendant swung from it and he looked at it for a moment as it hung from his old hand, his face a picture of regret, then he tossed it into the pit. It landed on the hilt of the blade.

The sun was falling behind the trees as they filled the hole with soil, entombing Rouland in the cold earth.

When they had finished they both stared at the mound of soil, breathing hard. Jack ached all over, and his shirt

317

was moist and filthy. Eventually Sexton pulled out a small coin from his pocket and flipped it to Jack.

'For going home.'

Jack stared at the silver coin in his hand, the familiar seal of the First World engraved into its face, and understood that he was returning alone. He wondered where his home really was now. Could he go and live with his aunt after all this?

The old man coughed loudly to clear his throat. 'Will stay, to watch over him.'

Jack gazed up at Sexton's wrinkled face. 'Sexton, I have to warn you—'

The old man held up a firm hand. 'Is this about my death?'

'Well, yes.'

'Don't want to know,' Sexton barked firmly. 'Stupid to know.'

'But you can avoid it. You can—'

'Can the ground avoid the morning sun?' Sexton's eyes sparkled as they studied Jack. His fierce stare softened into a warm smile as he dabbed his forehead with a filthy handkerchief.

Jack nodded reluctantly and held his hand out to Sexton, who stared at it awkwardly. The handshake was the briefest of things, but Jack smiled anyway, then with a nod he turned on his heels, back towards the church. As he stepped inside he looked back at Sexton one last time, and laughed to himself as he closed the door behind him.

The junction chamber was dim and still, stranger now that Jack was here alone. He stepped into the centre of the room and held up Sexton's coin. A gentle tingle caressed his fingertips and he let it go. It did not fall; instead, it floated gently in front of him and rose towards the dark stone ceiling. In a flash the coin disappeared and the anonymous room was transformed as the ceiling gave way to a large circle of water. Jack floated up. There was a momentary flash of white light and then he disappeared.

As his eyes adjusted to the shifting light Jack saw that he was standing in a pool of water which lapped over his shoes, yet he remained completely dry. He was back at the Grand Junction, deep below St Paul's Cathedral. He checked for other travellers before he ran back towards the stairwell up to the crypt. The Sorrowline was there, waiting for him, and he left 1805 behind.

The crypt of 2008 rushed towards Jack as he fell from the Sorrowline. He opened his eyes and he saw Eloise and Davey with Jo-Jo. All were safe, and a giddy relief swept over him.

'Jack!' Jo-Jo laughed to see him again.

'You're alive!' Davey shouted.

'And so are you!' The pair smiled and embraced awkwardly. Whatever was to come between them, for now it was forgotten. Davey groaned; his body was tender and bruised from Rouland's attack.

'Where are the Paladin?' Jack asked.

'Dunno,' Davey replied. 'After you vanished with Rouland they disappeared too.'

'The Grimnire despatched them,' Eloise said gruffly.

Jack's eyes went to Eloise. She looked drained, her pale face covered with dried blood. Davey had bandaged her chest with the sleeves of his shirt, and her sword glowed softly as it returned the stolen energy to her. She looked up wearily at Jack, her face full of tension. 'Rouland?' she asked. 'I cannot feel him.'

'Contained,' Jack replied. 'He's buried in the ground in 1805.'

'That will not stop him for long.'

'I put the sword into his heart.'

Eloise's dark eyebrows lifted as she understood that the threat of Rouland was over. He was contained, frozen by the Paladin sword. Sudden tears filled her eyes. Thick drops of water fell from her eyes as she allowed herself a brief exhausted smile. Jack studied her weary face, wondering if she still wished to end her life. She looked up, as if reading his thoughts.

'I have been dead,' she said. 'Now, I might live a while.'

Jack gestured towards his younger self. 'How's he doing?'

'He seems unharmed,' Eloise said. 'He has an energy about him. He makes me feel well again.'

*The power of the Rose*, Jack thought.

320

From out of the shadows an unearthly shape emerged, timeless and ancient. The Grimnire glided up behind Davey, its long finger beckoning again, this time to Eloise.

'Yes,' she said, as if in reply to some silent command. She turned to Jack. 'It wants me to go with it. Me and Davey. Our destiny in 1940 has yet to be played out.'

Jack looked at the Grimnire, its features hidden deep inside its smoking hood. 'You're going back to 1940? But you're already there.'

'I am entombed there, yes. But a Grimnire cannot be denied. Destiny cannot be denied. I am required there, and so is Davey.'

Davey shivered. 'We're going back to 1940? With that?'

Eloise smiled warmly. 'Don't worry, Davey, you've suffered worse.'

Jo-Jo came to Jack's side, his grubby face breaking into a toothy grin. 'Can we go home now, Jack?' Jo-Jo asked, eyeing the Grimnire nervously.

'Yes. I'll take you home,' Jack said.

'And then what?' said Davey.

'I don't know yet.'

Davey frowned. 'Will I see you again?'

Jack recalled his encounters with David as an old man. He knew he owed a debt to his grandfather. He knew he must try to help him somehow, for his mother's sake. He hoped the future – Davey's future, his family's future – was not set in stone.

'I hope so,' he said uncertainly.

The two embraced again.

Eloise and Jack exchanged a hug too. 'You are braver than you know, Jack,' she whispered in his ear. Then she turned to Davey with her hand outstretched. The Grimnire stepped closer, gaining height as it opened its feathered cloak to cover Davey and Eloise. The pair stepped inside and faded away, engulfed into the darkness, leaving the Grimnire standing alone for a brief moment before it folded in on itself, escaping inside its own cape, until nothing remained.

# 31

## ARRIVALS

Jack found himself outside his parents' flat once more. He could barely recall his journey from St Paul's back to Whitechapel. He had walked in a dazed state as his conscious mind hopped frenetically from one event to the next, trying desperately to process all of the things that had occurred. He barely noticed Jo-Jo by his side, holding his hand tightly, becoming more tired with each step.

When he returned to the flat he found the front door unlocked. Inside, all was still and empty like a frozen tomb. His father would return soon from the night shift and would find his wife missing, leaving only anger and unanswered questions where once a loving family had been. And so would begin a spiral of events that would lead his desperate father to a life of crime. He had not changed his mother's destiny, but the details were different. In his timeline she had been found dead in the flat, a botched robbery that had gone fatally wrong. But now the Grimnire had taken her, he knew not where, and things were different now.

He stepped into his old room, exactly as he remembered it, placed Jo-Jo into the bed and covered him with the quilt.

The child rolled onto his side and took a deep breath. His eyes gazed up at Jack, his face looking puzzled. 'Will I see you again?'

Jack almost laughed. 'I'm certain of it.'

'Good.'

'You're tired, go to sleep,' Jack soothed. 'Your dad will be home soon.'

'What about Mum?'

Jack hesitated. 'You can dream about Mum.'

Jo-Jo closed his eyes and snuggled into his pillow, content for perhaps the last time. Jack stood over him, watching, listening, wondering. He felt connected to his younger self through the Rose, their minds entwined as one. It was a simple thing to enter his thoughts, to calm and control Jo-Jo, easing the horrors that the young boy had witnessed. Then Jack understood why he did not recall tonight's events. Like a skilled surgeon he was removing the worst of it from Jo-Jo's mind, one memory at a time, unravelling the terrible images until all that remained was the ghost of a nightmare, half-forgotten in the dawn sunlight.

He shivered. Was this how it was to be an Operator? he wondered. Was this the corrupting power that his mother spoke of? It would be a simple thing to abuse such a gift.

324

He watched Jo-Jo until he was asleep, then decided it was time to leave.

As he returned to the living room he was startled to see the Grimnire standing silently by the sofa, its dark cloak draped over it. It pulled the cloak away to reveal his mother's body. In spite of her obvious injuries she looked at peace. With a regretful smile Jack understood that all the pieces of the jigsaw had been put back into place, the Grimnire policing destiny, ensuring its correct path. His mother wouldn't end up in the catacombs of the First World, but in the cemetery here in this world so her son and husband could mourn her.

He knelt beside his mother and kissed her goodbye for the last time. The pendant around her neck shone out to him. He gently removed it and lowered it over his own head, a final keepsake to remember her by. He stood to leave and saw that the Grimnire had disappeared again, its work completed.

Jack waited outside until his father arrived an hour later, making sure he entered the flat and found his younger self asleep. The coming weeks and months would not be easy for his father, or for Jack. That tiny flat would be filled with grief and desperation and agony.

Jack walked towards Whitechapel Cemetery with his heart full of remorse for what could have been.

* * *

When he returned to 2013 the summer was at an end, and the leaves on the trees were turning vivid shades of brown in anticipation of their fall to earth.

He realised that somewhere along the way he had turned thirteen. It hardly seemed to matter any more. He had been gone for only a few short weeks, and yet he was irrevocably changed. He could not now go back to his old life, to live with an aunt he hardly knew. His father was now in Pentonville Prison, wondering what had happened to his son, and Jack was chalked up as a young runaway, lost to the vices of London, an evacuee running from a life bombed out.

He had returned home and found it empty, their few belongings sold, he guessed. He was detached from this life, without a home, without a family.

He thought about going to visit his father, to put his mind at ease. But how could he tell him any of this? How could he go there without surrendering himself to a life of care with strangers? Even his aunt was a stranger compared to the friends he'd left behind in 1940. He needed time. Time to think. Everything he cared about now belonged to the past, and so did he. There was work to do there also – he knew the gift inside him could be used for good, and he needed somewhere safe to explore his new abilities. Somewhere amongst friends who understood him.

He vowed to visit his father soon. Tomorrow. There was always tomorrow, waiting for him with eternal patience.

He sat in the cemetery, the enormity of his adventure only now sinking in. Unconsciously he pulled out the book he had stolen from 1813: *On the Nature of the Concealed Realms* by Magnus Hafgan. It had guided him to his mother and the Rose, it had shown him a way to defeat Rouland, and he was certain more secrets lay within its small pages, waiting to be discovered.

He turned to the back page and the handwritten cryptogram inserted there. He looked at the letters for several lonely moments before he realised what it was that drew him back to it again and again. The symbols were neat, formal, and yet so familiar to him that he wondered why he had not seen it before. He knew the hand that had written these letters: it was his own.

Jack smiled to himself wearily. He knew his adventure was just beginning, and this little book was at the centre of it all. One day he would contribute a page to its sought-after contents, a page that would lead him, via the circle of time, to this moment. For now he closed the book and returned it to his pocket.

He sat there in the cooling breeze and wrote a letter to his father, telling him he was well. He gave no hint of what had happened to him, of the things he now knew, but reassured him that he would see him again soon. He fished out his mother's wedding ring from his pocket and placed it, and the letter, into the envelope. He addressed it and took it to a nearby letterbox and dropped it inside.

As he did so he felt his last tenuous connections with 2013 falling away, leaving him like a man adrift, out of time. But the sensation did not fill him with fear. After all, he was unique. He had a way out of his despair, back to a better time. He was going on a journey again, back to 1940, back to his friends, back to his family. It was all he had left now.

He walked through the familiar graveyard until he found what he wanted. He touched the stone with his fingertips, and smiled to himself as he disappeared into it.

# ACKNOWLEDGEMENTS

Every book starts with an author and an idea. For a time, author and idea work together in a blissful cocoon of isolation, each growing and changing, learning and evolving. But the time comes when the author must throw the door open and invite others to share in the idea. This is when things get complicated. Because each new person adds to the idea, helps shape it, makes it grow in ways the author never expected. Sometimes this can be a painful process, but it's necessary, and the idea becomes stronger, larger. A living thing. So it's only right that I thank the people who helped me take the idea of *Sorrowline* and bring it to life.

To my brilliant agent, Juliet Mushens from PFD, for her tireless enthusiasm, funny tweets and being a friend. To my editors at Andersen, Charlie Sheppard, Ruth Knowles and Eloise King, who asked all the right questions. To Philippa Donovan at Smart Quill for her incisive notes, and to Sam Copeland for pointing me to her.

A huge thank you to Liv and Claire from New Writing North who made a grown man cry, and kick-started me down the path to publication. The financial support of New

329

Writing North and the Northern Writers Awards (supported by The Leighton Group and Sunderland University) have meant a great deal to me.

To good friends who supported me: Curtis Jobling, for enthusing and egging me on; Paul Birch, for subliminal lessons in grammar; Dougy Pincott, for reading an early draft; and Chris Chatterton, for being funny and interested, even when I dragged him round bookshops taking pictures of covers.

To friends who never knew they helped: Bryan Hitch, Dean Roberts, Gary Dunn, Tim Watts, Uli Meyer, Gordon Fraser and Richard Dolan. To Kevin Cecil and Andy Riley for supporting and encouraging me when I said I wanted to write.

If *Sorrowline* is about anything it's about the bonds of family, so I must acknowledge the contribution of my own. To my parents, Enid and Al, who let me read comics and burn holes in the garden, I am what I am because of you. To my other parents, Mary and Albert, who always made me feel welcome, even though I didn't have a 'proper job'. To the two Davids: grandfather and uncle, both sadly missed. To Sarah, my first target-audience reader, for her honest feedback and enthusiasm, and to Megan, for listening, liking, and asking for the next chapter.

Finally, to my wife, Diane, who has read *Sorrowline* more times than she'd care to remember. She's been by my side every step of the way. Her considered feedback,

her unwavering support, has made this book – and me –
far better than I ever could have hoped.

Niel Bushnell

2012

# ABOUT THE AUTHOR

When I was ten years old I made a long list of things I hoped to achieve later in life. One of my main ambitions, lodged in between becoming an astronaut and drawing comics for a living, was to write a novel.

The plan was to do this before I turned thirteen, but it's taken me a little bit longer than that. My early love of comic books eventually took me in a slightly different direction: a career in animation. I've worked as an animator on several features films, computer games – including *Harry Potter and the Philosopher's Stone* – and television shows. And now I run my own animation studio.

But I continued to write until my first novel, *Sorrowline*, was completed...some decades after my thirteenth birthday. I'd like to take the credit for it, but I swear there is something living under the stairs that whispers secrets to me when no one else is around.

I live in my native north-east England, where the voices under the stairs continue to influence my career path. And I still plan on becoming an astronaut and setting foot on Mars, but it might take me a few more decades to tick that one off my list.

Niel Bushnell
www.nielbushnell.com

COMING SOON

# *TIMESMITH*

The Ealdormen of Ealdwyc are dead.
Rouland is missing.
The First World is in turmoil.

A boy called Jack Morrow could be the only person who can stop this secret world from falling into anarchy. But Jack has his own problems: the powerful Rose of Annwn lives within him, and he doesn't know how to control it.

The Paladin seek the one thing that might lead them to Rouland's hidden body, the one thing that might bring Rouland back from the edge of death: his sword, Durendal.

With Jack, Davey and Eloise separated in war-torn London and hunted by the lethal Paladin, it seems victory is short-lived, and the return of sinister Rouland might be at hand.

Can Jack find his friends and seize Durendal before the Paladin? Can he stop Rouland's return? Can he save himself from the terrible power of the Rose?

*Timesmith* is the epic sequel to *Sorrowline* and continues the adventures of Jack Morrow as he falls deeper and deeper into the mysterious First World city of Ealdwyc.

READ ON FOR
A SNEAK PREVIEW OF
*TIMESMITH*

The man buried in the cold earth screamed a motionless scream.

He had long since given up trying to move, his body was rotten and useless. Every message his angry brain threw out went ignored by his wasted, pathetic frame. Yet he felt everything.

Worms moved through him, wriggling, feeding, persistently tearing at his human remains. Moisture formed about his darkened flesh, seeping in with needles of ice cold indifference that cracked his calcified bones. And the sword, even after all this time, he felt the mocking metal of the sword impaling his inert heart. In all the time since his demise the pain had not diminished. Unimaginable, never-ending pain.

Nothing worked any more, only his soul, his very essence prevailed somewhere deep within. He felt the passing of time like the slow, maddening drip, drip, drip of a frozen waterfall. Seconds laughed at him for decades. Decades scorned him for an eternity. He was buried in time.

And yet Rouland endured it all.

One burning thought kept him going. It was a thought about a boy, a boy who had beaten him. Rouland was immortal, unstoppable. He had never been beaten before.

The boy's face came into his mind and a new wave of hatred consumed him.

Jack Morrow.

He had bested Rouland. He had plunged a sword through the centre of his heart and suspended his eternal existence. He had buried him in this patch of earth and left him to rot, to die like a mortal man.

But Rouland was no mortal man, and his rage sustained him through the lonely, dark years. Rouland waited, and plotted, and schemed. He knew his day would come. His followers would find him and restore him and he would have his terrible revenge on Jack Morrow.

For one brief moment Rouland pictured his victory, and he forgot about the pain. He was satisfied. Then as the notion subsided the pain returned, stronger than ever. Inside the prison of his mind pain condensed into pools of terror and Rouland's soul screamed.

IF YOU HAVE ENJOYED *SORROWLINE*,
YOU MIGHT ALSO ENJOY
THESE OTHER TITLES,
AVAILABLE NOW AND PUBLISHED BY
ANDERSEN PRESS...

# THE
# APOTHECARY
## *Maile Meloy*

'An absorbing and original historical thriller with
a Pullman-esque feel' *The Bookseller*

Fourteen-year-old Janie Scott is new to London and
she's finding it dull, dreary and cold – until she meets
Benjamin Burrows who dreams of becoming a spy.

When Benjamin's father, the mysterious apothecary,
is kidnapped he entrusts Janie and Benjamin with his
powerful book, full of ancient spells and magical
potions. Now the two new friends must uncover the
book's secrets in order to find him,
all while keeping it out of the
hands of their enemies – Russian
spies in possession of nuclear
weapons.

'If you read anything this summer,
this book should be the one'
*Telegraph*

9781849395069 £6.99

# HAUNTED

**A FANTASTIC COLLECTION OF GHOST STORIES
FROM TODAY'S LEADING CHILDREN'S AUTHORS**

'A chilling slice of horror. An excellent balance of
traditional and modern and a perfect pocket-money
purchase for winter evenings.' *Daily Mail*

Derek Landy, Philip Reeve, Joseph Delaney, Susan
Cooper, Eleanor Updale, Jamila Gavin, Mal Peet, Matt
Haig, Berlie Doherty, Robin Jarvis and Sam Llewellyn
have come together to bring you ten ghost stories:
from a ghost walk around York; to a drowned boy,
who's determined to find someone to play with; to a
lost child trapped in a mirror, ready
to pull you in; to devilish creatures,
waiting with bated breath for their
next young victim; to an ancient
woodland reawakened. Some will
make you scream, some will make
you shiver, but all will haunt you
gently long after you've put the
book down.

9781849393218 £6.99